Joseph W. Bebo
Hudson, MA, 01749
Email: joewbebobooks@gmail.com
Editor: James Oliveri
Cover Design: Elyse Zielinski
Proof Reader: Paul Kelloway

Library of Congress Cataloging in – Publication Data
Joseph W. Bebo
Forever Fearless /Joseph Bebo – First Edition
Fiction, Crime Drama

ISBN: 978-1-7339308-7-1
Fiction, Crime Drama

This trilogy, 'The Lawless Chronicles', is dedicated to my father. Dad was one of the earliest readers of the first book, 'Almost Dangerous', back in 1984. It was called 'Almost Sometime' back then, and was my first novel. It was full of errors and tangential subplots, with gross violence and foul language (yes, much worse than it is now!), but Dad loved it. Not necessarily because it was well-written or edifying, but because it had a lot of action and took place in our hometown. Also because it was autobiographical in a bizarre way like many first novels are. Dad gave me the encouragement I needed to continue. This trilogy is the result.

Prologue

He had been stalking her for months. She was ripe for the taking. Young, naïve, restless, and bitter, she was a girl looking for a way out of her sad, boring life. He promised her freedom and fun, a combination she couldn't resist.

His emails were bland and discreet. No hint there of his real intentions. From what he gathered, she didn't share them and no one seemed to care. Her parents were divorced, an ugly affair still being talked about in the small New England town.

She lived with a mother too busy to do much more than wash her clothes and cook her meals. She was too caught up in her own world of sadness and resentment to care much about her daughter. His phone conversations promised her things she could only imagine, things she had only dreamed about, that, and much more.

Today he was meeting her for the first time. She had sent him her picture. He told her she was stunning and showed a lot of promise. He was going to take more pictures of her today and show them to a producer friend of his, who was looking for young models to help advertise his next picture. He was sure Alicia would be perfect. Unfortunately for the young, foolish fifteen-year-old, no producer would ever see her pictures. As a matter of fact, there was a good chance no one would ever see Alicia again.

Chapter 1

I had been on the job about a week. It was my first one on arriving in town, a missing person's case that promised nothing but heartache and grief. However, I was too hard up to turn it down. I should have listened to my better judgment, but I've never been one to listen to advice. Not even from myself. Some people just don't learn. Like me, they keep making the same mistakes and living with their regrets, those lucky enough to make it out alive, that is.

I guess you could say I'm lucky in a roundabout way, lucky just to be here to tell the tale. But here I am, and I aim to stay no matter what some psycho, knife-wielding maniac or pack of wacko terrorists have to say.

I thought I had reached rock-bottom when I first got back to my hometown after dropping out of school and hitting the skids in Boston. That was before I lost my wife and kid, before I had killed my first human being. There must be something wrong with me. Every decision I made turned out wrong. Like the decision I made to come back home. I thought living among familiar surroundings and friends would be a good idea. I might as well have gone to hell for all the good it did me.

If I could have only seen into the future, like one of those old prophets you read about in the Bible. That is if you read the 'Good Book', which I never did, not until recently. The Bible can teach you a lot. Like what happens when you break the commandments. I broke them all, so I should have known what to expect.

The world is made so that mankind can never know what's going to happen. That would ruin the "Big Plan", I guess. But it sure makes it tough on us poor humans, who have to stumble through life blind waiting for the next axe to fall.

I couldn't have foreseen the string of ugly murders I'd become involved with, or the madman I would kill. At least I thought I killed him, but then I'm not too sure. That's when I met Suzy, the one good decision I made in my life. She changed things. At least I thought so at the time. However, it was only a temporary blip on the radar-screen of my miserable existence. I soon made the inevitable bad decisions again, one after another, until I lost everything.

Me and my big dreams, I should have settled for bank clerk or computer programmer. No, I had to be a tough guy. I had to be the guy who solves the crime and gets his man, no matter what the consequences. I had to be a hero and save the world. All it got me was heartache and pain, that and a bad back. Not to mention the divorce and custody battle, but that's water under a toll bridge.

It's just as well I didn't get custody of Bud. I'm not fit to be a father. I'm barely fit to be alive. Yeah, I beat the odds. I survived, but at what cost? I've killed and killed again. Once is bad enough, no matter what the reason, even if it's for self-defense. You might as well be married to the dead person, for they'll be with you the rest of your life - there when you wake up in the morning, there when you go to bed at night. Some people are no better than animals, dangerous predators that have to be caught and put away. I used to think I was the one that had to do the catching. Let me tell you, once you go down that road it's damned hard to turn back.

I finally had to leave my hometown in Upstate New York. Not because I broke any laws, but because I upheld them, upheld them to the max. I did what I had to do to save my wife and child, but in the process, I lost them. Even the cops who gave me the commendations for heroism in bringing down a dangerous terrorist organization, looked at me like I was some sort of demon from the pit, as something not quite human. Who can blame them? I left a trail of death in my wake not even the terrorists could match, though they probably would have done much worse if I hadn't stopped them. Like before, I only did what I had to do. Maybe if I keep telling myself that I'd believe it.

Boston was the only place I could think of going when I left the 'burgh'. Not a big city by New York or Chicago standards, but big enough for my needs. I went to school there at Northeastern, majoring in Criminology. That is before I crapped out. It's a long sordid story. I'll spare you the details.

Even though I never got my diploma in the subject, I've dealt with enough criminals and lawbreakers to earn a degree of sorts. It's the kind of degree you get on the streets. I stared death in the eye and death blinked first. I still see those eyes staring at me sometimes.

The first thing I did when I got back to Beantown was get a place to live and put an ad in the papers. I didn't have a penny to my name. Suzy and Little Bud got everything. If it wasn't for the money my dad left me, I'd of been in dire straights. Though what little I had wouldn't have lasted long if I didn't get work.

I found a room in the home of an elderly woman in the North End near Hanover Street. Her husband had died recently and her son, a Boston cop, had moved out years ago. She needed the company as well as a tenant. I must have made a good impression because she rented me the room there on the spot. It probably had something to do with the fact my mother and she had the same first name, Rose.

I bragged and told her how good my mother's sauce was. She took that as a challenge and made pasta for me the first night. It was a match made in heaven. During dinner she asked me why my mother married a non-Italian like Lawless and gave me a name like Jason, Jay for short. I couldn't answer. It must have been love.

I sold my drums before I left the 'burgh' so couldn't hire myself out as a musician. I put ads in the papers for self-defense instructor and private detective instead. I got a few students who I taught karate in the basement of Mrs. Corrado's house. It was dark and dusty and had too many poles holding up the ceiling, which was a bit low. After sweeping the floor a half-dozen times, however, and putting up posters, pictures, and pads around the place, it didn't look too bad. The small, slat windows could be open onto the street to let in some air. I even put down a carpet that I got in a garage sale down the road.

My students were two women, Grace and Linda, and a teenage boy named Tom. He was the son of a friend of Rose's who was always being bullied in school. The women saw my ads in the paper and signed up. The ad included an old picture of me doing a flying side-thrust kick. It wasn't something I'd try on the street, but it was impressive enough to attract the attention of a would-be student. I even hung a heavy bag from the ceiling. For an extra ten bucks a week, I taught the women tai chi in the park. It always attracts onlookers and sometimes prospective customers. I didn't get any calls for my detective services, even though I included a long list of credentials and references. That is until that Friday night.

It was a woman. She sounded distraught.

"You've got to help me," she said. "My daughter is missing. She left school yesterday afternoon and I haven't heard from her since."

I looked at my watch. It was 5:06. Twenty-four hours had elapsed.

"Have you called the police?" I asked reasonably. "If you haven't, I'd have to. The police have to be notified in all missing person cases. You daughter might be in danger."

"That's why I called you. I don't want the police involved."

"Why?" I asked, suddenly suspicious.

"I have a feeling my husband's behind this. We're divorced and I have custody of Alicia. That's my daughter's name. He wants custody. He'll do anything to get it. I'm afraid if I go to the police he'll use it against me in court to take her away from me. He'd say I'm negligent or incompetent or ill-treating her or something, although all the time he's the one behind her disappearance."

"Still," I replied, not wanting to turn away my first prospective client, but having a bad feeling about it the more I heard. "You're going to have to report your daughter's disappearance to the police. How long did you say she's been gone?"

"A little over twenty-four hours. I last saw her when she went to school on Thursday morning."

"What was she wearing?" I took out a notepad and began to write.

"A plaid skirt and purple sweater, with long matching socks"

"Real school-girl outfit," I said, thinking of a Penthouse foldout I had seen recently.

"What?" asked the woman.

"Nothing," I answered. "How old is your daughter?"

"She just turned fifteen. You've got to help me find her."

I then gave her my spiel, the one I use because I don't trust anyone who would hire me.

"Where'd you get my name?"

"Under the want ads in the paper. I saw the karate ad on the preceding page and put them together. I figured you'd be a good guy to have around if my daughter's in trouble or with that creep husband of mine."

"I charge thirty dollars an hour plus expenses," I replied, off the top of my head, half hoping I would scare her away. I hadn't thought much about my fees, but figured that was about what a city detective made and that was good enough for me. It would pay the rent and let me save what was left from my inheritance. She said OK.

"I'll need a recent photo of your daughter," I told her, "and the address of your ex-husband, if you have it."

"He lives in Florida."

"That will cost you extra if I have to go down," I said.

"Whatever it takes to get my daughter back from that monster, Mister Lawless."

"Is your husband violent?" I asked on hearing her statement. "Will he, or has he, ever harmed your daughter?"

"No, not exactly, not physically, but he can be very hurtful in other ways. He's just using Alicia to get back at me."

"For what?"

"That's nothing you need to know, but he's a cruel, vindictive man. I wouldn't put anything past him."

"You really should go to the police. You could get into trouble for not doing so, and I could lose my license." It had cost me $500 and a favor from the captain of the State Police in my hometown.

"No, there can't be any publicity. That's just what he wants me to do. He'll use it against me. No, the silence will drive him crazy."

"If it was your husband. There could be a number of other explanations for her disappearance. How has she been acting lately? Do you get along with your daughter? Have you had an argument recently that might cause her not to come home? Is there anywhere else she could be? What about friends?"

"No, nothing out of the ordinary. She's just a normal headstrong teenage girl who wants to grow up too fast. I can't imagine where she could be. She doesn't have that many friends."

"Has she mentioned anyone following her or watching her?"

"No."

"Do you and your daughter talk?"

"No, not really, Mister Lawless. You're right, it could be any of those reasons for her being missing. Just find her, please."

I wasn't sure, but the cash register was ringing in my ears. She gave me her address. I said I'd be there first thing in the morning. She told me to come that evening.

Chapter 2

A half hour later I was crossing the bridge to Charlestown. It was almost eight o'clock and still light, one of those perfect, long spring days. The golden glow of the sinking sun made even the dirty streets of Charlietown look attractive.

I quickly got lost. Rounding a corner I came to the Bunker Hill monument. After a few helpful directions, I found my way from there to Alicia's mother's apartment. The building, a three-story, three-family wooden house, had a nice view of the city from the heights across Boston Harbor.

The woman who answered the door had red-rimmed, tired eyes, and a drawn-down mouth frozen in a frown that looked like it hadn't cracked a smile in twenty years. Her hair was dirty-brown. Not yet gray, but it might as well have been. I immediately felt sorry for her and repulsed at the same time. I wondered if her disposition had something to do with her divorce and the runaway daughter.

She showed me to her daughter's room and gave me a picture of her. Alicia was a pretty, shy-looking girl with long brown hair and exotic eyes. After viewing the photo, I asked her if I could sit alone in the room.

"What?" she replied perplexed. She probably thought I was some sort of pervert.

"I'd like to sit in Alicia's room for a little while. I won't take anything unless I ask you. I won't even touch anything. I'm not psychic. I'm not trying to pickup vibes or anything. I just want to try to get to know your daughter, familiarize myself with her things. It might help me get some insight into where she might have gone."

She thought the request strange, but if it helped find her daughter, she would agree to anything. She left the room to brew a pot of coffee, to which I said I'd be much obliged.

When she went out I sat on the bed and looked around the room. The first thing I noticed was her record collection and the posters of the raunchy rock stars she had on the walls.

The bed was covered with stuffed animals and teen magazines. The contrast was striking, still a little girl, but striving to be a woman. The closet held an odd mix of conservative dresses and too short shorts with tiny halter tops. One set was obviously purchased by the mother. The other bought by the young girl with the intent of attracting attention. If only she knew what type of attention she might attract.

There was a small computer on her desk. I switched it on and looked around the room when it prompted me for a password. I'm no computer geek or hacker, but some of my friends, like John Rothburg back home, are. I've learned a thing or two. I started entering the names of the rock stars whose pictures decorated the walls. The third try, the lead singer for the 'Red Hot Chili Peppers', got me in. The computer chimed her name and said she had mail. I opened it.

There were several advertisements for various products, from hair rinse to car insurance. There were also some emails, all of which I read. She didn't seem to have a lot of friends. I wrote down the names of the message senders. There weren't many replies from her. Some of the emails were a bit catty, but nothing I would deem cyber bullying. None were from boys. There was one email from someone who signed themselves, 'Captain Kelly'. It read like advice from a teacher about how to get into the modeling business. What books to read, what schools to look at, what agents and agencies to contact. I was about to try to find out who it was from, when Mrs. Fleming came back with the coffee.

"What are you doing?" she demanded sharply. "Who said you could run her computer? You said you weren't going to touch anything without asking."

"Do you monitor her contacts, her emails and things, who she's communicating with over the Internet?" I asked, not answering her question. "It's a virtual portal into the world. Messages can come from anywhere and anybody if they're not filtered."

"I don't know anything about that or computers," replied the mother of the missing girl.

I felt like telling her that if she had spent more time talking to her daughter and paying attention to what she was doing, Alicia might not have gone missing like this. However, I had decided long ago, when I learned they had to be celibate, not to become a priest. I wasn't going to change that now, so I gave no sermon. I just asked her for a $500 retainer fee to secure my services for the next week.

Chapter 3

After leaving the Fleming residence and finding my way out of Charlestown and across the bridge, I drove into downtown Boston. The lights of the city attracted me, as I supposed it might a lonely, yearning teenage girl running away from a boring, overly-restrictive home. I pulled into a parking garage, took a ticket, and walked out into the glittering night.

There were people all around me, rushing to their appointments and parties. Not a few of them were young girls about Alicia's age. Most of them were in groups, but a few were alone. They walked with their arms folded and their heads down like Alicia in the picture her mother gave me.

I strolled through the Common and along Boylston Street, watching the crowds. I was looking for anyone who resembled the girl in my picture, which I glanced at often. I followed a few until I was sure they weren't Alicia. They met their friends or their date and went on their way.

At some point I drifted downtown to Washington Street and the combat zone. At least what had been the combat zone when I was there last, thirty years before. It had been cleaned up considerably, but still had its share of dingy bars and hookers, all a bit more discreet than in my day.

There weren't many teenage girls in this area of town. The ones there were, were working. They were dressed in clothes like I saw hanging in Alicia's closet. Not the nice dresses and suits her mother had bought her, but the raunchy, revealing things hanging next to them. There were plenty of young men about, young punks from the neighboring boroughs making up for the lack of college boys. They prowled the streets in search of a good time.

One young girl attracted my notice. She looked nothing like the one I was searching for, but her provocative manner grabbed my attention like a praying-mantis grabs its prey. She was petite, with curly, short blonde hair and blue eyes. Her pouty lips were painted red. Her stomach was bare as were most of her legs right up to her pert rump, thanks to her mini-shorts and halter-top. She was chewing gum, and as her eyes caught mine she blew a big bubble. I smiled. Stopping on the street corner next to me, she drew out a cigarette and asked for a light. She cupped my hand in hers as she lit it.

"No matches?" I asked.

"I lost my lighter," she answered.

"Where from?" I inquired, wondering if she was from out of town. "Springfield, Missouri?"

"How'd you know?" she answered back sarcastically.

"Your accent. That twang gives you Midwesterners away every time."

"Naw, I was just kidding. I'm from around here and I don't have a twang."

"You waiting for someone?"

I was at least thirty years older than the girl, who couldn't have been a day over sixteen.

"No, nobody in particular. I come here all the time."

"You haven't seen this girl, have you?" I asked, handing her Alicia's picture.

"You're not a cop, are you?" replied the girl, looking quickly at the picture.

"No," I said, "just a friend of the family. Here, take a good look."

I thrust the picture into the girl's face so she had to look at it.

She took it and studied it for a minute.

"No, Mister, I haven't seen her around here."

No longer interested in my lighter or me, the girl suddenly became nervous and said she had to go. I must have hit a nerve. Maybe there was someone like me out looking for her. Then I noticed the cop on horseback coming up the street.

"Thanks for the light," said the petite beauty and started walking away.

"How old are you?" I asked.

"Too young for you," she quipped as she skirted around a corner.

"Ain't that the truth," I said to no one in particular.

I walked down the block toward the theater district, then up to Tremont and toward the Commons again. I was standing on the corner of Boylston and Tremont when someone spoke to me from behind. I turned to see a policeman on horseback.

"Are you following that young girl?" inquired the officer.

"What?" I said, a bit startled. "Who?" I looked around and noticed the kid I had been talking to only a few yards away up the street. "No," I stammered. "I haven't been following anyone."

13

"I saw you talking to her earlier. What are you up to, loitering around like this?" he asked.

"I'm working, if you must know, officer," I answered. "I'm looking for someone."

"Who are you looking for," he said, even more suspiciously.

"This girl," I replied, pulling out Alicia's picture and handing it up to him.

He took the picture and held it up to a street lamp to study it.

"She hasn't returned home from school since Thursday. Her name is Alicia Fleming. She's done this before and usually shows up in a few days. Instead of calling the police and embarrassing everyone this time, the family has decided to call me. I handed him my card, which seemed to annoy him even more.

"Missing persons is a police matter," he told me. "The family needs to report this to the police. We can't have ..."

He was about to go down a familiar road. I decided to head him off.

"I'm fully aware of my obligations under the law. It hasn't been forty-eight hours yet. I have another twelve hours before I have to report this. If you let me do my job, the police won't have to be bothered for this trivial family matter. Sometimes it's best for all involved to settle things quietly. Despite what you think, I'm an experienced professional."

I showed him my license and dropped a few names. That seemed to satisfy him, although he didn't seem too pleased to have me on his beat.

"I'm on your side, officer," I said, pocketing my credentials and the picture. "I'd be the first one to call you if I thought the girl was in any danger. We've been through this before with her."

The cop ignored me and moved on as if I wasn't there. He almost ran me over with his horse, which defecated on my shoes as it walked by. I swore, cursing the horse and rider with some of the more colorful phrases I picked up in the Bible. There's nothing like those Old Testament prophets for drumming up a curse on somebody. Then I tried my best to clean my shoes off on the grass. I didn't have much use for Boston's finest at that moment.

Lingering in the park, I saw nothing but a host of lonely, desperate teenagers, boys and girls. I don't remember that much angst when I was young, but then my memory is kind of short and getting shorter the older I get. Now that I think of it, I *was* one of those kids walking the streets at night looking for something, yearning for the meaning of life perhaps. Well, I got news for you, there's no meaning to life. It's just one absurd, cruel existential joke. One minute you're here. The next you're gone. If you're not careful, it might be a lot sooner than you think. So stop searching and start laughing, 'cause the joke's on you.

I knew my chances of finding her by combing the streets of the city randomly were slim at best. It was as good a way as any to get started, however. The girl I was looking for appeared to have few friends. Where else would a runaway with no associates go, but the streets of the city?

I drove back to the North End and sat in my room going over the names on my list from Alicia's computer, thinking. As I thought, I sipped a glass of Scotch on the rocks. I hate the stuff, but it's the only way I can drink without doing too much.

I kept coming back to the mysterious 'Captain Kelly', the guy with all the advice about modeling. Could it be a teacher, or maybe an older boy, perhaps someone out of high school? The modeling line is always a good one with runaway girls who want to be stars. The fact that whoever sent it obviously went through some trouble to hide his true identity was even more suspicious. Just like something a cyber predator would do.

I don't know much about computers, but I was in a town full of people who did. I made some notes of things I wanted to do the following day, people to call, leads to follow. Then I tried to take my mind off the case. Last thing I needed was a sleepless night following phantom leads in my dreams. Not having a TV, I opened a magazine.

Mrs. Corrado had rented me her son, the cop's, old room. There were still some books and magazines on criminology lying around. I recognized some of the text books on drugs and related law enforcement topics I had read in college. Some of the magazines had good information about forensic techniques. Some even included grisly morgue shots of dead victims and criminals, if that's what you're into. I've seen enough of the real thing to last me a lifetime, thank you.

One of the magazines I flipped open happened to have an article on white slavery and human trafficking. This is where gangs of individuals - anything from African pirates and Arab terrorists to the Sicilian mafia and Russian mob - kidnapped young women for work in the underground sex trade. Much of this took place in Southeast Asia and places like Mexico, but also, as it turned out, right here in the good old U.S. of A.

What I read was interesting and compelling, but also disturbing, and made it difficult to fall asleep. Was it possible that what I was reading about might have some relevance to my own missing person case? I prayed not.

Chapter 4

Unable to sleep after an hour of trying, I turned on the light and got dressed. It was 12:15 a.m., a good hour to be roaming the streets if you're looking for a runaway teenage girl. I figured I could get a nightcap at some sleazy downtown bar, and see what I could pick up - in the form of information, that is.

I headed back into town for a second try, the missing girl's picture in hand. I figured I might as well earn my money. Most runaways end up on the street. So that's where I searched. I found a spot to park along the Commons. I guessed it was my lucky night. As usual, I was wrong.

I sauntered through the park and down Charles Street to the theater district, then down Stuart Street to Chinatown and what used to be the combat zone. I asked anyone and everyone I saw who didn't look like they'd shoot me if they had seen the girl in my picture. Groups of kids, girls on the corner, bartenders and bouncers, cabbies and winos, pimps and pushers, panhandlers and punks, I asked them all the same question. I went into bars and taverns, upscale clubs and corner dives, showing Alicia's picture.

"Have you seen this girl?" I asked.

Most people were polite and tried to help. Many avoided me and walked by as if I wasn't there. I couldn't blame them. A couple wanted to fight. I avoided all confrontations and kept moving. No one was stupid enough to chase me.

It was getting late, almost two in the morning, and most establishments were closing. So far I'd had no luck. I was discouraged and tired. Seeing life on the street had only depressed me. I needed a drink. Looking up I saw a street sign. It indicated I was on LaGrange. A bright neon sign across the road announced the 'Glass Slipper'. The full-length poster on the marquee promised more than just a drink. I went in.

It was dark inside, with a red, plush interior. A half-naked girl danced on the bar. There were a few girls dancing at the tables as well. I didn't see any lap dancers, but there was a VIP room where I expected such activity took place. I took a seat at the bar near the door and ordered a Scotch, never taking my eyes off the girl on the pole.

When the bartender returned with my drink, I showed him Alicia's picture as I handed him a five. He hardly looked at it and muttered a hasty, "Ain't seen her," leaving my tip on the bar. I turned my eyes back to the girl. She couldn't have been over twenty-one, not quite young enough to be my daughter. At least she had that going for her.

She was slim and athletic, with a dark, tanned body and matching eyes. Her hair was long. It was hard to tell what color with the low, red lights. She gyrated around that bar like a trapeze artist, hardly touching the ground. She was obviously strong and in good shape. She probably worked out and ran. It looked like she was dancing just for me, although the bar was crowded.

I checked my wallet - $45. I'd need most of that to get me through the week. Then I remembered the $500 check Mrs. Fleming gave me, Alicia's mom. I made a point to smile at the dancing girl as I put my wallet away. She came over after her set and sat at the bar a few seats away from me, where the waitresses ordered their drinks.

"I enjoyed your set," I said after a few moments. She had lit a cigarette even though there were no smoking signs all over the joint. "You move very well. You make it look easy. Are you a trained dancer?"

"No," she answered, moving closer to me and stubbing out her butt on the heel of her shoe. She had on a short dress that she had obviously pulled over her head as she sped from her dressing room. She probably only had on what she left the stage with under it, which was nothing. "I taught myself from watching other girls dance."

"Well, you must be a natural."

"Thanks. You from around here?"

"Yeah, I live on the North End. Can I buy you a drink?"

"Sure, thanks," she replied, smiling. She had an accent and dark exotic looks. I instantly thought Eastern European or Russian. If so, she had been here a long time.

"Where are you from?" I asked. "You have an accent."

"I was born in the Ukraine, but I lived most of my life in Lynn with my parents and brothers."

"Well, you'd hardly know it from the way you speak. The only way I knew you were from some place else was because of your stunning looks. You must be a struggling actress."

"You got the struggling part right, but no. I just like to dance."

"Have you seen this girl?" I asked as her drink came.

She took the picture and studied it closely.

18

"No, I don't think so. She's kind of young, isn't she?"

"Yes, her name's Alicia Fleming. She's just fifteen."

"A runaway?"

"Yes, at least I hope so. The parents are divorced. I don't think she had a very good family life."

"Hmm, poor kid," responded the dancer.

I was putting the picture back in my shirt pocket, when I noticed a look of alarm on the girl's face. She was looking immediately behind me. I caught a rushing, blurring motion out of the corner of my eye, over my right shoulder. Instinctively ducking to the left, I pulled my shoulder in. As I did, a large man lunged over me. His fist missed my ear by a fraction of an inch. He landed on the bar between me and the girl, spilling the glasses over the bar. The girl screamed.

I brought my elbow back into his face, snapping his head back. Without stopping, I swung around with a hard left hook. Jumping off my stool, I knocked him backward with a right. He was big and burly, but totally off balance. I caught him by surprise, although the way he swung at me for no good reason he should have expected something. I must have been talking to his girl. Maybe she was smiling too much.

Using his momentum, I continued to move him backward with a series of hand strikes to his face, neck, and body. Right-left-right-left, I knocked him through the door and out of the club. As we hit the sidewalk, he missed the step and went down, hitting the pavement hard. His head bounced off the cement like a bowling ball. He didn't get up.

I hardly had time to turn around when two of his bouncer friends rushed out of the club like mad bulls. They made right for me, as if I was a red flag. Drawing my right foot back into a stance, I put up my fists. They were both big bruisers. I hoped they weren't trained, or if so, not well. The first guy pulled up short right in front of me, not sure what to do. The unconscious man was bigger than both of them. They all had on the same black pants and t-shirts with the club's insignia.

"I don't want any trouble," I said, still in a defensive stance. "This guy attacked me from behind. I wasn't doing anything but spending my money."

"You must have done something, you little punk," said one of the bouncers. He started to go for me. The man on the ground was groaning and beginning to wake up.

"You better help your friend," I suggested, putting down my hands and turning to go. "He might have a concussion. He tripped on the step there and fell when we came out of the club."

"Hey, you," the first guy yelled as I walked away. "We're calling the police."

"Go ahead," I replied, still moving away from the club. They followed me. A crowd of bystanders, all waiting for a fight, followed as well. I didn't get far. The two bouncers cornered me along an adjacent building.

"You ain't going anywhere until the cops get here," said one of them.

"OK," I replied.

I turned and headed back to the club.

The bigger of the two took a clumsy punch at me. It had some power, but was telegraphed and wild, like his adrenalin had gotten the better of him. I didn't even have to move, but just pull my head back and to the right a little. He was off balance and leaning forward as he punched.

I brought my right up quickly with an uppercut that hit him square on the jaw. It wasn't that hard of a blow, but it caught him as he was stretched out and bent forward, knocking him off his feet. He flipped over backward and landed on the back of his head.

At that moment, his buddy grabbed me from behind around the shoulders. He had all his weight on his forward foot as he grasped me. I dipped my shoulder and ducked my head, pulling his arm out and downward. Using my hip, I flipped him over my shoulder. He hit the ground feet first, landing right on top of his buddy who was just getting up.

This last move is one I've been doing ever since bullies started grabbing me from behind, which was just about as soon as I could walk. I learned it in the third grade when a visiting teacher from Japan gave us judo lessons. I can't tell you how many times a bully ended up on the ground looking up at me with surprise after trying to grab me from behind. I guess you could say I'm a natural at flipping people, go figure.

The first guy, the one who had tried to sucker punch me in the club, was on his feet again, but in no shape to rumble. He was being helped back into the bar by a couple of his friends. The other two sat on the ground. One complained of a broken shoulder. The other held his head. A crowd had gathered and was having a good old time, cheering and clapping with every punch.

"That was just like on TV," one onlooker, a young male, observed.

"Yeah, just like TV," I said, walking back down the street toward the car. I made it back to my parking spot without further incident. I was exhausted by the time I got home, and fell asleep with no problem after taking two aspirin. Even though I worked out often, I wasn't in competitive shape. I made a vow that if I was going to be walking the streets of Boston at night asking questions, I would change that.

Chapter 5

The next afternoon I called Alicia's school and made an appointment to talk to some of her teachers. I told the principal that Miss Fleming had run away from home and I had been hired to help find her. I also asked her if I could talk to the girls who had sent Alicia the catty emails. She told me I'd have to talk to the parents for that.

"The summer recess started this week," she informed me. "The students are no longer in attendance at the school. Why haven't the police been notified?"

I told her the family was trying to keep it out of the papers. That seemed to be enough of an explanation.

I was about to go down to the library to use the computers. I wanted to look up the names of the people on my list to see if I could get a phone number or address. If worst came to worst, I could try emailing them.

Just as I was about to leave the apartment, there was a knock on the rear door. The small efficiency apartment I have is on the second floor of Mrs. Corrado's house. It has a private entrance in the back, which opens onto a small porch. I'd never had a visitor, but figured my landlady would direct them around the back if I did.

When I opened the door there were two men standing there. From their size and the shabby suits they were wearing, I immediately recognized them as city detectives. I was wondering what they were doing at my door when I remembered the previous night.

"Mister Jay Lawless?" the first man inquired.

"Yes," I answered. "Can I help you?"

"We have a surveillance video from the 'Glass Slipper' nightclub that shows you in an altercation with some of the club's employees. They've issued a complaint. You'll have to come down to the station with us."

"Are you arresting me?" I replied. "If you saw the film, you know I was defending myself. I was attacked!"

"The video shows you coming out of the place chasing one of the victims and knocking him down. Then you did the same to the other two bouncers."

"Yeah, after the guy attacked me! I was coming back to wait for the police when the other two came after me. It's all on camera. Are you arresting them too?"

"We're not arresting anyone, Mister Lawless. We only want you to come with us so we can clear this matter up. We know you are a private detective. The captain wants to talk to you. If you want to keep your license, you better come with us."

A half-hour later I was in one of the local precinct houses in Boston.

If I wasn't under arrest, it sure did feel that way. They asked me questions and took my fingerprints. They even had the nerve to ask if I would take a drug test. I said the fingerprinting was intrusive enough. I then sat in a hallway for twenty minutes waiting to see the captain.

"Hello, Mister Lawless," he said when I finally was shown in. "You seem to have caused quite a bit of trouble at the 'Glass Slipper' last night."

"That wasn't my intent, I assure you," I replied. "I was just having a drink and talking to one of the dancers. That's the whole idea, right? Buy the girls a drink while they talk to you. That's how they make their money. There was no call for that bouncer to come at me like that out of nowhere."

"Are you saying the man attacked you first, for no reason?"

"Yes, sir, that's exactly how it happened."

"Well, that's not the way they told it."

"You have the videos don't you? They speak for themselves."

"We only have the pictures from the outside surveillance camera. They show you chasing this guy out of the bar and hitting him. Then it has you doing your karate tricks on his buddies when they came to help. They didn't give us any video from inside the club."

"Well, ask for it. It will show you that it was an unprovoked attack and I was the victim."

"And what were you doing with this girl, the dancer?"

"Nothing! She came and sat at the end of the bar next to me after she got through dancing. I asked if I could buy her a drink. She said yes. Then I asked her if she knew this girl."

I took out the picture.

"I'm trying to find this runaway. Her name's Alicia Fleming. She's fifteen. Her mother doesn't want any publicity, but I might as well report it to you now. It's been thirty-eight hours. I was looking for her, asking some questions. I certainly wasn't causing any trouble. Ask the

23

dancer. This guy came out of nowhere and attacked me from behind. He didn't give any warning or reason. He just tried to sucker punch me in the back of the head."

"What, you have eyes back there or something?"

"Yeah, sort of. I saw the girl flinch and something out of the corner of my eye. I ducked just in time. The rest, well, you saw the rest."

"You made pretty short work of them."

"That's the idea."

"Well, I've heard all about you, Mister Lawless. I talked to the captain of your local state police force. He says you're quite the hero up there. Says you singlehandedly wiped out most of a terrorist cell. Said it was a regular bloodbath. I hope you're not planning more of the same down here in our city."

"No, sir. Just the opposite. I came here to get away from all that. I'm just trying to make a living. I'm not a law breaker. I'm an upholder of the law. I work with the police, not against them."

"Well, it seems wherever you go there's trouble. And I don't want any of your trouble in my town. You understand, Mister Lawless? You're treading on thin ice. If we hadn't had a lot of problems with that place before, I'd be inclined to believe them and take your license away. But since they don't have a lot of credibility with us, not that you have, I'll give you the benefit of the doubt this time. I'll have those indoor surveillance videos subpoenaed. In the meantime, I suggest you keep your activities to tracking deadbeat husbands."

I showed him the picture of Alicia Fleming again. He promised to put an amber alert out for her, and told me I should have done that in the first place. I asked him if I could still follow a few leads, since I had already been paid half my fee.

He didn't answer, but told me to follow him. He had something he wanted me to see. To my consternation, he took me downstairs to the morgue.

"What's this about, Captain?" I asked.

He said nothing, and took me into the autopsy room. There were several tables with sheets on them.

"This isn't a job for amateurs," he told me, pulling the sheet off one of the tables. There on the slab was the young girl I had talked to the previous evening, the one I had lit the cigarette for.

"Damn!" I swore.

She looked so small and pitiful. The lipstick and mascara were gone, but the blue eyes and dirty-blonde hair were the same. She had bruises about her body and welts on her neck. I swore again.

"See what happens when you get involved in this business? People get hurt."

"How'd it happen? I inquired. I figured if I had to look at this, I could at least learn something.

"Some John got his rocks off by beating and strangling her. She's only fourteen years old. A runaway like yours, living on the street, trying to survive the only way she knows how."

"When did it happen?"

"Late last night or early this morning. We found her in an alley in the theater district. Why? This isn't your girl, is it?"

"No, but it could have been. I saw this girl last night, around nine or ten. I talked to her. I lit her cigarette for Christ's sake. She was acting provocative, but I didn't take her for a hooker. I showed her my girl's picture. She said she hadn't seen her."

"What else did she say? Was she waiting for someone? Did you see anyone around her?"

"No. I was showing Alicia's picture around. She asked me for a light. I forget where she said she lived, but it was local. I didn't get the impression she was a runaway, just a tough kid from the neighborhood. She seemed to know her way around."

"You didn't see anyone eyeing her or following her?"

"No. As a matter of fact there was a cop on horseback. He was giving me grief because I talked to her. She disappeared when she saw him. We were on the corner of Tremont and Washington. The cop's horse shit on my shoes."

"So, you're the one. The animal has good instincts. Lucky for you we have you on video at the time of her murder, otherwise I'd hold you on suspicion."

Seeing the corpse of the young girl made me even more determined to find Alicia. I was beginning to feel like I knew her. I felt responsible for her, even though she wasn't my kid and I had never met her.

"You guys have to worry about every runaway in the city," I told him. "I've only got to worry about this girl. Let me help and do my job."

"OK, Lawless, but make sure you don't get into any more fights."

"That is my fervent wish, captain."

Chapter 6

It was three o'clock by the time I got home. It was almost time for my appointment at Alicia's school at four. The day was shot. I was thinking of taking a second shower to wash away the stink of the police station, when there was a knock on the door. I wondered if the police had changed their mind and decided to arrest me after all. When I opened the door, I received an even greater shock. It was my twelve-year-old son, Bud.

Neither of us said a word for several moments.

"Bud," I stammered finally. "What are you doing here? Where's your mom? Why didn't someone call?"

"Hi to you, too, Dad. I'm glad you're so happy to see me."

"Sorry, Bud, but I'm a bit surprised, that's all. No one mentioned you'd be coming."

"That's because you're never home to take our calls and too poor or stupid to get a cell phone like everyone else."

"There's no reason to be rude, Bud. Come on in."

If ever a kid was not a chip off the old block, it was Bud. We were about as different as a pea and a peanut. When he was young I had tried to show him karate, thinking like most six-year-olds he'd like to kick and punch like Daddy. He wanted no part of it. He just wasn't interested and would start to cry and run to Mommy if I tried to push him. He wasn't cut out to be athletic. He much preferred reading and playing on the computer, even as a young kid. He didn't play sports, which bothered me, but by then I was no longer living at the house.

I'm sure the trauma of being kidnapped by terrorists didn't help. He seemed to be scared of me after that. I can't say I blame him. My wife, Suzy, didn't go out of her way to help him understand. She didn't understand herself. She never forgave me for getting them involved in the whole mess, although it wasn't entirely my fault. Things sort of crept up on me and the next thing I knew I was in the middle of a terrorist plot. I was lucky my family and I survived. A few didn't, like my friend Jerry, the chief of police. But that's an old story and I'd rather not go there. Suffice it to say, my relationship with my family was never the same after that.

"How's your mom?" I asked. I hadn't talked to Suzy since the previous Christmas, and that was a short, stunted phone conversation that lasted five minutes. I hadn't seen my son since a couple years before when I attended his tenth birthday. Suzy discouraged visits and I didn't push the matter. I'm afraid I was a disappointment to both of them. That's why I left town. I was sure there was some pent-up resentment on my son's part where I was concerned. Again, I couldn't blame him.

"As if you care," he said.

"Hey, watch your tone, young man," I answered. "I'm still your father."

"You don't act like it."

"That's because your mother and I are divorced. We thought it better that way."

"Better for who?"

"Better for you, for one."

He didn't answer, but looked out the window.

"So what happened? What's going on? Where's your mom?"

"Mom's on her honeymoon with her new husband. She tried to call several times when the plans changed. They had to go earlier than expected. I was supposed to stay with mom's parents, but they can't take me until next month. So here I am."

"Married!" I exclaimed. "She didn't tell me she was getting married. I didn't even know she was engaged!"

"It all happened kind of sudden. What, you think she was going to sit home and pine for you?"

"No, but at least I thought she'd keep me informed. After all, I have a right to know."

"You do? I thought after you left us you gave up all your rights."

"That's not so. First, I didn't leave you, and second, you're still my son. I haven't given up the right to be your father. And I never will."

"Well, you could have fooled me."

"Boy, you're just full of wisecracks, aren't you. Have you eaten?"

"Yeah, I had something at the bus station earlier."

"How long you staying? I have no room, you know. This is it."

"I'll sleep on the couch. It's only for a few weeks and I'll be out of your hair."

"What if I don't want you out of my hair?" I replied, tousling his long, brown locks.

"Quit it," he said, shaking my hand off as if I had cooties. He never did like any kind of physical closeness, except with his mother.

"Where's your stuff?"

"I left it downstairs on your front porch. The landlady directed me up here. She said I could take it through the house later."

"What's that?" I asked. He had a black case under his arm.

"My computer. I brought my laptop. I didn't want to leave it out front with the other stuff. It's got all my music and things. "

"And all your games, I suppose."

"Of course. I don't leave home without them."

"Just like your American Express card."

"What?" he said.

"Never, mind. That's a line from an old commercial. Hey, I've got an appointment in a little while. I have to interview some people for a case I'm working on."

"You still doing that detective stuff? I thought you quit that."

"No, I just couldn't find work back home. You've really got to be in a big city to do the kind of work I do."

"Kill people?"

His words almost stung me to tears. All I ever did, I did for him, including saving his life. I didn't expect him to thank me. He was too young to really appreciate what happened. It all must have been like a dark, scary dream to him. But he didn't have to be mean.

"Why, have the kids been ragging on you at school or something? You know I did what I had to do to save you and your mother."

"Mom says none of it would have happened if you weren't investigating sleazy people and pushing your nose into everything."

"You sound just like her, but without the sense of humor."

"Mom doesn't have a sense of humor."

"Well, she used to."

"Yeah, before she met you."

"Oh, that's a good one. You got any more insults for your old man? That's not a good way to start things off if you want to stay with me, you know."

"What makes you think I want to stay with you? I'm a twelve-year-old kid. What choice do I have?"

I couldn't believe the gulf that had risen between us. It wasn't that I never thought about him. I thought about him all the time. I just figured he was better off with his mother. As far as I knew they were doing fine, although this marriage thing threw me for a loop. It probably had a similar effect on Bud.

"I know, Bud. This must be hard on you. Let's make the best of it. I'm actually very glad to see you. I've been thinking about you a lot. I just wish I'd had some warning."

"Yeah, me too."

"Well, we're in this together. Let's try to have fun. What do you want to do while I go to my meeting? You can come with me if you want. I'm going to visit a school in Charlestown. Hey, I have an idea, why don't you set up your computer here."

"Do you have a wireless connection?"

"What?"

"Do you have computer service here? You know, to the internet, some provider like Verizon or Comcast?"

"No, no one here has a computer."

"Then I doubt there's any WIFI available in the area. Is there a library or YMCA around here? I can probably get a connection there."

"Yeah, there's a Y just around the corner. I can drop you off on the way to my meetings. I was going to go there anyway. I was thinking of asking if I can teach a karate class."

"Hey, I wanted to talk to you about that. I was thinking of maybe taking it up."

"What? You want to study the martial arts? That's great!"

"Don't go getting all excited. I don't want to become a black belt master like you. I just want to know enough to take care of myself, so I don't feel intimidated by bigger guys."

"Tell me about it. I was picked on all my life."

"Now you do the picking."

"No, not at all. I come to every situation with peace in my heart."

"Is that why you killed all those people?"

"I can see we're going to have to have a long talk, but now is not the time. Let's go."

We took Bud's bags up to my room after introducing him to my landlady. She was kind enough to invite us both to dinner that evening. Then we headed to the local YMCA, where I let him off so he could work on his computer. It seemed like the perfect place to leave him. He gave me his cell phone number and told me to call him when I was through.

Chapter 7

I found my way to the high school in Charlestown, a nondescript brick building on a busy city intersection. It took me almost as long to find a parking space as it did to get there, and that an illegal one. I was fifteen minutes late for my appointment. The principal was not happy with my tardiness. Even though the students had left for the summer, the faculty was still here closing things up and finalizing grades.

"This is highly unusual, Mister Lawless," she began after seeing my credentials and license. She had called Mrs. Fleming, who confirmed that I was working for her. She had obviously shared her doubts about me with the equally dubious Diane Sullivan, the principal.

"I know, ma'am. I would not be doing this if it wasn't absolutely necessary. The police have been notified and there is an Amber Alert out for Alicia. I gave her picture to the authorities. I think it looks better to have a regular guy like me here asking questions than a bunch of cops hanging around."

"I agree, Mister Lawless. I'm sure Alicia has gone down to Florida to see her father."

"Oh, have you heard something? Has he contacted you?"

"No, but she used to talk about him all the time with the other children. I'm afraid her bragging about him didn't make her too popular."

"So you're saying Miss Fleming was not popular?"

"I wouldn't go that far. She's a shy girl and finds it difficult to make friends."

"What do you know about her home life?"

"Not much. I try not to pry, as long as a pupil has a good attendance record and has no disciplinary issues with drugs or boys. Things like that. Alicia had none of those problems. She was a good girl. Kept to herself mostly."

"Did the other kids bully her?"

"No, Mister Lawless. We have a zero tolerance policy on bullying here, I assure you. There was nothing like that going on."

My talks with Alicia's teachers were equally unfruitful. No one seemed to know anything. I got the impression they hardly knew she was in their classes. She didn't seem to hang with the cliques, but there were many who didn't. None of her teachers had anything particularly

30

good or bad to say about her. "Nice, quiet girl who kept to herself," seemed to be the quote of the day. No one knew or had heard of a Captain Kelly.

I concentrated on the two male teachers, a math teacher and a history teacher. Neither of them said much, nor recollected her being interested in theater or modeling. However, the math teacher observed that she'd probably make a good model as she had nice features. No one knew of any teacher who was connected with or taught such a subject. I left the school knowing little more than I knew when I arrived.

I was back at the Y by 5:30, forgetting to call my son's cell phone. It was too much trouble trying to find a pay phone. I pulled into the parking lot across the street and went in.

I hadn't been in one of these places in thirty years. It still had the same smell of chlorine and sweat I remember from when I was a boy. As I approached a long counter in the center of the lobby, a crowd of boys burst out of a side room, chattering and laughing. Many had towels around their necks or over a shoulder, obviously fresh from some athletic endeavor or other. There was no one behind the counter, where I lingered, not sure what to do. The sign over the door the boys came from said, 'Gym and Pool Area'. I doubted Bud would be in there.

"Hello, can I help you?" said a young woman who had come out of the door after the boys. She had on sweatpants and a sleeveless t-shirt that showed plenty of well-formed arm and shoulder. Her eyes were blue. Her light-brown hair was in a pony tail. She was young and athletic, but not so young I couldn't take an interest in her without feeling pathetic.

"Yes, I'm looking for my boy. He was going to try and find a WIFI I think it was, so he could work on his computer. I was supposed to call before I came to pick him up, but as I don't have a cell phone it's difficult. Have you tried to find a pay phone on the street lately?"

"No, but it's probably just as hard as finding a cop or a mailbox when you need one. Your son is probably in the library-study area, just down the hall and up the stairs to the left."

"Thank you. Do you teach a class here or something?" I asked, thinking I could kill two birds with one slingshot, get a date and find out about setting up a class.

"Yes, I teach the boys and girls swimming classes."

"Oh, I bet the boys enjoy that."

31

"So do the girls, Mister …?

"Lawless, Jason Lawless. My boy's name is Bud. He's going to be visiting for a few weeks. Maybe he'll join your class, if it's not too late."

"I don't see why not." She took a large register book out from behind the counter and began thumbing through it. "I think I have an opening in my seven p.m. class."

"Great, I'll talk to him. I don't mean to be rude, but once he gets a look at you, I'm sure he'll want to sign up. You know teenage boys."

"I sure do, I have one myself."

"No," I said, honestly surprised. "I'm sure you hear it all the time, but you don't look old enough."

"I hear it all the time, Mister Lawless. And if I took the men who said it serious, I'd have a big head."

"Well, you certainly don't have that. I was wondering about teaching a class here myself. I had my own martial art school in upstate New York for several years. I even had a school in this area back when I was in college. Anyway, I've been doing it awhile. Thought it might be nice to teach the kids in the area. I could make it very inexpensive for them. Much less than what I usually charge."

"Drum up some business on the side?"

"It never hurts. Giving an eight week class at the Y is always a good way to get regular students to sign up."

"I understand, Mister Lawless. I'm more or less in the same boat. I also run the competitive swimming club. And those students pay. The director's not here right now. He would have to approve your application. You can fill out these forms in the meantime."

She handed me a few sheets of paper, which I folded and tucked into my shirt pocket.

"Thanks," I said.

"Mister Hancock is free tomorrow morning if you want to stop back then with the forms filled in. He'll discuss the details with you and help you set up your classes.

"Will you be signing up, Miss…?"

"Miss Judy Sales. You can call me Soupy. All my friends do."

I laughed. "Like Soupy Sales, the old kids show comedian? I haven't heard that name in years."

"I used to watch it all the time with my brothers and sisters. There were six of us, and the neighbors used to tease all of us with the name, but with me it stuck."

"Well, Miss Sales. It is a pleasure to meet you."

32

I shook her hand over the counter. I was about to turn to go down the hall to the study area, when Bud yelled out behind me.

"I thought I told you to call? Why didn't you call me? I've been waiting for hours."

I gave the girl a resigned look and turned to face my loudmouthed boy.

"Do you have to yell? I couldn't find a payphone. It was easier just to drive back here without stopping. And you couldn't have been here much more than an hour all together, so quit your griping."

"Well, you strand me here with no money and no food. I'm starving. You've got to get a cell phone, Dad. There's no way to get in touch with you."

"I kind of like it that way. And let me remind you, until a few hours ago, no one ever had to get in touch with me."

"Well, now I do. How can you run a so-called detective business if you don't have a cell phone?"

"I've got a landline to my apartment with a message machine, which, I should add, your mother never bothered to use. Who needs a cell phone? You need contracts, and there are all these special rules. It's a rip-off. It's too complicated and too expensive."

"Dad, I'm a twelve-year-old kid and I can figure it out. Get with it, man."

He sounded hurt and disappointed. I wondered if I was that disillusioned when I was his age. I couldn't remember, but chose not to think so. Bud seemed older than his years, at least more cynical. I blamed myself.

"I'm going to be teaching classes at the Y here. Maybe you can sign up. It will be a good way to get started, with a group of kids your own age."

"Yeah, maybe. We'll see," he answered, noncommittally, as if his disappointment with his father spilled over into his judgment of me as a potential karate teacher.

"Hey, you might want to signup for their swimming class too. See that knockout young lady over there?"

I pointed discreetly to the woman behind the counter who was now busy with a group of kids. We had moved closer to the exit as we talked and were now out of earshot.

"She's the teacher."

"I know," he said, hardly looking. "I've already checked it out. You should see her in a one-piece."

33

"You say that like you've seen a lot of girls in bathing suits."

"I've seen my share."

"I'm sure you have. Let's go eat. Mrs. Corrado has dinner for us. She's a great cook and she serves big helpings with seconds and thirds if you want. But I'd save some room for desert. How does that sound?"

"Great!" he said, sounding excited for the first time since he arrived.

Chapter 8

That night Mrs. Corrado pulled out all the stops. She cooked rigatoni al dente just as I liked it, with a killer sauce and sausages. It was an Italian son and his hungry boy's culinary fantasy, and Rose Corrado was a master. She had fresh Italian bread to sop up all the sauce and hand-shredded parmesan cheese to smother it.

Luckily, Bud was remarkably subdued, maybe because my landlady did most of the talking. She reminisced with us out-of-towners about what it was like in the North End in the old days when she was called little Rosie Greco. She used to go with her mother to the garment district, where she helped her stitch clothes in the factories. She had dozens of stories about her family and the neighborhood, and Boston in the day. She even knew someone who had died in the Coconut Grove fire, one of her uncles' friends.

I got a little worried when she started asking questions about our hometown and Bud's life. I was afraid he was going to blurt out something like, "Oh, did you know my dad killed a dozen people with his bare hands a few years ago?" Mercifully he just gave his name, rank, and serial number. He dutifully told her what grade he was in and informed her that he liked music and would spend most of his time at the Y on the computer while he was here. And nothing else.

"My, it's amazing what they do with computers these days," she observed, shaking her head. "It's hard to imagine what we'd do without them now."

"We did fine without them," I replied. "I have trouble imagining what good they are." I should have held my tongue. I had apparently hit a nerve.

"I have trouble imagining how you can be such a throw-back," Bud said, staring back at me with a contemptuous look.

To change the subject, I asked Rose if she knew of Anna Fleming, Alicia's mother. "From Charlestown. Her daughter's the one I've been looking for. They think she may have run off to be with her father in Florida. They're divorced. I guess it was pretty ugly."

"Hmm," said Rose Corrado. "I'm not sure I know the name, but the story sounds familiar. I knew of an Anna Rossi from Revere. She's the wife of Tony Rossi, a notorious mobster from the area. He was investigated for several crimes, including murder, but never convicted.

They ran him out of the state. His wife divorced him when he almost went to prison the last time. They had a kid, a little girl, but I don't remember her name."

"Alicia," I said with a sinking feeling.

"Yes, that's it, Alicia Rossi. They had a picture of her in the papers. A cute little girl. Poor thing, to be in the middle of all that. No wonder she ran away. Too bad if she went to her father, though."

"You haven't met her mother."

"Hmm-hmm," was Mrs. Corrado's only reply.

"How old was she?" asked Bud.

"She just turned fifteen. And she hasn't been killed yet. She's not a *was*."

"How do you know?"

"I don't, but I hope not. Until I learn differently, I prefer to speak of her as if she's still with us. I'd appreciate it if you do the same."

"And I'd appreciate it if you stuff it."

"Bud!" I shouted. "Apologize for speaking like that at Mrs. Corrado's table."

"I've heard a lot worse at my tables," said Mrs. Corrado, trying to sooth the situation.

"Still, I won't have him speaking disrespectful while he's a guest at your table."

"I don't mean to be disrespectful to Mrs. Corrado, but you can't tell me how to think. I think she's dead and there's nothing you can do about it. You read about it everyday in the newspapers, about how some girl is murdered. Why do you think your girl is any different?"

"That's enough, Bud!" I ordered. I couldn't believe this was my twelve-year-old son. "You sound like an ex-con and that's where you'll end up with that kind of attitude."

"What do you know? You weren't even around most of my life. Then you disappear when I needed you most. Well, I don't need you now."

"That's not fair. I was around all the time, least at first. You wanted to be with your mother. Christ, I went through hell for you."

"And I went through hell with you. Where were you when I turned twelve? You promised you'd be there."

"You know very well I had to stay away. Your mother didn't want me there."

"Yeah, and you always listen to her, right? You only do what she says when it suits you."

"My, you boys do carry on," interjected Rose Corrado. "You remind me of Lou and our boy. The way they used to argue with each other."

"Ah, what do you know about it?" Bud burst out.

"Bud! Apologize. She knows a lot more than you do, that's for sure."

"I apologize, for being here." He got up, threw his napkin on the table, and stomped off to our room. I barked after him, but he ignored me.

I apologized to Mrs. Corrado, who shrugged the whole thing off.

"I don't know what to do with the boy," I confessed. "His mother dumped him on me unexpectedly. He just showed up here today, as you know. I had to leave our hometown a few years ago after an incident that happened on one of my investigations. I ran afoul of a gang of terrorists. They took Bud and my wife and threatened to kill them if I didn't turn myself in to them. In the process of trying to rescue them, I killed several of the terrorists. The police gave me a citation, but it's a small town, and people talk. My wife ended up divorcing me. It wasn't ugly or anything like that. We stayed friends, more or less. She just didn't want me around the kid, which makes it hard in a place like we lived in. I figured it'd be best for everyone if I left."

"That must have been so hard on the poor boy."

"Yeah, I guess so. He seems to have a lot of pent up anger and resentment toward me."

"Ah, we all have our cross to bear. I'm sure if you talk to him, he'll come around."

"Yeah, but everything I say to him he turns around and uses against me."

"I'd say you have a smart boy there."

"Maybe too smart for his own good."

"He just needs to be guided, that's all. He needs his father."

When I got to my apartment, the lights were out. Bud was on the couch making a big show of snoring loudly. I went to my room without saying a word, but spent most of the night rehashing dialogue to myself while I tried to fall asleep.

Chapter 9

The next day broke gray and dismal. I only got half a night's rest and was in a foul mood. I lingered in bed longer than usual, trying to adjust my attitude and think of the right thing to say. I decided on something simple like, "I love you." He was my kid, after all. Trying to instill discipline in the boy at this point would have been fruitless. I needn't have bothered with the soul searching. By the time I got up, he was gone.

There was a used cereal bowl in the sink. The cheerios box was opened on the table along with the milk. I swore as I put things away, smelling the milk to make sure it was still good. The carton was cool. He couldn't have left long before. He sure was quiet. Probably didn't want to wake me. Now I had the added worry about where he could have gone.

I dressed in a panic and ran down the back stairs to the street. Looking up and down to see if I could spot him, I wondered where he could have gone. I was scanning the horizon for clues when Mrs. Corrado came out to her porch to get the morning paper.

"If you're looking for Bud, he's inside having breakfast."

"He's already had breakfast!" I replied.

"Not a real breakfast," she said. "Something you should try sometime."

"He shouldn't be bothering you like that."

"I don't mind at all. Besides I invited him. I've got eggs and sausage, with French toast if you want some."

"That sounds good." I said. I wasn't particularly hungry at this time of morning, but wanted to talk to my son.

"One breakfast wasn't enough for you?" I said on coming into the kitchen and finding Bud at the table filling his face with French toast, drowned with butter and syrup.

"I'm having second breakfast," he replied, with his mouth full.

"What are you, a Hobbit?"

"Bud made the nicest, most gentlemanly apology this morning," Mrs. Corrado informed me. "He explained how yesterday was a very difficult day for him, with all the travel and lack of sleep. The last thing he wanted was to be rude to me. Isn't that right, Bud?"

"Yes, Ma'am," said Bud after he finished chewing and wiping his mouth with a napkin.

"What are you boys doing today?" she asked.

I'd been so concerned with Bud and his sudden disappearance that I hadn't thought much of what I was going to do. I had some leads to follow and people to talk to, but I was more or less resigned to pounding the pavement and trying to find Alicia the old-fashioned way.

"I was thinking of stopping by the Y today," I answered. "You want to join me, Bud?"

"Yeah," he replied. "I want to join that swimming class you told me about."

"Good. I'll be down in a half-hour. Finish your second breakfast," I said, grabbing a sausage on the way out.

A half-hour later we were on our way to the YMCA.

"How do I know you're doing your school work while you're here?" I asked him as we drove.

"School's over," said Bud smugly.

"These years are very important you know. I hope you're working hard. You'll be in the eighth grade next year. Don't screw up now or you'll never catch up in high school."

"Don't worry. I don't want to end up like you."

"I'm happy to see I'm a reverse role model."

That ended the conversation until we reached the Y.

"Do they have computers in there?" I asked as I pulled into the parking lot.

"Yeah, if they're not all being used."

I left Bud at the counter where he proceeded to sign up for a swimming class. I went down the hallway and up the stairs to the study room. It was early on a weekday, but there was still a good-sized group there. Two computers sat along the wall. One was occupied. The other was free.

I sat down and started to browse the web. I don't have many computer skills. Not the kind that would allow me to hack into other computers like the RMV or public school system like John Rothburg could. I wouldn't have even known about Google if John hadn't showed it to me one day as a convenient way to look up zip codes and street locations.

I Googled the name 'Captain Kelly' and got a few hits. One was for a seafood place. Another was an ex-astronaut. I doubted either of these had anything to do with Alicia's mysterious e-mailer. I also entered the names of Alicia's two male teachers, but got nothing except a couple of addresses, which I wrote down, and their pictures.

I had nothing to connect the names of Alicia's two male teachers to the mysterious captain except a vague hunch. I wondered how much effort I should expend looking for this connection given the odds Alicia was with her father in Florida. Under that hunch, I decided to check out the local bus, train, and plane stations to see if anyone there recognized the missing teenager.

I headed back to the reception area. Bud was still there talking to some kids.

"I've got some things to do," I told him.

"OK, call my cell when you're through. I'll either be here, at the apartment, or somewhere in between."

I didn't like leaving him alone in the city, but I didn't have much choice. I couldn't drag him around town with me all day on a vague hunch or as I staked out the combat zone. I'd have to trust him to be where he said he'd be. I hoped I wouldn't be sorry. One missing teenager was enough.

"I'm getting a cell phone today," I informed him before we parted. "We need to stay in touch."

"Get one like mine," he suggested. "If you give them my number we can be on the same network. We can talk for free. On second thought, why don't you give me the money. I'll get you the phone and set it up."

"Where?"

"I noticed a Verizon store on the way here. I can walk home and stop by there on the way. Give me a couple of hundred bucks."

"A couple of hundred bucks! What do you think I am a money tree? I'll have to go to the bank."

"Give me your credit card."

"You're crazy if you think I'm going to give you my card."

"Suit yourself. Get your own stupid phone."

"Here," I said, giving him five twenties, my whole budget for the week. "Get the cheapest, dumbest phone you can find. They can bill me for the service charges to set it up."

"OK, that should do," he said, taking the money. "Maybe they have cheap ones for old fogies."

"There you go. Now you got the idea. Let's try to hook up around noon for lunch."

"Naw, call me at four. I'll either be at your apartment or here."

Then he left the lobby with his friends.

I was going to stop at the front desk and ask the person behind the counter, a heavy-set, middle-aged man, about my application, when someone tapped me on the shoulder. I half thought it was Bud, and turned around ready for one of his wisecracks. It was Judy Sales.

"Hi," I said, forgetting her name. Then I remembered and almost said Soupy. "Miss Sales, nice to see you. I was just going to ask about my application."

"I was hoping to see you," she replied, flashing me a stunning smile. "The director would like to set up a time to talk. As a matter of fact, he's free now if you have a few minutes."

"That would be great," I said. "Perfect. I'll be busy the next few days and I'm not sure when I can come back. We can get the preliminaries out of the way and hopefully get started."

"Of course, Mister Peabody, the Director, has to approve all applications. Did you sign the waiver? Once you've done that he can conduct a background check."

"I included a list of references with the forms. It's not like I'm getting paid a lot of money or anything. I hope he's not too choosy."

"He has to be careful, with the kids and all. You'd have thought I was applying for a job in the CIA the way they grilled me."

"Not you? Not with those innocent blue eyes."

"You'd be surprised what these eyes have seen. Good luck, Mister Lawless. I've got to go teach a swim class."

"My boy, Bud, signed up this morning. He's twelve going on forty."

"I know the type," she said, "a healthy young boy. Just go down the hallway and take a left at the top of the stairs. He's the first office on the right. Tell him I told you to come up. He'll be delighted to meet you. Good luck." She smiled again and walked away

Her smiled floored me. It was not only the upturned mouth and alluring lips, the flash of pearly white teeth, but the inviting sparkle in the eye. For a moment, I almost forgot where I was going.

I followed her directions to the Director's office and knocked on the door. A thin voice said, "Come in."

Mister Robert Peabody was a small, rather rotund man with his hair parted in the middle. He wore steel-rimmed glasses and had a small, thin, feminine voice. It reminded me of the little lady's in the movie, 'Poltergeist', the one that says, "Go to the light."

He welcomed me into a straight-backed chair facing the desk.

"Nice to meet you, Mister Lawless. Thank you for offering your services to teach at our institution. That's an impressive martial arts resume you've got there. You come highly recommended."

"Oh, how is that?"

"Captain Richards of the Boston police speaks very well of you. He says you are a highly-trained expert, very competent to teach our self-defense course. You understand we have to be careful. The last instructor we had was teaching kick boxing to the students. We had several injuries, including a broken arm. We can't have anything like that happen again."

"I assure you, Mister Peabody, nothing like that will happen in my classes. First of all, there will be no contact allowed. This will be an eight-week introductory class, teaching the basics and fundamental aspects of the arts - stretching, breathing, balance, a strong stance, and a good kiai. We will concentrate on how to defend against grabs and punches, and how to fall without getting hurt. I'll teach them how to avoid situations, and how to get away. Second of all, I teach my students to respect the art and each other. The students bow to one another and meditate before and after class. They are taught self-control. If they want to learn kick boxing, they can sign up for private lessons with me."

"That sounds very good, Mister Lawless. That's just what we're looking for. When can you start? We have two nights a week scheduled for adult self-defense classes."

"Next week, I suppose. Just let me know the times."

"We also have two hours a week open for children's classes. We were looking for something athletic. Would you be willing to teach a children's class?"

"Sure, no problem. I had plenty of kids of all ages in my school, from as young as seven up to fifteen and sixteen. Of course, the kid's classes would be a little different. You have to keep it fun for them, yet teach the art. We focus a little more on the basics. I stand them in a line and have them practice their punches and kicks in unison. We try to make a game out of it. We used to play dojo ball in my school, where they have to do a technique when they get to the base. If they don't do it correctly, they're out. There is more stress on teamwork and exercises that have them working together."

"What did you want to charge?" he asked, tentatively.

"You can charge what you want. I'll take half. The rest can go to the Y. I usually charge thirty dollars a week for group classes, and forty for private lessons. You can charge half that if you want, or less, whatever you think fair. I'm not in this for the money, although I hope to pick up some full time students in the process. I'll write up a waiver that protects me and the Y. They will have to sign it to take the class, the usual thing."

"That sounds wonderful, Mister Lawless. We are very fortunate to have you with us. I'll inform the board and the staff. We'll have everything set up for you when you come in next Tuesday at 7:00 p.m. We already have six people signed up."

"Great," I replied. I stood and shook his hand. "I look forward to my first class then."

On the way out I looked for Judy, the swimming instructor. She was not in the lobby. I was tempted to take a peek in the pool area to see if I could glimpse her in a bathing suit. Thinking better of it, I left the building without a look.

Chapter 10

I spent the rest of that day visiting all the bus depots and train stations in the city. Greyhound, Peter Pan, the MBTA, Amtrak, I asked ticket takers, conductors, and drivers - anyone who would talk to me - if they'd seen the girl in my picture. No one recognized her, at least not the ones who didn't tell me to take a hike. I almost got in a couple of fights, but remembered the captain's warning and meekly left like a scared whelp.

I ended up at Logan Airport at the end of the day, the worst time to go in or out of the tunnel. Once there, I went from terminal to terminal, airline to airline, showing Alicia's picture. Finally, around 5:40 with no luck and feeling discouraged, I headed back to the North End. Again, I forgot to call Bud. I was lucky I could get home in the thick, rush-hour traffic let alone find a phone booth to call from. I got to the Y around 6:20, forty minutes for a fifteen minute drive. He was long gone. No one had seen him for hours.

I hadn't called or talked to him all day. I'm embarrassed – no, mortified – to say I completely forgot about him. Well, not completely. Every now and then, when I was between stops or at one destination thinking of the next, he'd pop into my mind. I'd make a note to find a payphone, then forget about it as I dealt with the next round of questions and half answers. It was a frustrating, fruitless day, and now I had lost my son again.

I hoped he had been true to his word and gone back to the apartment. I headed home in hopes of finding him there. We were due for supper again with Mrs. Corrado at seven. I had tried to say no, which I'm usually pretty good at. She's a lonely old woman and loves to cook. She can be needy at times, but with Bud around I needed her support. So I found it difficult to deny her requests to come to dinner.

I got there exactly at five to seven and knocked on the front door. Mrs. Corrado answered and said she hadn't seen Bud all day. My heart dropped. I ran back out and up the back entrance to my room. I wasn't sure what I was going to do if Bud wasn't there.

I needn't have worried. He was sitting at the table, a bowl of half-eaten cereal and an open carton of milk in front of him, tinkering with a cell phone.

"Don't leave the milk open," I ordered, snatching it off the table and putting it in the fridge. "It will spoil."

"No it won't," he said, without looking up.

"OK, Mister Know-it-all. You can buy the next carton when this one goes sour."

"Why didn't you call me? You were at the bus stations and train stations, the airport. I bet they have dozens of payphones at those places."

"They do. I just wasn't around those places when it was time to call you. I was stuck in traffic, sitting in the tunnel like an idiot when I should have gone the other way by Revere."

"You're the big city detective. I thought you were supposed to know your way around."

"I do, but there's so many ways to go sometimes you pick the wrong one."

"You wouldn't have that trouble if you had a smart phone or a GPS system."

"I know. I gave you a hundred dollars to buy me a cell phone. I hope it's the one you're playing with."

"Here," he said, flipping it closed and handing it to me. "If you want to call me, just click the button in the upper right and scroll down the list to my name. I put mom's number in there, too, and her cell phone number, but you better not call that one. That's for emergencies only."

"Great!" I said. I was thrilled to finally have a cell phone, and it was already set up. "What's my number?"

"Here," he said. He showed me how to pop up the number, which I soon had memorized.

"I'll have to get cards made up," I said.

"There you go," he replied, turning his attention to the TV, which I had recently purchased at his request with some of Anna Fleming's money. It was on too loud.

"You're a pretty smart kid. Maybe I'll hire you as my secretary."

"You can't afford me."

"That's true. At least let me take you out to dinner tonight. What do you say we do Italian?"

"OK, but you're not getting off that easy. We're going to dinner with Mrs. Corrado tonight, remember? You can take me out for Chinese tomorrow night, at the big place they talk about up on the hill overlooking route 1. I saw an advertisement for it on the tube."

"Yeah, I know the place," I replied, recognizing it from his description. "But I know an even better place that's been here a lot longer and has much better eggrolls."

That night, after another masterpiece from the kitchen of Mrs. Rose Corrado, Bud and I had the first real father and son talk that I can remember. He was well-mannered during dinner and made no outbursts or sarcastic remarks. As a matter of fact, he said he had a great day and spent a long time describing Miss Sales, the swimming instructor. He told me she was going to teach him competitive swimming.

"She promised to take seconds off my stroke," he said, enthusiastically.

He even asked about the beginners' karate class I was giving at the Y. I told him he could join my private group classes too. That way he could learn more before he had to go back home.

That night I informed him I might have to leave town for a few days.

"I can stay here, can't I?" he asked.

"That depends," I answered. "Mrs. Corrado might not have time to take care of you and feed you every day."

"She won't mind, ask her."

"I will. It also depends on you. Can I trust you to behave yourself and not get into trouble?"

"I did today, didn't I? Anyway, what choice do you have?"

"Don't get wise, buster. That's not going to help your chances."

"Honest, Dad. I won't get into trouble. I'll confine myself to the Y and here. If I want to go with friends somewhere, I promise to ask Mrs. Corrado. And you too! Remember, you have a phone now. We can talk any time, at the press of a button, for free."

"I'll think about it. I might not even go," I told him.

"Pop, why don't you carry a gun?" he asked out of the blue.

It was the first time he called me 'Pop', and the first time he asked me about guns. The juxtaposition stopped me for a moment.

"Why, does it look like I need a gun?"

"No, but maybe if you had one you wouldn't have had to kill all those people back home."

"You mean like if I got the drop on them or something? Your Granddad did that and look what happened to him."

"They shot him?"

46

"Exactly. What if something happens and you don't have the gun? You can't take it everywhere, you know. I can't forget the art. You can't leave home without it. I might forget it after fifteen or twenty years of not practicing, but it's something that's always with you."

"But in your line of work, being a detective, don't you need one? All the bad guys have them. They can shoot you before you even get close."

"Then let's hope they don't see me coming."

Chapter 11

The following morning I called Alicia's mother, aka Anna Fleming, the ex-Mrs. Rossi, whatever you prefer, to tell her my hunch.

"Have you received any sort of ransom note or call?" I asked in case it was a kidnapping.

"No, it's nothing like that. I'd have gotten something by now. My ex would know if it was anything like that."

"Then I think I should check out your husband in Miami, see if Alicia's with him. If she is, you can have the police pick her up. Maybe he's breaking some law by bringing her there."

"He has visitation rights, although he's never acted on them. He doesn't dare step foot back in the state."

"It will cost you another $500 for expenses," I informed her. "I have to eliminate this possibility. There's a good chance she's there, although no one at the bus depots or train stations remembers seeing her. I canvassed the airport as well. Same result - nothing. But that doesn't mean she didn't take a bus, train, or plane and go down."

"Fine, Mister Lawless. I was going to suggest that myself. I'll write you a check. You can stop over and pick it up."

"OK, I'll come by on my way to the airport tomorrow. Say, is there any chance I can have Alicia's computer for a few days? I have a friend who might be able to hack her email, find out the identity of who's been mailing her under an alias."

"I thought you said you think my husband's behind her disappearance?"

"Yes, but there are other possibilities. The idea is to eliminate them all until you're left with one, hopefully the real reason behind her disappearance."

"You're the professional, but I'd rather not give you her computer. That's her personal possession."

"That's why I'd like to look at it more closely. It could hold the key to her disappearance."

"My husband's the key to my daughter's disappearance, Mister Lawless. You're on the right track. Just check him out."

"Have the police in Florida talked to him? After all, we have an Amber Alert out on her."

"The police are probably afraid to bother him. He's more than likely got them all paid-off. He had the ones up here in his pocket."

"Why didn't you tell me about him? Why did you lie to me?" I asked suddenly.

"I knew you were from out of town and didn't know about Tony. I was afraid you wouldn't take the job if you found out. That's why I took my maiden name back. I don't want to be associated with the man."

I tried to get more out of her about her ex, but she told me little, except his last known address and to watch myself. "The little prick is mean."

The next day, after stopping by the Fleming residence to pick up another check, I drove to Logan. I purchased a ticket for the cheapest, fastest flight to Miami, Florida I could find - coach on an American Airline supersaver. I flew down on Friday and stayed over Saturday. That would give me plenty of time to check out Mister Tony Rossi and see if his fifteen-year-old daughter was staying with him.

Mrs. Rossi may not have told me much, but Mrs. Corrado, my landlord, was a fountain of information. For example, she told me Tony liked the races. On any given day he could be found at the nearest track betting on the afternoon Trifecta. He was also a ladies man, who liked to work on his tan by the pool and frequent dance clubs in the evening.

"Tony Rossi's retired," Mrs. Corrado informed me. "He may do some consulting once in a while, if you know what I mean, but he's not active anymore. He probably doesn't have anyone reporting to him or working for him. He might have a loyal lieutenant or two he takes care of, but that's it. He won't have a lot of soldiers around."

Every little bit of intelligence helps and Rose knew a lot.

The plane was crowded. The passengers were jammed into their coach seats like oily sardines. We no sooner took off when the big palooka sitting in front of me slammed his seat back. He did it so hard and fast, he almost crushed my legs. I was about to give him a short right to the side of the head, when the flight attendant came up and asked him to move his seat forward. I smiled and thanked her when she bent down to ask if I wanted a drink. I ordered a scotch. Our hands touched as our eyes met. I asked her if she was staying over in Miami. She said she was. When she came back with my drink, she had written her number on the napkin. I pocketed it and smiled, happy to suffer a crushed leg for a night with a beautiful woman any day.

I sipped my scotch and gazed out the window at the New Jersey shore 27,000 feet below. I wondered exactly what I was going to do if I found Alicia with her dad in Florida. He hadn't abducted her as far as we knew. That wasn't his style. He might have lured her down and paid her fare. Perhaps he was the mysterious Captain Kelly. It didn't appear he was breaking any law, at least as far as his child was concerned. Still, there was an Amber Alert out for her in Massachusetts. That might be enough of a pretense to at least take the girl into custody and bring her home to her mother. In any event, I resolved to inform the authorities both in Florida and Boston if I found her there, which I hoped I would.

I thanked the pretty attendant again as I got off the plane, and told her I'd give her a call that evening. She was a slim brunette, with short, curly hair, a bit taller than me. She had an inviting smile that promised much and dark eyes that said even more.

I got a cab and went straight to my hotel, a place on South Beach called the Royal. It had rooms for $190 per night and wasn't far from Rossi's luxury apartment. I didn't waste any time, but went directly to his address after checking in.

He lived in the top floor of a high-rise, the beach only a hop-and-a-skip from his front door. I pretended to be looking for an apartment and checked the place out. I had on my one expensive suit - a heavy dark one unsuited to the climate – and my dad's gold watch. It was the only thing I took from his things when he died. It gave me some class, which I otherwise would not have had. I hoped I looked like a wealthy out-of-towner searching for a place to live.

The attractive office manager was a snappy redhead who reminded me a bit of Suzy in her younger days. She was most attentive and helpful. If I hadn't already had a date, I would have asked her out. She showed me a number of different style units from their brochure. I asked if there were any studios. They started at $5000 a month, she answered. I asked if I could look at a couple and spend some time in the establishment. She said yes, and suggested I check out the pool and nightclub areas.

"You'll never have to leave the premises," she informed me. "We have everything you need right here."

"I can see," I said, smiling and looking at her pert breasts, busting out of the top buttons of her blouse.

I was able to walk the hallway in front of Rossi's apartment. I made a point to identify the general vicinity so I could locate it from

50

the outside. Then I went to the pool area, had a drink at the bar, and hung out. I asked the bartender questions a perspective customer might ask. I also queried him about the vivacious redhead at the front office. He told me she was as wild as she was hot. I filed the information away for future reference.

It must have been my lucky day. I hadn't been there twenty minutes when I heard some loudmouth jerk behind me bragging about some dame he had just laid. He was talking about her like she was some prize buck he'd just bagged. I glanced up at the paneled mirror behind the bar and recognized Tony Rossi from pictures his ex-wife had given me. He was in a loud bathing suit with an equally strident Hawaiian shirt. The shirt was open to expose a hairy chest and a heavy gold chain. He was thick-set and short. He had two large goons with him. All three of them looked like gangsters out of some Goodfellas movie. I sipped my drink and ignored them. They complained about the lousy service, bought a round of drinks, and went back to the pool. I found another seat further toward the end of the bar, in a corner where I could watch them unobtrusively.

It was obvious that Tony liked to play the big man and throw his weight around, as well as his money. He whistled at the girls and made wisecracks when they didn't respond. He pretty much made a nuisance of himself, but no one seemed to be bothered. I'd have to be careful. I didn't want to be seen watching him. If he had his daughter staying with him, there was no indication he had let that change his habits.

I hung around the complex the whole day watching the trio. They spent most of the time going back and forth between the bar and the pool. It didn't look like his daughter was with him. I decided to stake his place out anyway. I had dinner at the restaurant where I could keep an eye on the suite of elevators and the lobby. Tony and one of his associates left around 7:00 p.m., just as I was leaving to start my observations.

Earlier that day, when I picked up my rental car, I had noticed a parking garage on a side street, kitty-corner from Rossi's building. I parked the car in a spot at the top. It had a clear view of his apartment only a couple hundred yards away. With my military field-glasses - a gift from my dad - I was able get a partial view into his apartment through a large, plate-glass door leading from his balcony. I couldn't see the floor, but I could see most of the opposite wall and ceiling, and the balcony, clearly.

The lights were on. I could see furniture against a wall, and a lamp. There was a telescope on the balcony looking out over the city. I watched for some time, but saw no activity. Then after almost an hour, someone walked by the glass panel. It was a large man. He went back and forth several times. Then he disappeared again. Perhaps Rossi's daughter was in one of the darkened rooms sleeping. Perhaps she was too small to see through the window. More than likely she wasn't there.

I sipped my coffee and sat in my car, watching the window through the glasses. I had a good spot, and no one seemed to notice me. Then I remembered the phone number in my pocket, and the fact I had a possible date with a beautiful woman. I also remembered that I had a cell-phone in my pocket as well. Ah, the wonders of modern technology. I was instantly connected with what would have been a fleeting encounter I otherwise might have missed. I took out the crumpled napkin and dialed the number. A female voice answered after the sixth ring. I was almost about to hang up.

"Hello," she said.

"Hi, Elisha," I replied, looking at the name on the napkin. "We met on the plane today. I was wondering if you wanted to get together for a drink."

No sense beating around the bush when you're on a stakeout.

"Oh, yes," she said. "The man with the deep, brown eyes."

"As long as you don't say cow's eyes."

"I like cow's eyes."

"Moo. Are you free tonight?"

I figured I'd seen enough of Mister Tony Rossi's apartment. Alicia did not appear to be there.

"I'm sorry," she replied. "I'm busy tonight, but I'm not doing anything tomorrow night. What did you have in mind?"

"I don't know. I'm thinking of renting an apartment on the beach," I lied. "They have a hot club there with live music. Do you like to dance?"

"Yes, I love to dance."

"Good," I said, giving her the address. "I'll meet you there around 10:00 tomorrow evening. Bring your dancing shoes. I'll take care of the cab."

I hung up and continued to watch Rossi's apartment until he arrived back at the place around midnight. They had girls with them. I got a good view of Tony as he grab-assed with his playmate on the balcony. The way he was banging her, I thought he was going to knock her off the railing. I began to seriously doubt he had his fifteen year old daughter staying with him.

Going back to my hotel, I had a nightcap in the lounge. I thought of the redhead at the apartment sales office, and the stewardess I had a date with. If only one of them was staying at the Royal. I fell asleep thinking of the possibilities.

Chapter 12

The following morning I was up early and back at the apartment complex. I went to the restaurant, where I sat in my favorite seat and had breakfast. I was in the middle of my waffles and bacon when Rossi and his two associates came down the elevator and left the complex. Rossi handed the doorman his keys as they walked out. He had on a light blue Armani suit, with matching socks and a lot of Jewelry. I ran back across the road and got into my rental car. I was sitting on the street double-parked when they drove out of the entranceway and sped down the road. I followed.

Perhaps he had his daughter stashed in another place, figuring his wife would come looking for her. Maybe they were on their way there now. I followed them south along the beach road, past my hotel. We drove for about forty-five minutes, until we reached a large racetrack/casino complex. The sign said, 'Gulf Shore Park'. They weren't going to see his daughter. They were going to the races.

I stopped in a spot not far from where Tony's man parked their Caddy, in a huge parking lot about a mile from the stadium. I waited until they moved off, then got out. I wanted to keep them in sight, but wasn't sure what watching them would buy me. The girl was obviously not with her father, unless he was keeping her at the racetrack. Then again, he could have her under lock and key back at his apartment.

I followed them as they made their bets and went to their seats. It was easy to elude detection in the mass of people. I was dressed as unobtrusively as possible in t-shirt and jeans, a Marlins baseball cap, and sunglasses. Once I was certain they were there for the duration, I darted back to my car and headed to his apartment building.

I didn't know much about breaking into computers like my friend John Rothburg. However, I've learned a thing or two in my day about picking locks, especially the old-fashioned pin-and-tumbler kind. Even the most sophisticated hotels and apartments still used them. I always had a pin and thumb wrench with me for just such devices.

The doorman recognized me. I still had my guest pass, compliments of the attractive office manager. I asked if she was in and was told the office was closed on Saturdays.

"She might be by the pool," the doorman informed me helpfully.

I raised my eyebrows.

"That I'll have to see," I murmured in my best Groucho voice, and hurried off in that direction. When I reached the elevators, I made a detour and went up to the top floor and Rossi's apartment.

I scanned the hallway for cameras. Other than one in the floor's lobby where the elevators opened, I could see none. I wondered vaguely if the door was alarmed. I could see no indication of a security system. I tested the lock with my pin as I leaned against the door as if drunk, looking up and down the hallway. The lock was 'pickable'. I continued using my pin and thumb wrench to open it, lifting the lock-pins until the knob turned. Not much security, I noted, as I slipped inside.

My heart was beating fast. No matter how many times I've broken and entered someone's place, I still get the heebie-jeebies. Time becomes an obsession, a palpable thing you can almost feel ticking away. It pounds in your head like an incessant hammer. Every second is one more instant closer to your demise. Anything could happen. These weren't accountants I was dealing with, retired or not. What I had to do, however, wouldn't take long.

The apartment was dark except for a light in the hallway leading to the bathroom. The place was large, with three bedrooms and two full baths, plus a large, sunken living and dining area.

I called her name softly as I walked around the apartment, from one room to another.

"Alicia! Alicia, are you here?"

It was silent as a tomb, which it was beginning to feel like. Unless she was bound and gagged in a secret panel, the missing girl was not here.

Then I wondered if I had been tricked somehow. I left the apartment without being spotted and raced back toward the track. I got there about half-past noon and panicked when I saw their seats were empty. I was worried they had given me the slip and gone to where Alicia was hidden. Backtracking, I searched the stadium and picked them up a few minutes later at the casino restaurant, where they spent plenty and tipped little. I felt bad for the waiter, but good that they hadn't eluded me.

I was almost certain the girl wasn't with her father. That was the good news. The bad news was it meant she could have been abducted. She could be anywhere. The chances of finding her had just been astronomically reduced.

I spent the rest of the day dogging them, before following them back to Rossi's apartment around 5:00 p.m. I didn't bother trailing them all the way. Stopping at my hotel, I got ready for my big date. I figured I'd take her to the nightclub at the apartment complex. That way I could do some more spying while I boogied the night away with an attractive stranger.

I grabbed supper at a diner down the street. It served greasy burgers cooked in butter, and fries so smothered in heavy fat that each one felt like a full plate of dumplings. Then I stretched out and relaxed for a couple of hours watching an old movie on cable TV until it was time to go. I almost fell asleep. I jerked to attention around 8:00 in a panic I had missed my date. My cell phone was ringing. It was Bud.

"Did I wake you?" he said. "You sound groggy."

"Yeah, I must have dozed off. I was out late on a stakeout last night."

"Yeah, 'Have-no-gun, will travel.'"

"Very funny," I laughed, hearing one of my own lines parroted back to me by my twelve-year-old son. "How you doing? What have you been up to?"

"Oh, not much. I can't wait for my karate lesson."

"I'll be home by noon tomorrow. I can give you a quick class then. We'll go over some basics."

"I'm really enjoying the Y. Miss Sales is great. She's a fantastic swimmer. She's the fastest person I've ever seen in the water, even for a guy."

"Good! I'm glad she's helping you, but don't forget this is all temporary until your mom gets back."

"Don't worry. I haven't forgotten I'm only temporary. By the way, I invited her over to dinner tomorrow night. She's going to give you some pointers on your classes."

"Oh boy," I said. "Just what I need."

I felt guilty for going out on a date when Bud mentioned Judy's name. I wondered why. I hardly knew the girl. I had a feeling that would soon change.

After talking to Bud and a quick shower, I looked in my meager wardrobe for something to wear. All I had were t-shirts and jeans. I selected a clean pair of each, both black, and grabbed the heavy, dark suit jacket I had used in the interview earlier. I didn't look too bad as I gazed at my image in the mirror, kind of like a forty-something Al Pacino. It was after nine when I headed to Rossi's apartment complex.

Chapter 13

I was waiting in front of Rossi's building when my date's cab arrived at precisely 10:00 p.m. That's an airline stewardess for you, right on time. I know the term isn't politically correct. I'm not sure why. It's supposed to be demeaning, I guess. But there's nothing offensive about the term stewardess as far as I'm concerned, especially when they look like Elisha. Believe me, it is a term I use with the utmost respect, adoration even. Flight Attendant just doesn't do it for me. Why use two words when one will do?

I was about to escort her inside, when we were accosted at the curbside by two large men in suits. They came out of nowhere. I recognized them instantly as Rossi's associates.

"You have to come with us," the biggest of them said, as they came up real close and personal like.

My immediate impulse was to lay these two old goons out cold. That would make a good impression on my date, and send a message to Rossi. In any case, I wasn't about to let them ruin my date.

"Who are you?" I yelled standing my ground. I thrust my face into his, making myself appear in inch taller. "I'm not going with you. Who the hell do you think you are? I'll call the cops if you don't get out of here. Leave us alone."

"We're the apartment security," replied the man, backing off a step. "You're under house arrest for breaking and entering Mister Rossi's apartment. We're the ones who will be calling the police."

"Yeah," said the other one, crowding behind him, "after Mister Rossi gets through with you.

"You aren't security," I responded. "You're Rossi's goons and you're not taking me anywhere."

The second man started moving from behind his friend. I stepped forward, around the first man, and quickly sidestepped the second one. I was past him and had taken my date's arm before he had time to react. We moved toward the entrance. She had been standing there with her mouth open the whole time, not sure what to do.

"It's nothing," I assured her. "These guys are playing policemen."

"Hey, you," the second goon said, coming up behind us. "Where do you think you're going?"

He grabbed me by the shoulder. I turned and slapped his hand away, getting into a stance. That just made him mad. He made a lunge for me. I blocked his arms, and using his momentum, spun him into the other man who was coming up behind him. The girl screamed.

At this point I figured I had a full-fledged fight on my hands, and it would probably be to the finish. That is unless I could nip it in the bud, or a squad of police showed up in riot gear. As I began to tussle with them, I wondered if that's what I really wanted. I remembered what happened last time I started something with someone who had 'associates'. The next thing I knew there was a string of dead bodies in my wake. It had been them or me, a fight to the finish. No, I didn't want to start something like that again. Besides, I kind of wanted to talk to Rossi myself.

"OK, OK!" I yelled as the man came at me swinging. I ducked and backed away with my hands up. "I don't want any trouble. I'll go with you. I wanted to talk to Mister Rossi anyway. Be cool."

"You be cool, mister karate man," he said.

He came at me with a whistling right, which I evaded, and a stinging left, which I blocked. I didn't counter like I would normally have done, but kept my hands up and open in front of me.

"I'm going with you. I don't want to fight."

"Well, I do, asshole!" he shouted.

He ran at me, his arms outstretched as if to tackle me. Again, I resisted the impulse to kick him in the head, or clothes-line him off his feet, or flip him forward on his face. I let myself be thrown to the ground instead. He landed on top of me like a half-ton turd. I kia'd to keep from getting the wind knocked out of me and absorbed the blow.

I didn't want to fight, but I didn't want this 200 pounder laying on top of me either. I grabbed his private-parts, squeezing and twisting as I did so. He screamed and reached down. As he did, I lifted my legs, and using my hands, threw him forward over my head. Squirting out from beneath him and hopping to my feet, I stood over him ready to stomp his skull.

"I said I don't want any trouble," I told them. "I'll go with you, so cool out."

He got up and was going to come at me again, ripping mad. It was just as I thought. Once you started something with one of these guys, you'd have to go all the way. I braced myself to get it over quick.

"Hold it Harry," said the first one, the bigger of the two. He was obviously the higher ranking of the old lieutenants. "Mister Rossi only wants to talk. He wants to know what you were doing breaking into his apartment. He wants you to give whatever you took back."

"I didn't take anything," I insisted relaxing. "Look, let me take the lady inside, buy everyone a drink, and then we can go talk to your boss."

"You buy the lady a drink. Then you're coming with us," declared the second man rubbing his sore balls.

I bought my date a drink and explained that I was really a private detective working on a case. She was more than ready to dump me by this time. Telling her I would not be long, I followed the pair up to Rossi's apartment. He was sitting on the couch watching TV when we arrived.

"Sit down, Mister Lawless," said Rossi as I was escorted into the room. He pointed to another couch adjacent to his at a right angle. "I hope we didn't interrupt anything."

So he knew my name. That couldn't be good.

"Just a date," I answered sitting down. "She'll never go out with me again. Nothing serious."

"Well, my daughter is serious," he replied. "Yes, I know who you are and what you're doing here. I know my wife hired you and that my daughter has run away. What I don't know is what you were doing in my apartment. Before I turn over the film from my surveillance camera of you breaking in to the police, I'd thought I give you a chance to explain yourself."

"If you know why I'm here, then you know what I was doing in your apartment. I'm looking for your daughter."

"Well, as you can see, she's not here. I haven't seen her, which is what I told the police when they came looking for her. What makes you think I'd take her?"

"Your wife seems to think so. She said it's your way of trying to get custody."

"My wife is an idiot. That's what I get for listening to my family. You've been watching me. Yes, I've known you've been tailing me since the first day you showed up at the pool asking questions. Does it look like I've got my daughter with me? Well, does it?"

"No, but you might have her stashed somewhere."

"This is my daughter we're talking about!" he yelled, standing up and leaning over me pointing his finger. "Not a lost piece of luggage. Instead of wasting time and my ex-wife's money snooping around me, you should be out trying to find Alicia, you sorry freaking son-of-a-bitch."

"I'm trying to eliminate possibilities, Mister Rossi, and this was the quickest and easiest one to do away with. Now I can concentrate on the other 999 possibilities.

"You find my daughter, Lawless, or you'll wish you never heard of her."

"You don't have to threaten me, Rossi. I'm being paid to do a job and I'll fucking do it, but it won't be easy. She could be anywhere."

"Find her," he said softly, sitting down again, as if sorry for his outburst. "Despite what you may have heard or what you might think of me, I love my daughter very much. I'm sorry our divorce and separation was so hard on her, but she's better off with her mother. I tried to tell her that."

"Did she ask to come here to live with you?"

"Sure, plenty of times, but I always told her no. Can I get you something, a drink perhaps?"

Now that we were on speaking terms, I accepted.

"A Scotch on the rocks would be nice."

"Harry, get Mister Lawless here a Scotch on the rocks. Use my best bottle."

"Can you think of anyone who would want to take your daughter? Do you have any associates or enemies back in Boston who might benefit from her abduction?"

"Naw, you're barking up the wrong tree, Lawless. It's not a power play, nothing like that. Everything's quiet. Besides, I'm retired. I got no power. No one would gain any advantage by taking her. Besides, none of those cocksuckers would dare. I made them, all of them. No, there's something else going on, someone new in the neighborhood, the Russians. They're taking young women off the streets and selling them into sexual slavery in the Orient and Middle East."

"Do you know this for certain," I asked.

"No, but that's what I hear. Look, the people I know, they may not be the politest group of businessmen, and they may run a few rackets and things, but they're not into this white slavery stuff. We know our competitors, though. Sex is big business, but there's enough money to be made legally. Eighty percent of what we dealt with was legit. A little off-track betting on the side, cigarettes and booze, but nothing dirty like kidnapping for sex. These are young girls we're talking about.

"The word is that there is a new player in town, in the northeast. They specialize in the sort of thing we're talking about. Blame it on fucking Perestroika, I don't know, but it's all international. There's just as many Russians operating in the U.S. now as there are Sicilians or Italians. We're a minority in our own land."

"Join the club," I answered.

"So what are you going to do to find my daughter?" he asked.

I couldn't answer him, but told him I'd do something.

Chapter 14

I left for home early the next day. I had gone back to the lounge to look for my date, but she was nowhere to be found. She must have hurried home, embarrassed and sorry to have ever met me. I hoped she'd be on the return flight. I was about to leave and go back to my hotel when I heard someone shout my name.

"Hello, Mister Lawless!" It was the redhead from the sales office. "So, what do you think?" she asked coming over from the bar.

"Very nice. Like you said, it has everything, including an exciting nightlife."

"You should do a promo for us. I bet you'd look good in a blowup."

"Not as good as you'd look. You're not a model on the side, are you? If not, you should be."

"Why, thank you, Mister Lawless. Can I call you Jay?"

"Certainly, Miss Dubois, if I can call you Beverly."

"Jay, if you buy me a drink, you can call me anything you want."

That was the beginning of a wild night that didn't stop until the sun came up and I had to rush back to my hotel and pack for an early flight home. God, I love redheads. In my mind's eye I recalled the night. Her pretty face was pushed so close to mine all I could see was a long eyelash, freckled cheekbone, and a flaming halo of red hair.

Tony Rossi had left me with some disturbing information. His sources had fingered a Russian white-slaver, the worse of my fears. Tony Rossi turned out to have very good intelligence and gave me some excellent leads. Why not? The guy was a made man, and had plenty of connections and associates, if you know what I mean. I certainly didn't want to be on his bad side. That meant finding his daughter alive.

He had no info on a Captain Kelly, but said he'd find out what he could. I told him not to hurt the ex-astronaut. He had nothing to do with it.

The flight back to Boston was long and monotonous. I looked for Elisha but thought of Beverly. Even though the latter was on my mind, I wanted to talk to the former and apologize for the night before. It certainly couldn't have been a very pleasant evening for her. When we were only a half hour from Boston, one of the flight attendants came over to talk to me. They were done serving and I wondered what she could want. It was too soon to put my seat up.

"Are you Jay?" she asked with concern. She had blonde hair tied back and high cheek bones, with a face like Faye Dunaway's.

"Yes," I stammered, wondering how she knew my name.

"Elisha was so worried about you." She had bent down and was now leaning on my armrest, her face only inches from mine. "She was afraid those men were going to hurt you."

"They only wanted to talk. I'm afraid it must have upset her. I told her I'd be right back. I was hoping she was on the flight this morning so I could talk to her."

"Oh, she got married today."

She walked off before I could ask any more questions. The plane landed at Logan a few minutes later.

The leads on Alicia's computer email and the mysterious Captain Kelly became more important with the elimination of her father as a reason for her disappearance. I was also interested in her math and history teachers. Did either of them have a connection to the mysterious handle? Or did this have something to do with the Russian mob and human trafficking?

I got into Boston around noon and was home soon after that. Bud was in the apartment making a ham sandwich. He made one for me. It was Sunday. We talked.

"You have time for a lesson?" he asked.

"Sure," I said, pleased that he was finally interested in the Art. It certainly couldn't hurt him.

I found an old pair of sweat-pants that fit him and a t-shirt, and brought him downstairs to the basement where my little impromptu dojo was setup. I had missed my usual Saturday class and had called my students to invite them over as well. I informed them about the classes at the YMCA, and told them they were welcome to come by and help if they wanted to. I mentioned it might win them some brownie points with their sensei. They were all busy that morning. I promised to meet them in the park later that afternoon for tai chi.

I started Bud's lesson off with the stance.

"One of the most important things in the martial arts is the stance. It is the most basic of the basics, the fundamental secret to everything. A good stance leads to good balance. A strong, balanced stance leads to a powerful punch. Balance is the key."

I pulled my right foot back in a fighting stance and put my hands up.

"You want your feet about shoulder width apart. Not too close together and not too far apart. You can also have your feet parallel, side by side, in what we call a horse-stance. Keep your knees slightly bent. That's it, like that. There you go. Keep your feet parallel. Don't hold you heels in like that."

I gave him a slight shove in the chest and he fell backward a couple of steps.

"See, you need to keep the feet parallel for maximum balance, like you're on a track, straight-ahead. No, now you're standing pigeon-toed."

I grabbed his arm and tugged him lightly. He fell forward a few steps, again off balance.

"Here, push me," I said, standing in a classic horse-stance with my fists at my sides, elbows back. He gave me a hard shove, but couldn't budge me.

"See, it's all balance and center of gravity. If your feet are firmly placed, you will have balance and your punches will have power."

I threw out a hard, straight right, snapping my left elbow back for added power and emphasis.

"Then, if you step back with the right like this, or your left like this, you have an even more stable fighting stance. You can kick from these stances as well."

I threw out a front kick. My pant cuff made a snapping sound with the motion.

"Gee," he said. "Can you show me how to do that?"

"Of course. Stick with me, kid. I'll have you kicking and punching like Bruce Lee before you go back to the 'burgh'."

"Who's Bruce Lee?" he asked.

"Never mind," I answered.

We practiced some basics.

"What do you do when someone grabs you like this?" he asked. He grabbed me by the collar with both hands, making two fists under my chin.

"This," I answered. I swung a short right and left hook at his temples. "A guy grabbing you like that is at a big disadvantage. His hands are full holding your t-shirt and yours are free to smack him. You can't even block my punches while you hold me like that. No, when a guy grabs you like that, you own him. Nail him."

64

"What if you don't want to hurt him? Or if he's too big?"

"Well, the trick to defending against a grab like that, or any type of attack, is reaction time. If you react quick enough you can counter his move before he really gets hold of you. If he's real big and strong, a grown-up who has no business grabbing you like that, you might have to kick him to make him let go. You know, kick him in the shins or knee, or the groin. You can also try to duck out of it, like this. Here, grab me."

I got on my knees so he was bigger than me. He grabbed me by the collar and tried to push me back. I snaked my right hand over his left and under his right, and slapped it hard with my left, easily knocking his hands off. He stumbled sideways.

"See, you didn't have a good stance when you grabbed me."

I showed him the maneuver and let him practice it on me several times, until he was slapping my hands away even as I grabbed him. I showed him how to kick my shins to make me loosen my grip, then use the move to duck out of the hold.

"There, keep practicing that. You can go to the park with us this afternoon if you want. Here, I'll show you one more good trick. Use this if one of your friends grabs you and you want to make everyone laugh. Here, grab me."

He grabbed me by the collar as bullies do.

"Grab me hard," I said. Then I reached my opposite hand over his and grabbed his thumb with my thumb and forefinger. Pinching them together on his thumb joint, I slowly applied pressure. He yelped and let go."

"Ouch!" he cried.

"Here try it on me," I said, showing him how to reach over and grab my thumb with the opposite hand and squeeze the joint. The thumb joint is a weak spot, and even I, with larger, stronger hands, had to relent and let go.

"Ow! That's it. There you go. Now you've got a couple breaks for that hold. And remember, you can always punch the guy while he's busy holding your collar, but make sure you have a good, strong stance when you do."

"Good! Can Miss Sales come to the park with us?"

"I don't know. You'll have to ask her. I don't suppose you have her number, do you?"

"Sure," he said, taking out his phone.

"I'm not so sure it's a good idea for you to be calling her like that."

"It's OK. She gave me her number so I could call her when you got back."

"Well, what do you say you give me her number and let me call. You can erase it from your phone so you won't be bothering her."

"Ah, Dad, I'm not bothering her."

"Erase it. You don't want her to get into trouble for helping you, do you?"

"No."

"Well, than do it."

"OK, but let me transfer it to your phone first."

A second later her phone number appeared on my contact list.

"How'd you do that?" I asked.

"You show me how to kick like you and I'll show you how to program your phone."

"It's a deal," I agreed.

I called Judy and invited her to the impromptu class.

"We're getting together to do tai chi in the park," I informed her.

"Great," she replied.

"Are you still planning on coming to dinner this evening?" I asked. "Bud mentioned he invited you."

"Yes, if it's still OK. He said you were returning from a job in Florida. I hope everything went all right."

"Yep, everything is fine. Bud says you're helping him with his swimming."

"Yes, he's a great kid. He could be a good competitive swimmer some day if he works at it. He's got the perfect build for it."

I wasn't sure I liked her talking about my boy's body like that, and resisted the urge to say something about her body.

I told her the place and the time and hung up. A couple hours later I was at the park in my gi bottoms and t-shirt. While we waited for the others, I showed Bud the stretching exercises he'd have to learn to be able to throw effective kicks. He was complaining royally about trying to touch his toes from a sitting position, when the first of my students arrived.

Judy showed up a few minutes later, wearing white shorts and a tan, sleeveless t-shirt. She looked just fine. She joined us for the stretching exercises and turned out to be more limber than all of us. She and Bud watched as the group, a man and two women, went through the tai chi form together, but left for a walk around the park after watching for a short time. I have to admit, I was a bit miffed when my son took off with the girl I was interested in. I soon lost myself in the slow, strenuous movements of the exercise, however. They were back before the long Yang-style form was finished.

After tai chi I showed Bud a few more basics. Judy joined in for fun.

"Maybe I'll take up karate," she teased, throwing out a few front kicks, half jokingly. They were actually pretty good. She came up and snapped the kick out from a raised position as if she'd been trained. This girl had potential in all sorts of areas. Later that evening, after stopping home to her apartment, Judy came to the house for one of Mrs. Corrado's meatball and spaghetti specials.

I was impressed with Bud. All that day and into the evening he was a perfect, personable little gentleman. Despite all that I and Suzy had done wrong, he had turned out OK. Not that I can really blame Suzy for our problems. Despite running the insurance business and travel agency, she was home every evening to cook for us and put Bud to bed. I did my best to cover for her, doing the housework and babysitting during the day. Sometimes I took Bud with me to the grocery store or the Laundromat or on a stakeout. However much time I spent with him his first six years, we had trouble relating to each other. I couldn't engage him and he pretty much ignored me. Then I hardly saw him for the next six years of his life. In spite of this, he was turning out to be a decent human being. I thanked my lucky stars.

Somehow, during dessert, the conversation got around to my current case, the missing fifteen year old, Alicia Fleming-Rossi.

"What do you think happened to her?" asked Judy as I reluctantly told something of what occurred in Florida. I kept my fling with the redheaded office manager out of my narrative. We hadn't even started dating yet, and I was feeling guilty.

"I don't know," I confessed. "I'm following up some leads, some things I found on her computer and things her father mentioned. She could just be a runaway like thousands of others, on her way to New York City by now. It's a big world out there."

"What, Tony didn't finger one of his old cronies?" commented Mrs. Corrado.

"No, he didn't seem to think any of them were involved. Anyway, what would they have to gain?"

"Revenge," replied the old woman, with vigor.

"Tony told me he didn't have any enemies."

Rose laughed. "Maybe none that's alive, but he had enemies, plenty of them. Who knows, maybe one's still kicking."

Judy didn't know what to make of the conversation. Bud laughed.

"I've been worried lately," said Judy, with a thoughtful expression. "One of my girls hasn't shown up for class now for two weeks. When I called and asked her parents they said she was sick. I talked to her younger sister the other day. She said she hasn't seen Dominique in weeks, and that she's run away."

"Have you called the police?" I asked.

"No. I just found out. I didn't know what to do. Do you think you could help?"

"I don't know," I replied. I wanted desperately to get into this girl's good graces. "I have an obligation to my current client. You never know, maybe they're somehow connected. Let's talk about it Tuesday before class."

"OK," she said, smiling, and changed the subject to Bud and his swimming.

All that night as I lay in bed chasing an elusive night's sleep, I thought of Judy Sales. She was naked and glistening and pinned beneath me on a black satin sheet. Needless to say where that led – God, what a pathetic jerk I am.

Chapter 15

The following afternoon I took Bud to the Y so he could do some surfing on his computer. The other two desktops were occupied. I went down to the lobby hoping I'd bump into Judy. She wasn't around. So I talked to the bearded, overweight geek with the glasses who stood behind the desk. It turned out he taught the computer class at the Y.

"Do you know how to hack computers?" I asked in jest, thinking of my buddy John Rothburg back home.

"If I did I wouldn't tell you," he answered, chuckling.

"What about a handle? Can you find out where an email came from if it doesn't have the name of the sender?"

"You mean an anonymous message where there's no URL or email address with it?"

"Yeah. How would you go about finding out where it came from?"

"Well, first of all, there are dozens of web sites you can go to where you can send an anonymous email. People use them all the time for advertising or sending a complaint to the police department. Stuff like that. You can also create an anonymous account under an assumed name on aol-mail or gmail. In both cases, you'd need a police order or court warrant to find out who sent the message.

"You can do things like use aliases, set up web proxies, and employ phony screen names. There are hundreds of ways to send an email message without giving away who you are or where the message came from. There are even services that will take your email and send it off as instructed with no questions asked. Their whole business is built on protecting their clients' privacy."

"Great," I said, instantly discouraged.

"Why?" he inquired.

"Oh, nothing." I wasn't sure how much to tell the guy. I sure needed an ally with computer skills. "I have a friend whose daughter is missing. They've reported it to the police, but they haven't made much progress finding her. I noticed an email from someone on her computer that had an alias for an address. I was wondering if I could find out where it came from."

"That's doable. Do you have the computer?"

"No, but I can get it." I hoped I wasn't lying. It was time to talk to the ex-Mrs. Rossi again.

I was about to leave and pound the pavement around town with Alicia's picture when I caught sight of Judy out of the corner of my eye. She was just coming in.

"Hi," she said noticing me. "I was hoping I'd see you here today."

"Hi, Judy. I brought Bud over to work on his computer. I was hoping to see you as well. I, er, I really enjoyed talking to you last night."

"I had a wonderful time, Jay. I wanted to thank Bud again for inviting me over."

"He enjoyed himself too. He was on his best behavior. You should come over more often."

"I'd love to, but first I have to reciprocate and have you boys over to my place for dinner. Mrs. Corrado is invited too."

"Oh, you have a lot of confidence cooking for a master chef like Rose."

"I loved her cooking, but I would never try making Italian for her. I was thinking of stir-fried shrimp or something."

"That sounds delicious, although I'm not sure Mrs. Corrado is ready for that." We both laughed.

"I wanted to talk to you about Dominique, my student. I didn't want to wait until tomorrow. I don't think it would have been appropriate to talk about it last night in front of Bud. I'm afraid something has happened to her."

"What makes you say that?"

"When I called her mother, she told me Dominique was sick, but her sister says that's not true. They have a bad home life. The mother lives with a younger man who the sister says drinks and yells at them. She said the night before her sister disappeared, she had a fight with her mother's boyfriend. The mother had to restrain him from hitting her."

"That's not good."

"Do you think you can find out what happened to her?"

"I don't know. Did you tell the police this?"

"No, not yet. I don't want to get anyone in trouble."

"If the girl's in danger…"

"I know, but, well, it's not something I want to accuse someone of lightly. I thought perhaps you could, er, you might…"

"What? Snoop around?"

"Yeah, something like that. That's what you do, right, as a private detective?"

"More or less. Yes, I'm a snoop."

She gave me the address and the family's name. I told her I'd check it out that very day, although I wasn't reassured when I read the Roxbury location. A white dude snooping around asking questions there could get in a lot of trouble real fast. I wasn't even getting paid. If it meant being helpful to a beautiful woman like Judy Sales, however, I was all for it.

I drove down Mass Ave to the address Judy gave me, toward Dudley Station. Pulling into a parking garage, I tried to be as inconspicuous as possible. As anyone who reads Sherlock Homes knows, part of being a good detective is being able to make a good disguise. I couldn't change my race, although I got pretty dark in the days before I was terrified of the sun. I could, however, morph into a bookish school official. Judy thought Dominique went to school at Boston Latin, so that's where I'd tell them I was from.

I wore my hair slicked back with a pair of black-rimmed glasses, a la Clark Kent. I had whitened my hair at the temples with talcum powder. This, together with my dark, wrinkled winter suit, made me look like an underpaid, middle-aged school administrator or a cop. I hoped the getup would give me the space to do what I needed to do.

"Hello, Miss Devereux," I said on finding the apartment and knocking on the door. "I'm from your daughter, Dominique's, school. She hasn't been in class for some time and didn't graduate."

"Yes, she's been sick," answered the woman, keeping the door open as little as possible. "I told that to the woman from her school who called last week."

"Yes, I know, but, well, we have to check up on her, make sure she's OK. Will she be coming back to school in the fall? She'll have to repeat the grade unless she goes to summer school."

"I don't know. When she's well, I suppose."

"Can I see her?" I asked.

"No, she's resting."

"Well, can I come in and talk? I have some questions I need to ask you about her. Has she seen a doctor?"

"Who's that, Stephanie?" said someone from behind the door.

"Someone from Domi's school."

"Well, tell him to go away."

"I have to go," the woman told me with a resigned look. "She has mono. She'll be back to school when she's better."

"Maybe we can arrange to bring her make up work to her," I replied, trying to stall for time.

"Where did you say you were from?" said the boyfriend. He stepped in front of the woman, crowding her away from the door. He was big and well-muscled and looked young enough to be her son.

"I'm from Dominique's school," I lied again, "Boston Latin."

"Dominique doesn't go to Latin," her mother informed us.

"Who the hell are you?" demanded the man, storming into the hallway fists at the ready.

"I'm a friend of her teacher. I'm trying to find out what happened to..."

The youth threw a right at me as I tried to finish the sentence. I put up a left and blocked the blow, knocking him off balance - so much for his stance. He looked surprised, and came at me again with another clumsy right.

Standing my ground, I drove the blade of my hand into his nose with the same motion I used to block the strike. The blow knocked his head back. His nose began to bleed. Before he could recover, I drove him back through the open door of their apartment with a quick series of hand strikes to his face, neck, and midsection. Once inside, I leg-hawked him to the ground, bouncing his head off the floor. Obviously, no one had taught him how to fall. As a matter of fact, no one had taught him much of anything.

I dropped a quarter-power knee onto his chest and forced the last bit of air out of his lungs. The woman screamed and ran at me.

"Hold it!" I yelled, "Unless you want me to crush your boyfriend's sternum you better back off."

She stopped and held her hands up to her head.

"I just want to ask you some questions," I told them. "I don't want to cause any trouble."

I pulled the boyfriend to his feet and shoved him into a chair. He didn't look so big now, trying to catch his breath and sniveling.

"Sit down!" I ordered the girl.

"I'm going to call the police," she replied, looking at the phone on the kitchen table.

"Go ahead," I said. "Maybe you'd like to tell them what happened to your daughter."

"I didn't do anything to her," insisted the boyfriend.

"Her sister said you had a bad argument with her before she disappeared."

"She was being disrespectful to her mother. We argued, that's all. She needed to learn some respect. I didn't lay a hand on her. That's not my style."

"I saw your style and I'm not impressed," I commented. "Her sister said you had to be restrained from hitting her."

"The little brat's lying," he replied. "I swear, I didn't lay a hand on her."

"That's the truth," the woman confirmed. She hadn't gone for the phone nor had she sat down. "Dominique left for school the next morning and never came home."

"Why didn't you call the police?"

"She's stayed out all night before. That's what she and Roy were arguing about. She was getting out of control."

"Why did you lie to her teacher and say she was sick? That doesn't do much for your credibility."

"We were afraid they'd think Roy did something to her," confessed the mother. "He has a record."

I wanted to say, 'You really know how to pick them.' Instead, I asked her if they'd heard anything from the girl since she left or knew where she might have gone. Before they could answer, there was a knock on the door.

"Stephanie, are you all right?" a voice asked. "What's going on in there?"

"Help!" she yelled. "There's a guy in here attacked Roy."

Just then a large black man burst into the room with two of his homeboys close behind him. He was short but wide and had a bat, which he proceeded to swing at my head.

I had jumped up when they came into the room. Grabbing my chair, I swung it up to block the strike. The bat thudded against the wooden seat a few inches from my head. As it did, I drove the ball of my foot into the big man's groin as hard as I could. He wasn't wearing a cup. As he doubled over in pain, I brought the chair down on his head. He was out for the count, but one of his buddies flew into me like a linebacker.

I went with it and rolled back on my heels. As I fell, I thrust my foot into his gut. Using his forward momentum, I threw him up and over my head. It was a move I had perfected long before learning the martial arts. He landed headfirst into a cabinet, dazed.

73

The third assailant was on me now, trying to kick me while I was down. I curled into a snake position. Spinning myself around with my legs like a crab, I kept him at bay with my feet. Noticing the baseball bat lying near me, I grabbed it and cracked it against his knee. He yelped in pain. I hit him in the knee again. He bent to grab his legs. I smacked the bat against the side of his head. He went down without another sound.

As I was fighting the intruders, Roy, the boyfriend, had grabbed a kitchen knife. He circled around the kitchen table toward me. I was still on my back. He jabbed the knife at me. I kicked the chair in his way and jumped to my feet. Without hesitating, I flew at him, swinging the bat in front of me, right, left, right, left, like a windmill. I hit him on the collar bone and head in succession. The blows were delivered so fast the bat was a blur. The first strike knocked the knife out of his hand. The last one left him bleeding unconscious on the kitchen floor. His girlfriend went to him screaming at me.

By this time there was an infuriated mob at the apartment door. Here was some honky in the hood, beating up 'brothers'. This crowd was thirsting for blood - mine. Several of them stood around the entrance glaring at me with deadly intentions. Seeing what had happened to the first four, however, had given them some pause. No one wanted to make the first move. I knew someone would show up sooner or later and start popping lead at me. I had to think fast.

I looked around the apartment. Two of my attackers were starting to wake up. Maybe I could grab one of them and hold them as a shield, threaten to break their neck if the mob attacked me. I calculated the odds of that working and thought better of it. It would have been chancy even if I had a gun. In any case, I made it a rule never to make threats that I don't actually want to carry out. I wasn't about to break that rule now.

One of the kitchen windows gave out onto a fire escape. The largest of the mob was making his move and coming through the door. I darted at him, moving so fast he didn't have time to react. My running at him was probably the last thing he expected.

Holding out his arms, he braced for impact. He was big, but his feet were too close together. He was already back on his heels when I hit him with a flying-thrust kick. The unexpected blow sent him stumbling backward through the doorway into the guys behind him. They went sprawling onto the hallway floor.

I quickly shut and locked the door, chaining it for good measure. A couple of my attackers were coming to. They got to their feet groggily. None of them attempted to stop me as I ran to the window and got out onto the fire escape.

I made it to the back alley with no problem and dropped the last few feet to the ground. Looking left and right, I decided to take the long way back to my car. I ditched the bat behind some trash cans. It was getting dark and starting to rain.

I made my way back to the parking garage under the cover of darkness using a roundabout route. There were still angry black men milling about, but I was able to get to my car without being seen. As I was leaving the parking garage someone spotted me. Several of them ran after me. One guy slapped my car as I sped past. Another threw a bottle after me. Soon, however, I was driving back up Mass Avenue and out of Roxbury.

It had not been a particularly successful operation. I wasn't sure what I expected or what I had learned. I was lucky to get out of there in one piece. While that punk Roy was nasty and dumb enough, I doubted he had done anything to his girlfriend's daughter. It was more likely that she had gotten fed up with the situation at home and bolted, like I hoped my Alicia had done. Still, there was a distinct possibility he knew more than he was telling.

.

Chapter 16

I went back to the Y to pick up Bud after his swimming class. I was early so I stopped by the pool where he was finishing his laps. He was cutting through the water like a dolphin. He moved with long, deep strokes, his feet kicking strenuously, churning up a small wake behind him. He only turned his head up on every third or forth stroke, keeping it submerged for maximum speed.

When he reached the end of the pool, he ducked under and spun around, kicking the wall expertly to push himself off. I couldn't believe it was my kid. There were others swimming with him, but he had easily outdistanced them. I could barely keep myself afloat in the water. Even though I was in good shape, I could not propel myself at any speed for long without getting winded. And I had to keep my head high out of the water the whole time. I had no idea he had such talent. Every now and then Judy would shout out a word of encouragement or instruction.

"That's pretty good," I told him as he came out of the water. "You look like an Olympian."

"He's not *that* fast," observed Judy, coming up and showing him her stopwatch. "But if he keeps working hard, he might make the team in high school."

"I wish I had someone like you back home to work with," he said, taking a towel and drying off.

"There's no one up there who can teach you?" I asked. "What about at the college."

"Not like Miss Sales," replied Bud. "The coaches at the college are too busy and want money for training you. Mom can't afford that."

"Have you talked to your mom recently?" I asked.

"No," he answered. "She's on her honeymoon, remember? She's busy."

"Too busy to talk to you?" I objected. Even if we *had* been divorced for five years, I was having trouble coming to terms with my wife on a honeymoon with someone else. Remarrying was so final. I just couldn't get my head around it. Not that I thought we'd ever get back together.

"She said she was going to call me Sunday. She must have been busy."

"Well, it's not right that she doesn't call you," I said. I seldom got the moral high ground where Suzy was concerned.

"Look who's talking," he responded, giving me a look. "You never call me. You're just peeved because she got married again."

"Well, can you blame me?"

As Bud changed up, I talked to Judy about her missing student. I enjoyed looking at her in a bathing suit. She didn't seem to mind. She was slim and athletic, strong but delicate at the same time, with a great figure.

"You were right about your student's home life," I told her. I recounted my encounter with Miss Devereux and her boyfriend, leaving out the fisticuffs. "It's pretty bad. The boyfriend is a nasty character, though I don't think he did anything to her. We had a nice man to man talk. He convinced me he hadn't touched her. He admitted to the argument, but said she was getting wild lately. He was only trying to help her mother out with her. Though for my money, he has no business getting involved with those kids. They said she ran away soon after that."

"Why didn't they contact the police? Why did they lie to me?"

"Seems the guy has a record. They were afraid the cops would think he'd done something to her. It wasn't the first time she had run away. I'll wager it's not the first time he's been involved in some kind of domestic abuse either."

"I think we should report this to the police," she stated.

"That's probably a good idea. I'll go with you if you want."

"Thanks, Jay. That would be great if you could."

"Sure," I said. "No problem."

About the last place in the world I wanted to be was the police station. However, if it made me look good in Judy's eyes, it was worth it. I was starting to like her. Standing there, talking to me in her bathing suit certainly didn't hurt her case.

I dropped Bud off at the apartment. Then I took Judy to the 1st precinct and helped her fill out a missing person's report. We were adamant in our opinion that the current situation at the home was not good. We also suggested the boyfriend should be questioned about the girl's disappearance.

We were about to leave when the captain came out of his office in a screaming hissy fit.

"Lawless!" he yelled. "What the hell did I tell you about busting people up in my town?"

"Hi, Captain. What are you yelling about? I haven't done anything," I lied, wondering how he found out about it.

"There was almost a riot in Roxbury today. You match the description of the troublemaker. The whole thing fits your MO to a T, Lawless. Four big, strong men beaten up by a karate master - kicking and punching, real kung fu boxing. Where were you between three and five this afternoon?"

"I'm not sure," I replied. "I'll have to check my appointment book."

"Don't get wise with me, dumb ass. I have a good mind to lock you up."

"Honest, Captain, I don't know what you're talking about. I was pounding the pavement, looking for that missing girl. I wasn't anywhere near Roxbury."

"Well, that's pretty strange, because you and your friend just filled out a missing person report for Dominique Devereux. She just happens to live at the address where they had the trouble this afternoon. Now do you want to tell me what's going on or do you want me to throw your ass in jail?"

I looked at Judy with an apologetic expression.

"I should have told you. I had a little trouble this afternoon checking out your student. I was helping Miss Sales here," I explained, turning back to the captain. "One of her students has been missing for over two weeks now. When she called and asked about her, the girl's mother said she was sick. She apparently said the same thing to the school. Judy here was worried about her. The girl's sister told her she hadn't seen her in weeks and that she'd had a fight with her mother's boyfriend."

"So you decided to go over and break heads," said the Captain.

"I only asked how the girl was and if I could see her."

"They said you told them you were from the school."

"I had to tell them something. The guy became belligerent and took a couple pokes at me. I didn't hurt him. I was just talking to them when these other three 'turkeys' busted in."

"That's not how we heard it. You broke some guy's collarbone! Anyway, what did you expect? A honky like you showing up in their neighborhood asking questions and lying is bound to start trouble. I would have tried to crack your head if you came to my house like that. You're a troublemaker, Lawless, and I don't want you beating up any more people in my town, you got that?"

"He was only trying to help me find this girl," said Judy showing him Dominique's picture. "I'm afraid something terrible has happened to her."

"Don't worry, Miss Sales," replied the captain, who seemed to have learned a lot in a very short time. "It's a police matter now. We'll take care of it. You better just be careful who you associate with. This guy's nothing but trouble.

He turned to me.

"I have a good mind to take your license. You can go for now, Lawless, but if I so much as hear about someone throwing a karate chop in my precinct, I'm taking you in and booking your ass. Now get out of here!"

"What happened?" asked Judy after we had left the police station.

"How far back do you want me to go?" I answered, embarrassed and in a sour mood.

"Just today would be good," she responded.

I should have simply done what she requested. For some dumb reason, I decided to tell her the whole miserable story of my life. From beginning to end, I recounted the entire sorry tale, starting with being thrown out of college. I told her about the knife-wielding maniac and the plot to bomb Washington, DC. I told her about the terrorist cell intent on blowing up the World Trade Center. I told her of the string of corpses I left behind me in my small hometown. I even included the recent brawl in the Boston strip club. Finally, I told her about the mayhem in the Devereux apartment. When I was done, she stared at me silently.

As I talked, we drove over the Mystic Bridge. The lights of the buildings and the boats below us twinkled like bright gems. We were now heading north on Route 1, past one restaurant or strip mall after another.

"Were you hurt?" she asked finally, as we passed a restaurant that looked like a ship.

"No," I said. "I was lucky."

"Do people have to be taken to the hospital after getting into a fight with you?"

"That depends how scared I get."

"How scared were you today?"

"Pretty scared," I admitted.

"I'd never want to make you scared," she said, looking at me with the same look the people in my hometown looked at me - like I was some kind of freak. I guess I am, a freak of stinking nature, a monster who should be caged, a poster boy for what not to become.

Judy was right to be worried about her student. It was a bad situation for a young girl to be living in, but it was a matter for the police now.

"You want to stop and get something to eat?" she asked.

"Sure," I answered. "I'm starved."

"Do you like prime rib?"

"Love it."

She told me to turn around and head back down Route 1 toward Boston. When a large neon cactus sign came into view, she told me to pull in and park.

We didn't talk much during dinner. She had a lot to digest and it wasn't all meat.

During what little conversation we did have, I asked her something that was on my mind.

"I thought you said Dominique went to Boston Latin? Everything went downhill when I mentioned that."

"Oh, I'm sorry. I was mistaken. Her sister said she goes to Charlestown High School"

"What? They send her all the way across town to school?"

"Yes. It's the legacy of forty years of forced busing, the desegregation of the Boston School system."

"That's funny," I said, feeling a jolt of adrenaline. "That's the same school Alicia Rossi went to."

Chapter 17

I finally had a significant break in the case. Alicia and Dominique, the two missing girls, went to the same high school. There was a definite connection between them. I had to find the missing link. Was it the mysterious Captain Kelly, the man with all the helpful advice on breaking into the modeling business? Too bad I had burnt my bridges in Roxbury. I would have liked to talk to Dominique's mother again. I'd have to leave that to the police. I would have helped them if the captain wasn't such an a-hole. Now, I was one step ahead of them. I wondered how many steps I was behind Alicia.

The following morning I called the school and asked to speak to the principal. She remembered me and asked if I had any information on the missing student, Alicia Fleming. I said no and mentioned Dominique's name, only to be informed she was out sick.

"Mono, I believe," said the school administrator.

"We have reason to believe she's actually missing," I informed her. "Her younger sister hasn't seen her for several weeks. The police are investigating."

"Oh, that's terrible," she responded.

"I wonder if I could speak to Alicia's math and history teachers," I inquired.

"You don't think it's one of them, do you?" she replied in alarm.

"I'm not even sure anyone has abducted them. They could both have simply run away. Heaven knows their home lives were bad enough. I'm simply trying to find out more about the two girls. Did they have anything in common? Could they have gone off together? I'm just trying to connect as many dots as I can."

"I suppose that's what you type of people do," she commented. The way she said, 'You type of people,' had a distinct edge of contempt attached to it.

"Did the two girls have any classes together?"

"Let me check," she said. I waited a few minutes until she came back on the line.

"They were both in Mister Sullivan's math class, although at different times."

"Can I talk to Mister Sullivan?"

"Mister Sullivan is no longer with the school," she informed me. "He's moved out of the state."

"When?" I asked, rather too vehemently. My suspicions rose.

"Just last week. He told us he had family business to attend to. His father had just died."

The news made my heart beat fast, as if the man was in sight and I was chasing him.

She gave me Sullivan's address in New Jersey. I hung up a short time later, after making an appointment to see Alicia's history teacher later in the week.

The fact that Mister Sullivan, the math teacher, had left town shortly after the disappearance of the two high school girls, both of whom were in his class, was definitely suspicious, at least to my mind. I wondered if the address he left was even real or worth a trip to New Jersey. More than likely it was an abandoned warehouse. Even if it was legit, what were the chances the math teacher would actually be there? If he was, would that eliminate him as a suspect? Maybe, if I had a chance to question him. And that was the idea, wasn't it? Eliminate each possibility until the real reason for their disappearance was the only one left.

"You look lost in thought," said Bud, coming into the kitchen where I was sitting at the table with my new phone. "What's wrong, your big case got you stumped?"

"Yeah, Mister Wiseacre. It's one big puzzle where none of the pieces fit."

"You're so backward I'm surprised you could solve anything. You need to get with the times. Get a computer or something."

"I've solved a few tough cases in my time," I bragged. "And I did it the good old-fashioned way. I pounded the pavement and talked to people. I didn't need a frigging computer. You're not going to solve a crime or find a runaway girl by sitting on your ass behind a computer."

"That's what you know," said my twelve-year-old son.

"OK, Mister Know-It-All. How would you find an address - see if it's bogus or not?"

"Ah, that's easy," he answered. "Take me down to the Y and I'll show you."

A half hour later I was standing over Bud as he logged into his computer and connected by WIFI to the internet. A second after that he was surfing the web, using the mouse like a boogie-board.

"You can get directions to almost anywhere you want using MapQuest," he told me. "But I like Google Map better. You can find any address in the world."

"I know that. John Rothburg showed me. Try New Jersey." I gave him the address I had obtained from Alicia's school. "Newark, on Spruce Street."

He entered the address and hit the search button. A map was instantaneously displayed of the eastern part of New Jersey, with a pink balloon over Newark. He clicked the mouse on an icon and the map began to grow, zooming in on the street. He grabbed the image and moved it up and down and to the side as he magnified it. He did this until the whole screen was taken up with Spruce Street. The balloon hovered over the address we had entered.

"Well, it looks like the place exists," I observed. "It's a real address."

"Yep," Bud replied. "Look at this."

He clicked another part of the display. The screen went blank for a moment. Then it reappeared with a picture of the street as if taken from a helicopter flying over the city.

"This is a satellite view of the same street we were looking at before," he informed me. "Look, you can see the houses and cars even."

"Cool," I said, mesmerized by the picture. "It's like we're flying over the place in a balloon."

"Exactly," he answered, maneuvering the image with the mouse to move along the street as if we were flying. "There's the place. Looks like an apartment complex of some kind."

"Yeah, looks like townhouses. Some place."

It looked like the whole area was made up of apartment buildings and blocks of townhouses. Now that I knew the address was real, I had to decide what to do about it.

"Can you look up a name using the address?" I inquired.

"Sure," replied Bud. Going back to the main Google page, he typed in the address. A list of names and addresses appeared as if in a phone book. The one with ours said Mr. and Mrs. John Sullivan of 5612 Spruce Street in Newark, New Jersey. The dates of birth, which Bud was also able to lookup, indicated they were both in their sixties.

"That must be his parents" I surmised. "Maybe this guy's on the level after all."

"What?" said Bud, looking over his shoulder.

"Nothing. Looks like I'll have to make another trip."

After leaving Bud at the library for his swimming class, I called Mrs. Fleming and brought her up to date. I told her I had a lead and had to go to New Jersey to check it out.

"You know what happened to Alicia?" she asked. I could hear the growing hope and spent tears in her voice.

"No, but I'm trying to eliminate the possibilities. One of her teachers has left the school recently. He may have also taught another girl who's gone missing. I need to check him out."

"Have you told the police? Maybe they should know."

"They'll be the first ones I talk to if I find the guy. It may be a dead-end, but even that would tell us something. Anyway, I'll need more money."

"Anything," she said. "Just find my little girl."

"I'm trying. By the way, have you thought about what I asked you? Can I have Alicia's computer? There may be some information on it that can help us. I want to have it analyzed, see if I can find out who was emailing your daughter."

There was a dead silence on the other end of the line.

"I don't know," she said finally. "I don't see what good that can do. You said you had a lead. What do you need the computer for?"

"So far all I've got are some vague hunches, just a bunch of unconnected facts. I need to tie them together. Alicia's emails may be the key."

"OK, if you think it's necessary. You can pick it up when you come over for the check."

I stopped at the Fleming house later that afternoon to pick up the check and the computer. I dropped off the latter at the Y, with the techno-geek I had talked to earlier. I met Bud there, as well as Judy Sales, who said hi and smiled sweetly as we left. I told her briefly about what I was up to. She wished me luck.

Mrs. Fleming had shelled out $1500 with little to show for it, except the certainty her ex-husband did not have her daughter. That gave her some consolation, but now she was more worried than ever about Alicia.

"You've got to find her," were her last words to me. I told her that I would give it another week.

"It will cost you an additional $500 bucks with expenses, $2200 total. After that, it will be on the house until I find her."

She thanked me and said she hoped I would find Alicia before that.

"So do I," I replied.

Chapter 18

I decided to drive to New Jersey that evening and arrive early in the morning. That way I could avoid the traffic and get the lay of the land. I went to bed soon after bringing Bud home, after a quick sandwich, around seven. I woke up about midnight. Finding my way in the dark, I stole from the house a half hour later. Bud had used the computer to mark the route on a map for me.

I started out on the Mass Turnpike heading west with a full thermos of hot coffee and a couple sandwiches Mrs. Corrado had made for me. After about an hour, I merged on to I-84 West toward Hartford. The roads were devoid of traffic, except for the trucks and an occasional car.

I made good time. After another forty minutes, I merged on to 91 and continued south toward New Haven. At that point I followed 91 and then 691 West toward New York. I crossed into New York State on Route 84 then followed 684 to Mill River Parkway, and then to the Garden State Parkway. At Route 46 I took a left toward Clifton. Following my directions, I took a few more lefts and rights and reached my destination around 4:30 a.m.

I was in a neighborhood of apartment complexes and townhouses, just like I had seen on the computer. I felt right at home. Finding a spot in a parking area of a large apartment complex, I surveyed the townhouses across the street. My eyes were heavy despite the gallon of coffee I had drunk. I could barely keep them open. I got out and walked around the block, reconnoitering the area.

It all seemed normal. Nothing was out of place. More than likely, the math teacher's story was on the level. He had gone home to help bury his dead father. I made a point to check the local obituaries. I got back to my car just as the sun was coming up and despite my best efforts, fell asleep almost instantly.

I must be getting old, because I've never fallen asleep during a stakeout before. Although there were a few times it would have been better if I had. I woke up some time shortly after eight a.m. feeling like I had let my best friend down. I was disoriented and for some reason out of sorts, like I had just blown the case. Of course, none of this was true. Nothing had happened while I slept except the newspapers had been delivered. I picked one up and read the obits. There was no mention of a Mister Sullivan passing away. However, that could have been old news. I decided to see for myself.

Leaving the car, I crossed the busy street to the Sullivan residence. It was the third townhouse on the left of a seven-family complex. There were flowers planted in front of it and along the walk, which distinguished it from the rest of the nondescript apartments.

I rang the bell and waited.

I was about to leave after ringing it two more times with no reply, when a small woman with gray-black hair and sharp features opened the door. She was bent and thin. She looked at me with a haggard expression.

"Hello," I said. "My name is Jerry LeGrande."

I hadn't given much thought to what I was going to say, but I wasn't about to give her my real name. At the last moment, I thought of my late friend, the ex-police chief in my hometown. I flashed my special New York State deputy sheriff's badge. It was more an honorary gift than a real sign of authority, but it came in handy when I had to show something flashy and official looking. She hardly looked at it, but eyed me suspiciously.

"Is this the Sullivan residence?"

"That's what it says on the door. What do you want?" she asked. "My husband's dead and buried. So if it's him you want, you're too late."

"I'm sorry to hear that," I replied. So far it looked like Alicia's teacher was telling the truth. "I wanted to talk to your son, Phil Sullivan. I want to ask him some questions about one of his students. She's missing. He gave this as his address when he left the school a few weeks ago."

The woman stared at me as if I had just told her she had an incurable disease. It looked like she was in a state of shock.

"Phil Sullivan is your son?" I asked, not sure I had gotten it right.

"He was," she said, tears welling up in her eyes. "He's dead. He's been dead three years now. What kind of cruel joke is this, Mister LeGrande?"

For a second I didn't recognize my cover name. I was in a state of shock myself at the revelation.

"No joke at all, Mrs. Sullivan," I replied, suddenly realizing the obvious. "Someone appears to be using your son's name. Can I come in?"

I felt bad for the old woman. She had recently lost her husband and was now alone in the world. The one person that might have been a comfort to her in her old age and widowhood had died three years before in an altercation.

"Phil wasn't the type of person who would get into fights," she told me.

But the other driver, who he apparently cut off, shot him anyway, and that was the end of it. They never did find the man who did it. She told me she believed the death of her son was responsible for her husband's sickness and death. She had watched him waste away with grief since that day he was told about their son's murder. There was nothing I could do but give my condolences, as I tried to find out as much as I could about the real Phil Sullivan.

I asked her if her son had any friends or acquaintances, anyone she could think of, who might want to assume his identity. She said no, just normal people who all still lived around the neighborhood. She showed me pictures of her deceased son. He bore a vague resemblance to the picture of the missing math teacher I had seen when I looked up his name on the web.

I left her place and drove back to Boston. My mind was abuzz with competing thoughts. All of a sudden, the math teacher, whatever his name was, had become a prime suspect. The guy had a connection with two missing young women. Why would he suddenly leave the school? And why would he assume a false name and address, unless he had something to hide? Two young girls maybe?

I got back to Boston around 4:00 p.m., exhausted, hungry, and sore. Other than a very disappointing hamburger somewhere on the highway between New York and Boston, I hadn't had a thing to eat all day. It would take a week to recover from my red-eye to New Jersey. I had found out a lot, however. Like the fact that Mister Phil Sullivan was not who he pretended to be. I promised myself I'd visit the captain and the 1st precinct, but not before I did some more snooping on my own.

I woke up around seven to the sound of a sitcom on TV. Bud was watching it from the kitchen as he heated up some soup. He had gotten home late, having gone out with some friends. I tried to engage him in conversation, but got the distinct impression he was trying to evade me. I wondered if I had done something to piss him off. Then I recalled I had forgotten to call him until I was almost back in Boston. He hadn't answered.

"Where'd you go today?" I asked as I grabbed a cup of soup and joined him at the table. I had forgotten what he had told me. I had been preoccupied of late. I knew it would only get worse the closer I got to the missing girls. I began to doubt whether I could work and take care of Bud at the same time.

"Nowhere," he responded, moving from the table to the couch with his bowl.

I followed him and sat down in a chair by the lamp, which I switched on. I tried to talk to him, but sensed he was trying to avoid me. He wasn't very communicable. I persisted, trying to make up for the last forty-eight hours of neglect. It was then I noticed the black eye and bruised cheek.

"What happened?" I asked, concerned. "Are you hurt?"

"Naw, it's nothing. Just had a little scuffle at the Y. Nothing serious."

"Fighting is serious, especially at the Y. What happened?" I repeated. I checked his eye and cheek under the light. "At least your eye's not swollen. You'll be OK. Who started it?"

"I don't want to talk about it," he insisted, getting up and going back to the table. I followed him.

"Well, I do, so start talking. What happened?"

"I was minding my own business, standing with some friends after my swimming class. We were all going to the show. There's this older kid. He thinks he's tough. He was making fun of me. Said I had a crush on the swimming teacher. One of the kids told him he'd better watch out, my father taught the karate class. Then he started teasing me, calling me the karate kid and doing punches and kicks at me. Then he punched me in the eye and pushed me down. That's how I scraped my cheek."

"How old is this boy?" I asked, my protective dander up.

"I don't know. Fifteen or sixteen, I guess. He's a big kid. Everyone's afraid of him."

"Well, you stay away from him. I'll talk to the people down there and see if they can't provide some adult supervision in that place."

"I told you, don't worry about it. It's no big thing."

"Just stay out of that bully's way. He'll get his. You're at a disadvantage right now while you're learning a new way of fighting."

"I didn't know that much to begin with," he said. "That's why I wanted to study with you."

89

"Just take one thing at a time and do what I teach you, and you'll be able to take care of that kid. But even then, I want you to stay away from him. I don't want you fighting, got that?"

"Look who's talking," he replied, as I should have known he would. "You fight all the time and you're a grown man."

"No I don't," I lied. "Who told you that?"

"Miss Sales for one. And Mom."

"Well, I don't want you talking to Miss Sales about me. It's not right."

"Neither is you telling me not to fight when you do it all the time."

"Do as I say, not as I do. I thought you said you didn't want to end up like me."

"I don't." he said.

"You're just like me."

"No I'm not!" he insisted. I was surprised how angry he sounded.

"Yes, you are. If you get into fights, you are."

"Shit!" he swore, shocking me into silence. He slammed his fist down on the table and stomped off to the couch, where he threw himself down. "I'm sick of taking orders from everybody. Why doesn't everyone just leave me alone?"

"I'll leave you alone. Losing is nothing to be embarrassed about, you know. I've lost plenty of fights. You pick yourself up, learn from you mistakes, and carry on. A really tough guy avoids fights because he has nothing to prove."

Bud turned up the TV to drown me out. I went downstairs to Mrs. Corrado's to catch up on the latest gossip and get some parental advice. I don't know what I would have done without that woman's help and sound guidance.

Chapter 19

The following day I went to the math teacher's old apartment. It was in Charlestown not far from Alicia's house. There was a 'For Rent' sign in the window. I rang the bell and asked the landlord about the room. She showed it to me and told me how much the rent was. It was a one bedroom, with a view of the street from the second floor. It was furnished and had a kitchenette, much like my place in the North End.

The landlord told me the old tenant, a school teacher at the high school, had left suddenly. He had broken his lease and she hadn't been able to rent the place yet. He didn't leave a forwarding address.

As she showed me around the apartment, I noticed a box of papers. They were old receipts and things that had apparently been left by the previous tenant. I pretended to check out the bedroom closets a second time, while the landlord waited by the door. In this way, I was able to snatch some old bank statements and bills from the box. Through these, I determined the name and address of Sullivan's bank.

I went back to my apartment and changed into my heavy, old blue suit. Then I headed to the mystery man's bank and asked the manager for assistance.

"Hi, my name's Jerry LaGrande. I'm investigating a case for State Farm Insurance." I showed her a card Bud made up for me at the Y that said as much. She looked at it and me doubtfully.

"How can I help you?" she inquired smiling.

"We believe that a Mister Phil Sullivan has an account with your bank. He's recently received a large sum from the company I represent. We have reason to believe his claim is fraudulent. The address he left appears to be false. We may need to have his account frozen."

"I'm afraid we can't do that," she replied. "We would have to get a court order for that."

"Of course, I understand. My company wants to avoid any unnecessary publicity. I'm sure your bank does as well. We do these things discreetly. Does Mister Sullivan have an account with your bank?"

"Let me find out," said the manager, checking her computer screen.

"That account has been closed, I'm afraid," she informed me after a few moments. "All the funds were withdrawn two weeks ago."

"Did he leave a forwarding address?"

"No, I'm afraid not. However, he still has a safety deposit box with us. There's a P.O. box here in Boston associated with it."

She gave me the box number. Now all I had to do was find the post office branch.

Leaving the bank, I picked Bud up at the Y. While I was there I talked to the computer geek who had Alicia's laptop. He told me the sender was anonymous.

"We'd need a warrant to find out who it is. They went through a lot of effort and expense to cover their tracks."

"It doesn't matter," I told him as I took the computer and left.

As we drove back to the apartment, I asked Bud a question.

"How do you find a post office, given a P.O. number?"

"It'll cost you," he announced.

"What?" I said, not sure I heard him correctly.

"It will cost you. What do you think, you can just use my services for nothing? It will cost you ten bucks an hour and that's cheap."

"OK, that's just about half of what I charge for private lessons. You owe me ten."

"That's not fair. You never said anything about charging me."

"Whoever said life was fair."

"OK, I want another lesson then. My price just went up."

We got home and suited up. It was my regular group night. The others soon showed up as well, but until they did, I worked with Bud one on one.

"The best way to fight is to not get hit. The best way not to get hit is to learn to block and counter. Here, throw a punch at me like I taught you. There, get into your stance, left leg forward. Spread your legs more. Bend your knees slightly. There you go. Now get your hands up in a fighting position. That's it, now step forward with your right. Good. Now do it again, a little harder."

He came at me with a right punch at my head. I stepped in with my left and slowly blocked it away, countering with a soft right to his nose, which I pulled inches before hitting him.

"See, block the punch and counter with your own. You try it."

We got into our stances. I came at him with a straight right to his midsection. He stepped in and blocked it, countering just like I showed him, and almost hit me.

"Watch your control. When you're working with another person at first, you need to go slow and only show the punch. You don't try to actually hit them or you won't have many punching partners. Once you show control, we can speed it up."

I had him do it again, slower.

"That's the idea. Now you know how to block a punch and counter. It seems simple, but a good fighter can counter off almost anything you can throw at him. It's an art, and can make things a lot easier for you in a fight. You don't want to stand there trading punches with some guy, especially if you're fighting a bigger opponent."

The others soon showed up. That night I made them work on reflex exercises - four-corners and the gauntlet. They were constantly having punches thrown at them from all angles and directions. They had to react. They had to block and counter. I hammered it into them for two hours before I bowed them out. It was a good hard workout and everyone, including Bud, enjoyed it.

Chapter 20

Later that evening I got my payment. Bud showed me how to use the computer to get the location of a post office branch from a P.O. Box, a city, and a state. I complained about how much he was charging for something so simple. He displayed a map leading to the very post office in question. So I coughed up a ten-spot and gave it to him.

The obvious thing to do was watch the bank to see if anyone used the safety deposit box. However, that would have been next to impossible. Banks can be difficult to stake out, even if I could have somehow kept an eye on the safety deposit boxes. I settled for watching the P.O. Box, a safer but less effective method.

There are dozens of ways to stake out a post office. I've used most of them over the years. It's a public place with plenty of coming and going. It's relatively easy to blend in and watch the place. They're not as paranoid as a bank. Gee, if you have enough quarters you can sit in front of the place all day in your car. I prefer standing in the anteroom, filling out forms at the table. You usually have a clear view of the P.O. boxes and are not visible from the desk where the workers and customers are standing.

Studying Phil Sullivan's picture, I resigned myself to spending a few days at the post office in the hope that the elusive high school teacher might stop by to get his mail. It was a long shot, but the best lead I had at the moment. I still hadn't gone to the police. I didn't feel too bad about it after the way the captain had treated me in front of Judy Sales. On hindsight, I probably should have.

I generally had on a cap and sunglasses on a stakeout. I'd wear nondescript clothes, usually drab gray or brown colors, nothing flashy. It was a cool, damp day, so I put on a light jacket. I got there early and stayed all day. Coming and going, I assumed various poses and activities. I read newspapers and filled out cards. I even pretended to talk on my cell phone. It's not only a convenience. It's a handy prop. Many people came and went, but none of them were Phil Sullivan, Alicia's math teacher.

The odds were slim at best that he would turn up there, but like I said, it was all I had to go on. The fact that the P.O. Box was associated with a safety deposit box at the bank gave me hope. After all, there could have been something very valuable in it. He would naturally want to keep tabs on any communications related to it.

The following morning I did much the same, but changed my clothing. In this way, one day passed into the next, until I had spent almost the entire week there. The drill was beginning to get stale and was leading nowhere. At my wits end, I was about to quit and go to the police, when I noticed a man standing at the table I usually stood at. He was doing much the same as I had done. He was taking his time filling out a form. Like me, he wore a cap and sunglasses.

I went to the counter and bought a book of stamps. As I did, I noticed him go toward the P.O. boxes. I stepped out of line and peeked around the corner. He appeared to go to the suspect's box. He was gone by the time I finished my purchase.

My heart was beating too fast for someone who had just bought stamps. I calmed my breathing - in through the nose, out through the mouth - as I got into my car. He was just pulling out.

Even though I hadn't lived in the city for long, my natural aggressive temperament and cat-like reflexes - not to mention the nerves of a stunt car driver – enable me to get through just about any kind of traffic snarl. I've never lost a tail yet, although most of those were in my hometown in upstate New York. I've done a bit of it in my day, though. Today I was following a kidnapping suspect, who would hopefully lead me to Alicia. My luck had turned up good despite all odds. I was on a roll. I was going to press it for all it was worth.

He was driving a black pickup truck. We headed north over the Mystic River Bridge. Not long after that I was following him up Route 1 to Revere. I followed at a distance, always leaving three or four cars in front of me. Soon we left the main drag and moved along a beachfront road. I stayed well behind, keeping his truck just in sight. We drove past small houses and cottages on the left. A short, stone seawall marched along our right. It separated the road from a long sand beach and the ocean beyond.

The truck made a left into the driveway of a small, white stone cottage. I drove by as the passenger entered the house with a bag of groceries. Continuing up the road, I came to a beach club. I pulled into the empty parking lot. The sign on the billboard said, The Driftwood, and what time they opened, which would not be for several hours yet.

The man did not appear to be Sullivan from the picture I had. Whoever it was, however, must have been in some way connected to the P.O. Box. At least I hoped so. I vaguely wondered if Sullivan still owned the box. Things like that can change fast. I even began to doubt, with a sinking feeling, that he had actually gone to the suspect's box. It was the only lead I had, however, so I clung to it like a man on a cliff.

I had to figure out what to do. Should I confront the guy, start asking a bunch of questions? I had a good idea where that would lead. Or maybe I should go to the police now with what I had, let them take it from there. That was sure to lead nowhere as well. Perhaps I should come back after dark and snoop around, see what I could find. That seemed like a good plan. I headed back home to get something to eat, take a nap, and get ready for a long night.

Bud was home, watching TV and looking smug.

"How'd it go today?" I said. "I hope you didn't have any trouble with that kid."

"He won't be giving me any more trouble," he replied, smiling broadly.

"Why? What happened?"

"I was standing outside the Y on the side street with some of my friends. Butch, that's his name, came up and grabbed me by the collar. I did just what you showed me, just like we practiced. He had both hands on me. I braced my feet and punched him in the head with my right fist. I knocked him right down. He got up and ran away. I thought he was going to cry. I've never seen anyone look so surprised in my life."

I was going to scold him for fighting, but from the sound of it, he didn't have much choice. The guy was asking for it and had been taught a lesson. Hopefully Butch's bullying days were over. Who knows, they might even become friends.

"Well, it's good you defended yourself, but don't go getting cocky. This boy may be ready for you next time. Try not to get into any more fights. Stay out of his way if you can. You don't want to get a reputation as a troublemaker. Once people think that of you, it's hard to live it down.

"I know. I don't want trouble. I just want that kid to leave us alone."

"Well, hopefully you've taught him a lesson and he's not vindictive."

"What's vindictive mean?"

"Like the kind of guy who's always out for revenge."

"If he does, I'll give him more of the same," he boasted.

"Just watch yourself, OK." With that I went to bed.

96

Interlude

The last of the day disappeared as another hellish night began. It was a far cry from the life she thought she'd be living. Instead of the glamour she was promised, there was only squalor and misery. In place of fun and money, only fear and wretchedness reigned. She had been chained and beaten, raped and choked, threatened with a thousand horrible things and dreaded even more. She had been assured fame and fortune, but she had been sold into a nightmarish life of slavery.

Every night he would come. Sometimes he would instruct them or read them the rules. Sometimes he would carry out the punishment for some infraction of those rules. Always he would train them in the art of sexual allurement and pleasure, where they would give and not receive, unless it was the back of a hand. He was the good one. He was the kind one that wouldn't burn you with his cigarette or stick you with a needle, although it was obvious he cared only for the merchandise and not the person. His only concern was that it fetch top dollar when the time came for trading. In the meantime, her living hell would continue.

A worse fate awaited her.

The rear door opened and closed. Someone came down the steps leading to the basement apartment where she was being kept with the others. The key was in the lock. The door handle turned. His steps - the sound of impending doom - approached through the darkness. She cried and bit her gag, sobbing quietly as he came near. She wished she was home with her mother, back in her old room listening to her records. Oh, why had she ever left?

Chapter 21

I woke up around midnight and literally rolled out of bed onto the floor. Crawling around looking for clothes so I wouldn't wake Bud, I found a black pair of jeans and a dark cotton sweatshirt. Putting on a short black jacket to protect me from the chill night air, I left the apartment. I was at Revere Beach a half hour later.

I pulled into the beach club parking lot. It was now packed with cars. I could clearly hear the band from the edge of the lot. Stealing across the street and over the retaining wall, I walked back up the beach toward the white stone cottage I'd seen the man from the post office pull into.

The reflection of the pale moon was visible on the surf as it washed onto the sand. I could hear the gentle sound of the waves a few feet to my left. Except for a few lonely gulls, the beach was deserted. I approached the cottage and knelt behind the wall, looking around.

The pickup truck was still parked in the drive. There was a light on in the front room. The rest of the house was dark with no outside illumination. That was a good thing. There were no dogs around either. That was even better. The houses were spaced well apart. The neighbor on the left was separated from the cottage by a wide hedge. On the other side there was a wire fence dividing the properties. Both were dark.

When I was sure no one was about, walking their dogs or strolling arm in arm, I stole across the road. Crouching next to the side of the house, I hid in the shadows and listened. There was a television playing in the front room. The windows were high so I couldn't see in without standing on something.

I crawled along the side of the house toward the rear, making a complete circuit of the building. There were bushes, which helped screen me from view of the street. I checked in the rear windows, which were closer to the ground and darkened. Several gave a view of the front room, where the light was on and the television playing. I could see no one. As I went around the building, I noticed there was a basement apartment with rather large windows. For some reason, they were covered with thick curtains, so I couldn't see in. I thought this was strange and decided I needed to take a closer look.

At the rear of the house there were steps leading down to the basement door. I ran back across the street and hunkered down behind the seawall. I planned to wait there until whoever was watching TV in the front room went to bed. Then I would break into his basement and have a look around. He obviously had something there he didn't want anyone to see.

Of course, I could have staked out the cottage for a few days. Perhaps find a spot further down the beach and spy on him with my binoculars. I might have watched who came and went and taken pictures. I had a feeling, however, that I could have watched this place all day and night for a month and not seen a thing. In any case, I might tip them off that way. In the meantime, my missing girls could be hogtied inside. I felt time was of the essence. I had thought this once before when a young woman's life was in jeopardy. My rather hasty action had saved a life. Perhaps it might do so again.

I don't know how long it was, but sometime around 2:00 a.m. the front light went out and another one went on. I assumed it was a bedroom lamp. It too, soon went out. I waited another twenty minutes. Then I made my way back across the street to the rear of the building. The night was quiet. Crickets chirped somewhere behind the backyard.

There was a clothesline and a small concrete slab that probably served as a patio, where a charcoal grill had been set up. I crawled along the bushes and listened at the rear of the cottage. Hearing nothing, I crept down the back steps to the rear basement door. Taking out my trusty pen and thumb wrench, I soon picked the lock and opened the door.

The air was stale and smelt of spoiled garbage. I flashed a small penlight briefly around the room and found myself in a kitchen area with pink walls. Moving past a table, I went through a narrow door, missing the step leading down to a sunken living area. Landing hard, I lunged forward and almost lost my balance. I stopped and turned on my penlight again. Something moved in the next room. I snapped off the light. Before I did, I noticed double glass doors with white curtains drawn across them.

I stood still in the darkness listening for the slightest sound. I could definitely hear movement in the next room. Crouching, I made my way slowly across the floor until I was almost touching the glass panel of the doors with my ear. I turned the knob. The door was unlocked. I opened it silently.

The stench of urine and feces hit me like a boxer's jab. My instincts, already on high alert, rose another notch. I heard a noise, aimed my penlight at it, and turned it on suddenly. Instead of finding a chained wild animal staring at me, there was a wide-eyed young girl. She was handcuffed to the bedpost with a gag on her mouth. Her clothing was torn and soiled. Her black hair was a long, tangled knot of curls. She had bruises on her arms. Her eyes were sunken and frightened. They screamed for her because she could not speak. They pleaded for me to help her. She was a delicate young black girl and she looked vaguely familiar. It was Dominique Devereux.

I tried to calm her down, but that only made her more agitated. There was another form lying inert in a nearby bed. I couldn't tell who it was in the darkness, but hoped it was my Alicia. It appeared that I had just stumbled on the missing girls. If not, it didn't matter. Whoever they were they were being held against their will. From the smell of the place, they had been made to go to the bathroom where they lay. It looked like they had been tortured, and I guessed raped repeatedly. With this realization and the sick feeling it caused, came the sound of someone stirring upstairs.

I had seen enough. There wasn't much more I could do at the moment, not with their captor alerted. He probably had a gun. I ran back through the apartment intent on escaping and calling the police. I had left my cell phone in the car. I was afraid someone would call it and give me away. I wished I had it now.

I made it to the kitchen only to hear someone running down the rear stairs. Finding the door unlocked, they burst into the darkened room. There were two of them. The first one was a slim man with a gun. He was the same guy who I had seen at the post office. The second man was larger. He trailed at the top of the stairs. They couldn't see me in the dark.

I hit the first one with the inner ridge of my hand as he ran into the room. The strike caught him under the chin in the soft part of the throat. He went down hard, as if he'd hit a clothesline riding a motor scooter. The gun flew from his hand. He was out for the count. The larger man was now at the door. He stopped and peered into the pitch-black room trying to see what had happened.

I didn't give him time to find out. I flew into him with a leaping double-front ball kick. It was the kind I liked to demonstrate on the bag. Normally, it's not a maneuver you want to try on the street. It's rather risky leaving the ground like that, and ineffective against a trained man. Coming out of the blackness, however, I caught him completely off guard. I hit him twice without touching the ground, first in the groin and then in the face as his head bent forward. He flew backward onto the stairs and lay stunned, holding his face and privates.

Not wanting him to get up, I pounced on his chest. I landed with the heel of my foot, twisting it on impact and digging it into his solar plexus. It knocked the wind out of him. He was a good-size opponent, but unprepared for my attack. He appeared to resemble the school photo of Phil Sullivan.

I bounded over him and up the stairs. I planned on making my getaway and calling the police. That's when the third man came at me.

He was as tall as Sullivan, but not as wide, built more like a quarterback than a lineman. I don't know where he came from. There was a second car in the drive, which he must have just arrived in. He came at me with a series of high, fast kicks that had me moving backward as fast as I could. I backed into the house, slapping the side paneling with my arms - not a very good position to be in. He threw a spinning-wheel kick. His foot missed my head by an inch, smashing against the siding of the building. He actually cracked it! This guy wasn't fooling around!

I ducked the kick and then another as I ran around him to more open ground. He moved to cut me off, unleashing a series of kicks and punches that backed me up some more. His last kick, another spinning kick, grazed my temple as I ducked out of the way. A jab caught me in the eye.

His kicks were powerful and high, designed to take my head off. He attacked again, this time with right and left hooks. They were expertly thrown, but easy to block and evade. I certainly didn't want to get hit with one of them. He wasn't giving me a chance to counter. He used his long reach to advantage, keeping me away.

He moved in again with a series of kicks, jabs, and hooks. The last one caught me square on the side. It felt like he had cracked my ribs. So far, his attack had been effective. He was moving me back like a trained seal. Good thing I can fight moving backward.

He came at me again with the same series of high, powerful kicks. This time I was ready for him. I recognized his pattern and intuitively knew he would throw it again. Why not? It was very effective. The trick was not to let him execute it.

This time I stepped into him in the middle of one of his beautiful spinning kicks. I caught him in midstride with an overhand right to the bridge of his nose just as he spun it toward me. I have to hand it to him. He stayed on his feet, but stopped dead and swayed. He was hurt and off balance.

Before he could recover, I stepped into him with a side-thrust kick to his floating ribs, knocking him off his feet. I thought he was done, but he got back up and assumed a stance. I had to admire his spunk, but this was taking too long. The other two might wake up at any moment.

I went right at him, moving in with a series of straight, hard hand strikes to the head and body. He tried to block and dodge, but he was dazed and couldn't handle me in close like that. He was taller than me, but not so tall I couldn't hit him in the head. My hands worked like pistons. When he blocked me high, I came in low with tight body shots. When his hands went down, I'd hammer his head, my punches coming from every angle.

Then, while still in close, I kicked him. One of the things I was known for in what little competitive fighting I did was my close in kicking. I could deliver a thrust kick standing an arm length away. Most people need more room to throw that kick effectively. I could snap them out standing close enough to slap you. My front kick came from nowhere. You couldn't stop it even if you knew it was coming.

I snapped one at his throat. Just missing, it hit him in the chin instead. It snapped his jaw shut and drew blood. I stood in close and didn't let him increase the distance between us. He was unable to use his long legs and arms to advantage. Then I caught him in an awkward, off-balance position, and hawked him off his feet – typical kenpo.

I still had him by the arm. Standing over him, I locked it at the elbow with my legs. When he continued to struggle, I snapped my knees together. I actually heard his arm crack. He yelled in pain, grabbed his appendage, and rolled on the ground. Then he bellowed in rage and started to get up again. I grabbed the nearby grill and brought it down on his head. That seemed to do the trick. If he didn't come to in a year, it would have been too soon for me.

I was about to breathe a sigh of relief, when the guy I used as the stairs, the guy that looked like Sullivan, grabbed me from behind in a head lock. Before he had a chance to apply any pressure, I grabbed him by the balls with my right. At the same time, I took him by the back of the hair with my left. Then I pulled his head back, and twisting my grip, lifted him by his gonads. He had to go with it or lose his genitals. Even as big as he was, he went horizontal and let go of my head. I slammed him to the ground on his back and stomped his face. I wanted to make sure he would not get up again any time soon.

Adrenalin was pumping through my system. I ran back into the house just as the first man was getting to his feet and groping for the gun. I could just see him in the darkness. It was good enough. I nailed him with a straight right and knocked him out again, just as he raised the gun to shoot me. Finding the switch with some difficulty, I turned on the kitchen light and located the gun. I held it on the three of them as they woke up one by one. By then, I had found some rope and tied them up. I had also found a telephone and called the police.

Chapter 22

The scene at the beach cottage was pandemonium. There were police cars and ambulances everywhere. I had been lucky. Except for a red, swollen, partially-closed right eye and possible cracked ribs, I would be OK. That is except for the doctor bills I didn't have insurance for.

Much to my regret, my picture, black eye and all, was plastered in the papers, along with those of the two kidnapped victims. One of them was Judy's student, Dominique Devereux. The other girl was a teenager who had recently been reported missing from Cambridge. Alicia Fleming-Rossi was not there.

I had all three suspects sitting or lying prone on the floor of the basement apartment, as the case may be. Some weren't doing too good. I didn't fight fair. I fought to win, especially when three goons were trying to put me down for good. I uncuffed the girls and was caring for them the best I could while I kept an eye on the suspects and waited for the authorities.

The other girl – I never did learn her name - didn't say much. She was pretty doped up and barely conscious. They were both suffering from malnutrition and physical abuse. Once Dominique calmed down, however, she was very talkative, and told me what had happened.

She said Sullivan had lured her to the house after promising to get her a modeling job. I asked her if she had seen Alicia. She said she hadn't, but there were two girls there just before she got there. She didn't know who it was. However, she had overheard one of her captors say they had been sold to someone in Mexico City. She seemed sure of this. I questioned her on it for some time. She didn't know the girls' names. I had to presume one of them was Alicia. Then the police arrived and that was the last I saw of her. I assumed she told the cops the same thing. I didn't bother to.

They were lucky I had stumbled onto their hiding place when I did. They were about to be shipped out as well, their training complete. I wondered if Alicia was one of the girls who had been here earlier. I had to assume that her disappearance, as well as Dominique's, was connected to the math teacher, alias Phil Sullivan. If so, why had she been spirited away and not Dominique? Maybe the timing of their abductions had something to do with it. The two girls were taken

104

weeks apart. And who was the other young woman that had been sold in Mexico? These and other questions plagued me in the aftermath of the rescue.

If it was publicity I wanted, I couldn't have done better. However, I wasn't so sure I wanted to advertise my involvement in this case. My client's daughter was still missing. Presumably she was a prisoner of the same people that kidnapped the two girls we rescued. A couple of the men involved were purported to belong to the Russian mob, not an organization I wanted to get on the wrong side of.

I was a hero of sorts. I even got an apology from Dominique's family, who gladly dropped the lawsuit they had filed against me. I should have been happy, but I knew it wasn't over until I found Alicia.

The authorities were elated. They not only recovered two kidnapped young women, they cracked a dangerous white slavery ring with international ties. Unfortunately, none of the suspects were talking. The man impersonating Phil Sullivan was the second man who attacked me that night. He was being questioned in connection with the murder of the real Phillip Sullivan three years earlier. The man's actual identity, determined by fingerprinting, was Neil Craig, wanted for child pornography and kidnapping in California. He and his friends, both with links to the Russian underworld, would be detained for a long time if Federal and State law enforcement had anything to say about it. The FBI had entered the case and questioned me as well. I told them and the police everything I knew, except for what Dominique told me before they came.

Despite the fact that I had saved two girls from a terrible fate, the captain down at the first precinct was less than happy with me. First of all, I had called the Revere police. They got all the credit for the arrests. Secondly, I had failed to report my findings to him or the whereabouts of the suspects.

"What are you, Lawless, some kind of vigilante?" he asked. "Why didn't you inform us when you learned about Mister Sullivan? You knew we were looking for those girls."

"I didn't think you took that lead seriously. You certainly didn't give it much credence when I told you he knew both of the girls and had left town."

"That's funny, I don't remember you telling us anything."

"Well, I told it to one of your guys. I can't be responsible for what your men tell you or don't tell you. I was just following up a lead. I didn't have anything solid. Things were happening fast. I didn't have time to go down and be drilled by you for just doing my job."

"You won't have a job if you keep that up, Mister Lawless."

I told him about my trip to New Jersey and what I had found out about the real Phil Sullivan. He became even angrier when he found out how much I had kept from him. I thought he was going to arrest me. As it was, he kept me at the station for four hours while he interrogated me. You'd have thought I was the kidnapper. Then he gave me to the FBI guys for another five hours, until they were all satisfied I had told them everything I knew in triplicate. None of this brought them any closer to finding Alicia, and I told them so. The captain didn't appreciate that either. We left on less than friendly terms.

"And stay out of police business!" was the last thing he said to me.

I wasn't sure if I still had a license, but it didn't matter. I still had a job to do. There was a lost girl out there. If what had happened to the two we had rescued was any indication of what was happening to Alicia, I had to find her fast. That is, if it wasn't already too late.

After my less than warm reception from the captain, I was happy I hadn't told him about Mexico. It was probably just the ravings of a hysterical young girl. She had more than likely repeated it to the police. If not, it was no concern of mine. They and the FBI didn't have jurisdiction south of the border, and by the time they got it, it would be too late for Alicia.

A couple days after the rescue, I got a call from Rossi in Florida.

"What's the idea, Lawless. I'm paying you all that money and you find two other girls?"

"I'm working for Alicia's mother. She's paying, not you," I retorted.

"Where do you think Anna's money comes from, you stupid shmuck? I'm paying you and don't you forget it. Do you know what happened to Alicia?"

"I think your daughter was there only days before. We just missed her. I have some leads to follow up."

"Look, I appreciate what you did. That was pretty impressive the way you handled those Russians. I could use a guy like you."

"I thought you said you were retired. How do you know your phone's not bugged?"

"It doesn't matter. Look, you've got to get Alicia back. I'll pay you anything you want. You should have called me after you found those bastards. I could have sent some boys up, maybe got some answers out of those guys you caught."

"I didn't have your number. I'm in enough trouble with the cops. I'll lose my license if I'm not careful, then I won't be any use to you or Alicia."

"Don't worry about your stinking license. You don't need one to work for me."

"Look, Rossi, I'll find your daughter if anyone can. Just stay the hell out of my way."

I hung up on him. While I hoped that was the last I'd hear from him, I wondered if I was being too hasty. Perhaps Tony could be of some help. After all, Mexico City was a big place. It might be nice to have someone watching my back. On further thought, however, the prospect of having one of Rossi's ex-goons dogging me made me realize I was right to go it alone. That way no one would see me coming.

I had little doubt that what Dominique had told me was true. I was almost certain the police were dealing with the same information. What would they do with it?

Later that day I called Alicia's mother. She told me her husband had told her to give me another $5000 to continue working on the case. I told her I'd be right over to pick up the check.

Anna Fleming was even more agitated and depressed than the last time I saw her. Looking like she hadn't eaten in days, she reminded me of the emaciated girls in the basement of the cottage. She didn't say much, the epitome of a defeated woman. The fact that I had just missed finding her daughter seemed to knock all the fight out of her.

Bud was excited to see my name and picture in the paper. That and the way he handled the bully had made him the big man on campus. I was told my karate class was now the number one class to join. I had enough new students to start a second group. They were even going to pay for my liability insurance. In addition, I got a couple calls for my detective services, which I had to turn down. I was already working on a job, and it was going to take all of my concentration.

With all the excitement and my preoccupation with the case, I hadn't had much time to pursue Judy. That didn't mean I wasn't thinking about her. While I contemplated the possibility of going to Mexico City, and the unlikelihood of anything good coming out of the trip, I decided to wash the car. I was standing in Mrs. Corrado's driveway hosing off the soap when Judy drove up. I had been thinking about her and was surprised when she appeared in the flesh.

It was a warm July day. I had my shirt off, enjoying the feel of the sun on my back. I was feeling better, though my ribs were still taped up. Bud was visiting with his friends.

"Wow!" she said, pulling up to the curb and getting out of her Pinto. "You sure have made a name for yourself around here. How are your ribs?"

"OK, as long as I don't laugh. The ribs aren't broken and doctor said there's no internal damage. I'll be good as new in a week or so."

"I'm glad to hear it," she replied, with a look of concern. Or was it something else. Her eyes strayed down to my chest, and then lower, to snap back up to mine. "It's nice to see you. I'm glad you're OK. It sounded dreadful."

"Not as bad of an ordeal as your friend Dominique went through."

"I know. Poor girl."

"Have you had a chance to talk to her?"

"No. She's not back in class yet. They're not letting anyone but family near her."

"I can understand why."

"I'm sorry you didn't find the girl you were looking for. What was her name, Alicia?"

"Yes. It's pretty frustrating to be so close and miss her. She was there only a few days before. Dominique said that there were two other girls at the cottage when she was brought in. She overheard the kidnappers say that they had been taken to Mexico City and sold to a VIP sex club. I'm going down."

"That's a long way to go on the word of a traumatized young girl, who was probably drugged up."

"No, I believed her. She wasn't drugged up. I admit she was a little freaked out when I found her, but she calmed down. We talked for awhile before the police came. I questioned her repeatedly about the girls who were sent to Mexico. She didn't know if Alicia was one of them, but she was sure what she overheard was true. They didn't know she could hear them. No, I'm positive. Whoever was there before Dominique was sold in Mexico City. I have to assume Alicia was one of them. It's too much of a coincidence that they both knew the fake Sullivan. It must have been her. It's a good a place to start as any."

"I guess you're right," she conceded. "It makes sense they'd be there. Ninety-eight percent of the people in Mexico live there and ninety-nine point nine percent of the sex trade resides there. But, well, it could be dangerous. I hope you're not thinking of going down too soon. I wanted to help you recuperate."

"What did you have in mind?" I asked.

"I hear water therapy is very beneficial."

She smiled and came close like she was going to kiss me. Then she grabbed the hose and turned it on me, soaking me to the bone. We laughed like kids as she chased me around the car. Who knows what might have happened if I wasn't living over a seventy-year-old woman with my twelve-year-old son.

Chapter 23

The next few days were hectic. I planned the trip and made arrangements with Mrs. Corrado to watch Bud. He wanted to come with me, but I told him that was out of the question. His mother had called him during this time – she didn't have the courtesy to contact me – and told him she would be in Hawaii an extra week. They had decided to see some of the other islands. I was glad to hear someone was having fun, no matter how irresponsible she was being.

So far, Bud had been doing OK without much supervision and staying out of trouble. I told him he was welcome to spend the extra week with me if he wanted. He said he'd ask his mom.

I read as much as I could about Mexico City from the brochures the travel agent gave me. None of it gave me a good feeling. As a matter of fact, just the opposite, what I read filled me with dread, with tourist kidnappings and hijacked buses.

I worked out hard the next few days, as much as my bruised ribs would allow. I trained as if I was preparing for a prize fight. Though I was past my prime, I was probably in the best shape of my life. I doubled my 100 pushup and sit-ups a day. Then, once I was mended, I doubled them again. Although too old to actually fight in a ring, I could hold my own with most fighters in my weight class for one or two rounds. Anything after that and my stamina would lose out to some twenty-year-old.

When I first got to Boston after leaving my hometown a second time, I hung around the gyms and dojos, working out with whoever would humor me. I worked with boxers, wrestlers, and other martial artists. We traded techniques and tips, and an occasional black eye or split lip. I was doing mixed martial arts long before it was on TV. It was great fun and there was plenty of mutual respect. I made some good friends.

My ribs were feeling better. I decided to see if any of the boys wanted to help me get ready for combat that I hoped would never occur. I stopped at the gym first. It was in Brighton on Holton Street. I took Bud with me. Smiley, the propriety and trainer, looked up from his morning papers with mild surprise when I walked in.

"Well, well, well," he said, in his gruff voice, "If it isn't the karate boy. I haven't seen you in a while. Where you been? Saw you're picture in the paper, some hero. You come in to get your ass whipped?"

"Hi, Smiley. Yeah, I came in for some ass-whippin'. How you been?"

"Good, good. Good to see you." He looked at my eye. "I'd hate to see the other guy. Who you got there with you?"

"This is my boy, Bud, visiting from New York, and there were three of them. One's still in the hospital."

"Typical Lawless. You better not hurt any of my boys."

"You just tell your boys not to hurt me. Who's around today that might want to spar?"

"Leroy and Andy are here somewhere. I'm sure they'd just love to work out with you."

He called to one of his trainers, who darted off to get the two boxers.

Leroy was a 200 pound heavyweight. He had won his last fight with a third round knockout, and was about as intimidating as they come. Big and fast, well-muscled, and black, he had a great game face, which helped him in the ring.

"You're not going to fight that guy, are you?" asked Bud on seeing him. "He outweighs you by fifty pounds. He'll kill you."

"It's the little one I'm worried about," I replied.

Andy was a light-middle weight, fast and strong, with a killer instinct. He could smell even a whiff of weakness in an adversary, and knew just where to hit you to hurt you the most. Andy was undefeated in his weight class after twenty-five fights.

Both men were great guys. They worked with me like dance partners. We traded technique rather than trying to prove something by taking each other's head off. Both of them were capable of it, as I was well aware. They were aware that their health depended on my following the Marquis de Queensbury's rules.

I worked with Andy first. Using my speed, I kept him at bay, jabbing as I moved backward and hitting him with hooks when he dropped his hands to block a body shot. I fought him with just my hands, working on my boxing technique. Of course, he got the better of me with his great combinations and footwork. Finally, I got tired of getting hit – although at half-power.

Finishing the round with a sequence of wheel kicks, I made him duck and back up out of the way. I got him in the corner on the ropes.

Then I hammered him with a series of half-power right and left hooks to the side of his headgear. He popped me in the nose as the bell rang. Smiley gave Andy the round after taking off points for using my feet to kick the opponent.

Leroy was too big and strong to keep at bay unless I kicked him in the knees or groin, and I wasn't about to do that. That would have made him mad, and I definitely did not want to make him mad. I worked him inside, using my speed and agility to advantage.

At one point, when he lunged at me with a hard right, I stepped in, and locking his arm, threw him over my shoulder. I really hadn't meant to. The move is so ingrained in my mind that I just did it out of habit when his big fist whistled by my ear. I couldn't resist it when I knew all of his momentum would carry him forward. Luckily he landed well and didn't get hurt. Smiley gave me a warning.

"That's illegal, Lawless. No throws," he yelled. "I don't want you hurting my boy." Leroy laughed as he got up. His next three punches whizzed by my ear like miniature cyclones, so I threw him again, this time over my hip.

"That'll teach you, Leroy," laughed Smiley. "What did I tell you about leaning in with your punches?"

Leroy was a little more cautious after that.

"That was great," said Bud when we were finished. "You wiped the mat with them."

"They were just sparring with me. Believe me, I wouldn't want to be in the ring with either of them for real. Those guys can take a punch as well as deliver it."

After the workout, we went to a local bar with them, where I bought a few brewskies. They thought I was crazy to go to Mexico City alone and volunteered to go with me. I was tempted, but told them I always worked alone. I didn't want to be responsible for anything happening to them. They both had families.

The next day I continued my training and called Kevin at the local wrestling club. He told me it was open mat day and to come down. Bud was busy, so I went alone. I got there around ten in the a.m., just when things were heating up.

In my book, a good wrestler will win almost any fight in a ring. Once they get their hands on you, like a good Aikido practitioner, it's all over. Of course, on the street it's a different matter. Without gloves, you can punish a wrestler mercilessly while he tries to grab you, cutting and blinding him with punches to the head and face. I should mention, however, that most of your wrestlers, as well as boxers, can take a good punch. In a ring, however, with gloves on, the boxer is at a distinct disadvantage against a good wrestler.

It's the same for a karate or kung fu man. If you've ever watched mixed martial arts fighting, a good percentage of the bouts end up with the fighters rolling around on the floor grappling with one another, trying to put the opponent into a submission hold. In most of these situations, the person with the best wrestling or jujitsu skills ends up the winner. They practice this as much as they practice the boxing and kicking, so I figured I would too. Remember, even mixed martial arts fighters have to follow rules. On the street, in a life and death situation, there are no rules. That's where kenpo excels. It's dirty fighting taken to the max.

Of course, like working with boxers, the wrestler has to cooperate. If not, things can get messy, in which case, someone could get hurt. That's why I didn't participate in the open mat bouts. I waited until someone I knew and had worked with before came in. I didn't have long to wait.

Stacy is a 250 pounder with a heart of gold. What looks like fat is all muscle, which I can attest. He loves to wrestle and he loves pain. The two go hand in hand. I would advise you to avoid that particular martial art if you are averse to pain. Most of the wrestlers I know love it, the more the better. They're just plain crazy!

When I first met Stacy, he was standing in the corner of the gym punching the concrete wall with his bare fists like most guys hit a punching bag. When he found out I knew karate, he asked me to kick him in the head. "Harder, harder," he would say, as I crossed into him with side-thrust kicks. I didn't kick him full power because I didn't want to hurt him, and hit him with the flat of my foot instead of the heel. I was kicking him pretty hard by the end of the exercise, however. He seemed to love it. I refused to grab him by the balls and squeeze when he asked me. Luckily, he found someone else to accommodate him.

"Harder, harder," he yelled as the guy squeezed his testicles. Now that's a wrestler for you!

Stacey was fun to work with. He didn't care how hard I kicked him or where. When I'd slap out of one of his holds, he'd just put it on harder and make me slap even more. I could keep him at bay for the most part, but because I didn't want to hurt him, he could get in on me whenever he wanted. When he did, I was pretty good at countering his moves, and strong enough to grapple effectively with him even though he was quite a bit bigger. I could tell he was going easy on me. He was an expert at throws, locks, and take downs. We bounced each other off the mat and attracted a crowd.

We ended the session lying on the mat taking turns putting each other into holds and trying to get out of them. Because of his size and strength, I found the arm-bar the most effective weapon against him. I grabbed his wrist with both hands and locked his arm at the shoulder with my legs. Then I applied pressure on the elbow. Once I got that on him, there wasn't much he could do. I countered most of his holds using aikido and jujitsu moves. At one point I even grabbed him by the balls.

"Harder, harder," he yelled.

Stacey didn't drink, so I bought him a burger at a nearby diner when we were through. He, too, wanted to go to Mexico with me. It was then I realized that all my friends were crazy. That must mean I was crazy too. What a rag-tag company that would have been. I fantasized about it all night, but knew if one of them got hurt helping me I'd never forgive myself, so didn't act on the impulse.

My class that night at the Y was packed. One of my private students showed up to help. Otherwise, I never would have been able to handle it. As it was, I wasn't able to provide much one-on-one instruction. It was good for them, however, to have a lot of different people to train with, punching and grabbing them. It's an excellent way to get ready for when someone on the street does it for real.

Chapter 24

My connecting flight to Dallas out of Boston was for Saturday morning. I had one more day to work out. I decided to spend it at the dojo of a friend from my hometown. Ray Miushi's father had taught us judo in the third grade. It was an exceptional experience and Ray was an exceptional martial artist. He went on to master several styles of karate and kung fu.

He had stayed in town and went to the college there, where his dad taught. Later, after his father died, he went out to LA with Ed Parker. Parker had come to town for Mr. Miushi's funeral. Seeing Ray work out one day, he asked him to go to Hollywood with him to train movie stars and choreograph their films. Ray had developed his physique while in college. He had muscles everywhere. You just had to look at him to know he was an elite athlete.

After working and training in California for several years, he went on the mixed-martial art circuit and did pretty well. He made a name for himself, and won enough prize money to open a string of karate schools in New England. Now he had the biggest chain in the area. His specialty was training fighters for the cage.

Ray was the same size as me. If anyone could give me a good workout, it was him. Bud wasn't doing anything, so I convinced him to come along and meet my old friend.

"He's one of the best fighters you'll ever see," I bragged

"Better than you?" Bud asked.

"Probably, pound for pound. He's certainly won more fights. He's a middle-weight mixed martial arts champion."

"Good," Bud said, "finally, someone who can kick your ass."

I drove down to Ray's main studio off Central Square in Cambridge. He was holding an advanced workout for some of his more high-ranking students. After introducing him to Bud, I suited up and stretched out as we brought each other up to date. He commented on the recent newspaper account of the rescue and told me I should think of going professional.

"If you're going to get black eyes like that, the least you can do is get paid for it."

"I am getting paid," I told him. "Anyway, I'm too old and smart to fight with any of your boys in the ring for more than two rounds."

"Two rounds! Why that ain't enough to work up a sweat."

"Exactly," I replied.

He started out showing me some new techniques he'd picked up. One was a nice maneuver to get your opponent in a front choke hold from almost any angle. It's a good move to use if some big guy tries to grapple with you. He then had his students surround me to simulate an attack by multiple opponents.

"Try not to hurt them," he told me. There were six of them. He gave each one a number and instructed them to attack me with assorted fists, clubs, and sticks when their number was called. We started off slow and sped things up as we went. By the end of the exercise I was bouncing people off the floor with trips, kicks, sweeps, and throws, as fast as they could get back up. I used Aikido techniques as well, to knock them into each other and fling them forward and back across the mat.

Finally, we got down to what I had come for, a good one-on-one sparring match with Ray. Taking off his gi top, he flexed his muscles, showing off for my benefit. Then he struck a pose, looking every inch like a kung fu movie idol, with bristling biceps and washboard abs. He threw a couple of almost vertical side kicks and cracked his neck.

"Ready?" he said.

I replied by snapping a flying front-ball kick at his head. For the next five minutes we threw just about every punch and kick you can think of. We worked seamlessly off each other's techniques. I came in like a Japanese fighter with a series of straight, hard front kicks, round-house kicks, and punches. He responded like a kung fu man with a flurry of circular wheel kicks, crescent kicks, and windmill strikes. It was exquisite. We were working together as if it had been choreographed, yet it was all spontaneous. It was like we were reading each other's mind.

Back and forth we went across the room. We were going as hard and as fast as we could without hurting one another. That was the beauty of it. Ray had pin-point control. He wouldn't hit me unless he wanted to. He was pulling full-power punches a fraction of an inch from my nose, and I was doing the same. After every flurry, Ray would stop and strike a different pose. I wondered if he was getting ready for a kung fu movie or something.

At one point he did a series of high, flying kicks. It looked very impressive. I let him show off his technique for awhile, but I didn't want Bud to get the wrong idea. These kicks were great for show, but

116

not too effective on the street. They were down right risky against a well-trained opponent.

He had forced me back across the room and was throwing one last high side kick. He left it extended in the air to emphasize his control and the perfection of the kick. I stepped backed, avoiding the strike. Then I grabbed his extended leg by the ankle with both hands and flipped him upward. He went flying backward head over heals. I was sorry as soon as I did it. I was afraid he'd land wrong and break his neck.

Wouldn't you know, that show off went over backward and landed on his feet! He struck another pose. I crossed over with a side kick and hit him in the midsection. His feet were too close together. It looked great when he landed, like an Olympic gymnast, but didn't help when my light kick struck him. He fell backward kiaiing as he hit the ground. Twisting himself back to his feet before I could stomp him, he struck another pose. Then he touched his finger to his tongue and licked it as if I had drawn blood.

"So much for those fancy flying kicks of yours," I said.

"You're just jealous 'cause you can't do them," he countered laughing.

"Wow!" cried Bud when we finished. "I've never seen anything like that before, not even in the movies. Dad, you were punching so fast I couldn't even see your hands! You guys are amazing!"

"Impressive, eh," I said sweating and breathing hard. "That was nothing. Wait 'til we get warmed up."

It was a great workout. I only got hit with one errant punch. Of course, it was to my bad eye. And Ray nailed me with a back kick I failed to get out of the way of, right in the ribs. They were just starting to feel better. But I got my share of good licks in. I may have broken his nose with a jab when he rushed in to punch me. All in all, other than the re-bruised bones, it was just what I needed to get me in shape for whatever awaited me in Mexico.

Chapter 25

The next morning I was on my way to Mexico City. Most people thought I was crazy. Trying to find a lost girl on the word of a hysterical young kidnapping victim was like trying to find a glass bead at the beach. I didn't even have an actual sighting. I was on a wild goose chase and everyone knew it except me. I had more chance of losing myself than of finding Alicia, but I was the only chance she had. The authorities would probably be mired in red-tape for the next six weeks. That is if they even knew about it.

I would have slept most of the way except for the young man sitting next to me. He chatted to his boyfriend in Spanish the whole way to Texas. That wouldn't have been so bad, but I had the sneaky suspicion they were talking about me. He kept turning on my skylight and being generally annoying. I flashed him a look that told him he was only inches away from being thrown out the plane at 30,000 feet. That didn't stop his incessant chatter, however.

I arrived in Dallas in a foul mood and found a restaurant to wait in until my connecting flight to Mexico City. I ate what would be my last meal in the United States. From here on in it was going to be tortillas and tacos.

Fortunately, my traveling companions were not on the connecting flight. Either they had missed the plane or were headed someplace else. I enjoyed their absence and got a few hours rest before we landed in Mexico City around six p.m.

I woke disoriented and confused, almost forgetting where I was and what I was doing. I still felt that way after grabbing my bags and going through Customs. The next thing I knew I was standing by the side of the curb blinded by the glaring sun.

There was a line of cabs with a knot of people standing by them. Everyone was shouting for attention. Baggage handlers carried luggage to and fro, looking for tips wherever they could find them.

I spotted a cab off by itself at the end of the line with no one standing near it. I sprinted for it, and thanked my lucky stars. I did wonder briefly what it was doing there all alone. I figured it had probably just let someone off. Not one to look a gift horse in the mouth, I seized my opportunity to get ahead of the crowd. It never dawned on me that I might be breaking the rules.

"The Hotel Presidenti Intercontenental," I told him. "On Campos Eliseus."

I had been practicing this line since I got on the plane. I repeated it to myself incessantly under my breath as I sat in my business class seat.

I had spared no expense. My U.S. dollars went a long way in Mexico. I had a fat $5000 sitting in my bank account from Rossi, and half of what Alicia's mother gave me in my pocket. I figured I might as well enjoy myself in style while I was there.

"Oh, senor, that is a fine hotel, La Presidenti, in Polanco. That's the rich section of the city, you know. You are very fortunate, senor."

"Thanks," I replied, hoping I hadn't made a mistake. The driver seemed nice enough and spoke good English. I had heard so much about people being kidnapped there, however, that I instantly became suspicious.

"Are you here on business or pleasure, senor?"

"Both," I answered evasively. "I hope to see some of the more exotic sites in the city."

I expected him to take the highway, but he drove by the entrance and onto a side street. Perhaps he knew a shortcut. We drove past one borough into another. I thought he might be taking the scenic route. After all, I was a gringo tourist.

We drove for some time in silence. My suspicions rose with each mile and dingy neighborhood. We didn't appear to be getting any closer to the center of town. We seemed to be lost in a sea of brown, dirty tenements and small store fronts.

"You won't see many neighborhoods like this where we are going," the cabby informed me. "You rich Americans only see the big hotels and expensive restaurants in Polanco. You never see how the real Mexicans live."

"Is this where you're from?" I asked, trying to be polite. I was getting more nervous by the minute.

"No, senor. I'm from the mountains to the East, but I drive through here all the time. There is less traffic."

"I figured this was the scenic route or something," I commented. "I'm surprised you didn't take the highway."

"No, not this time of day. This is a much nicer drive."

It didn't seem nice to me, but I didn't tell him that.

"Pleasant neighborhood. Lot of trees," I observed trying to be friendly as we passed a small park with a shaded ball court.

119

He slowed down at an especially dingy intersection and pulled into what looked like a deserted garage. I figured this was it, I'm getting kidnapped. I got ready to choke the guy out as soon as he stopped the car.

"My cousin, Fernando, works here," said the cabby. "They do car repair, things like that. He's got a gas pump in the back he lets me use."

It was getting dark. It was a perfect place to mug someone. We pulled behind the garage where it was even more secluded. I was ready for anything. There was an old pump next to a fence and a clump of hay weed. The cabby got out. I followed, keeping close.

"This is a bit unusual," I observed, "stopping like this."

"Not at all, senor, I do it all the time. My cousin, he is a good man to know. I will introduce you."

I decided to play along, see what I could find out. For all I knew, he might be involved in the human trafficking trade.

"You must know a lot about the city," I said as he filled his tank with illicit petrol.

"I have been around a long time, senor."

I tried to gauge if he was a real cabby or not. He sure looked shifty enough, now that I saw him up close, but not particularly threatening. Looks could be deceiving – I'm a case in point. Perhaps he had associates lurking in the shadows. I looked around cautiously and saw several places someone could be hiding waiting to jump me. I was on edge, but tried to keep my voice calm.

"I was hoping to find someone to show me the nightlife in the city. You know, a place with young girls."

"Ah, you want to see the senoritas while you are here, eh?"

"I hear they have the most beautiful girls in the world here and they dance very nice."

"Ah, si, senor, the senoritas are very pretty," he snickered.

His tank filled, we got back in the cab. It was now dark. I still wasn't sure if I was being kidnapped or not. Perhaps the guy was trying to decide that himself. I had no choice but to get back in the cab with him.

"How far are we from the hotel?" I inquired.

"Not far. The airport is a good distance from the main part of the city where you are going. Instead of taking the highway around to the other side, I have gone through its heart. The shortest distance between two points is a straight line, is it not, senor?"

"Si," I agreed. "You know best."

"Are you in a hurry, senor?"

"No, not really, and I did want to see some of the city."

"I want to show you something then," he said.

He drove me to the top of a tree-covered hill. Small, neat houses crowded together on both sides of the street. There was a nice guesthouse at the summit, with a large wooden fence at the end of the parking lot.

"This neighborhood es muy bueno," he informed me looking around, "It has many small, tidy one-family homes. It is what you would call lower-middle class, where people who work in the city, like me, live."

We got out and walked to the end of the parking lot toward the high, wide wooden fence.

"Down here, this is where the real poor people live," he announced. He stepped through a gap in the fence and pointed down into a valley. At first I thought I was looking at the city dump, where all its refuge had been heaped - paper, rags, tin, and cardboard, broken bicycles and dolls. Then I realized the tin and cardboard were shanties where people lived. The dolls were really children playing in the mud.

The last of the setting sun glinted on the image, as if a giant spotlight was being shown on the scene. I stared in disbelief and didn't say a word. The man looked at me with cloudy eyes as we silently got back into the cab.

He began talking cheerfully again, as if we had not glimpsed the most piteous view of humanity I've ever seen.

"I can show you some good clubs," he said as we drove through a few more shabby streets. Then suddenly, turning a corner, we merged with traffic onto a well-lit, upscale, multilane boulevard. There were high-rises and expensive stores, one selling Mercedes, another, chic men's clothes. A short time later, we pulled up to my hotel. A bellhop rushed out to get my luggage as I pulled out my wallet to pay the cabby.

"We'd still be stuck in traffic on the highway," he told me.

I was relieved to make it to the hotel without being intercepted by an international gang of kidnappers.

"You speak English well," I commented. "Where'd you learn to talk like that?"

"I grew up and went to school in Colorado," he answered. "I studied business administration at BU, in Boston. When my parents got divorced, I moved back here with my mother."

"Oh, I live in Boston. Are you going to be around later? I'd like you to take me around town. What's your name?"

"My name is Jose," he replied, shaking my hand. "And it would be my honor, senor, to show you the sights of our fine city."

Chapter 26

I met Jose later that evening after a long, hot shower and the best steak dinner I've ever had at a hotel restaurant. I waited outside in the warm, balmy night air. Jose showed up promptly at 9:00 p.m. So much for the stereotypical Latin disregard for schedules and punctuality, my Mexican cabby was right on time.

"How much for the evening?" I asked, wanting to get the formalities out of the way.

"For $100 American, you can have me all night."

"Sounds good," I said after doing some quick math. The cab ride from the airport took forty-minutes and had cost thirty dollars U.S. So a hundred bucks sounded about right for three or four hours of clubbing. I gave him fifty. "You get the rest when we get back to the hotel."

He took my money and we drove off. Weaving our way through traffic, we merged onto a large street with five lanes of cars all going in the same direction. There were bright lights and signs everywhere. The streets were crowded with people, tourists as well as Mexicans.

As we drove, I gave him my cover story. How I was scouting new talent for a dance club my associates were opening in Boston. We were looking for young girls from all over the world and heard the Mexican lap dancers were some of the best anywhere.

"Ah, you are looking for lap dancers, si?" he said.

"The younger the better," I replied.

He looked at me quizzically in the rearview mirror, but said nothing. We turned onto another broad thoroughfare ablaze in colored neon lights, and stopped at a large, red and green electric sign with a coconut tree and a martini glass emblazed on it. The name of the establishment was 'The Tahiti'.

"This is a good place to start," he announced. "I will wait out here, senor."

I had brought $500 dollars in cash to Mexico and another $500 in traveler's checks. I thought I'd be bringing money home with the exchange rate. That rate didn't seem to apply, however, to cabbies, gringos, and strip clubs. I realized that I'd be lucky if I wasn't in debt by the time I left Mexico.

The club was dark inside, with mirrors around the walls. There was a nearly naked young girl dancing on a stage. It had a sunken bar around it where men sat and watched as they drank. A large, burly guy checked my ID and showed me into the lounge. There were men in twos and threes, sitting at small tables surrounded by as many women. Other tables were occupied with lone men who had women sitting on their laps gyrating.

I found myself a seat near the stage and watched the girl dancing. She had dirty blonde hair. She looked hard and acted bored. I ordered a drink from a waiter and was soon surrounded by three pretty young women. All of them were smiling and wanted to sell me a dance. I bantered with them and smiled back.

I was surprised by three things. First, how young they all looked, second, how well they all spoke English, and third, by the fact that none of them were Mexican. I expected more ethnicity of the Latin variety.

"You want a dance?" asked a sultry beauty in a slip and panties. She spoke with an accent I couldn't place.

"From all of you?" I asked, looking at the three of them.

"If you want," said the first girl. She was a slim thing with green eyes and long legs - just my type.

"I'm afraid my heart couldn't take it," I replied.

"I'll dance for you," offered a second one, sitting on the arm of the chair. She put her hand on my shoulder.

This one was even prettier than the first one. The prospect of her sitting on my lap was very appealing. Apparently the first girl outranked her, however. After a few words in some language I didn't understand, the others went away and left me alone with the first girl.

"How much?" I asked, trying to get acquainted.

"Forty U.S.," she replied without batting one of her long lashes. I could have bought a steak dinner and taken a cab to the airport for that. I thought it was a good price.

"Where you from?" I asked, as if I hadn't decided if I wanted a dance or not. I looked around the room at the other dancers like a wise old shopper.

"Poland," she said.

"Poland?" I echoed. "What are you doing here?"

"A lot of the girls here are from Eastern Europe," she informed me.

"How'd you learn to speak such good English?" I fired off with my second question.

"I've been studying English since I was in the first grade. I know French as well as a little Spanish. Like many of the girls here, I am trying to get to the U.S."

"The U.S.? You're taking a roundabout way of getting there," I commented, starting to feel bad for the young woman.

"For some of us who can't get visas or green cards, it's the only way. Sometimes it's easier to get to the States from Mexico or Canada than from our home countries. The Americans have treaties with these countries that allow more people to cross over. And of course, the border is only a few hundred miles away."

I took out the picture of Alicia.

"Have you seen this girl? She disappeared from her home in Boston a few weeks ago. We have reason to believe she's here in Mexico City."

The girl recoiled from me as if I had grown gills.

"Are you with the police?" she asked.

"No, I'm just a friend of the family."

She looked up at some guy at the bar, who was staring at us rudely.

"Look, I can't stand here and talk all night, mister. Do you want a dance or not?"

"Sure," I said, as a slow, sexy song began to play on the club's sound system. The bored blonde was replaced on the stage by an energetic brunette with bouncing boobs. I watched the girl with the bouncing boobs as the young East European began gyrating on my lap. She was shy and hesitant. I could tell she was new at it, which made it all the more appealing.

"Hmm," I purred in her ear as she rubbed her bare boobs against me. She was on the thin side with delicate features, but athletic. I was starting to get turned on.

I whispered in her ear. "Have you seen anyone like the girl in my picture?"

She turned around to face away from me and ground her backside into my groin for awhile.

"No, there are no American girls here," she told me as she turned around and pushed her small breasts into my face.

I left the club a short time later nursing a boner. It was going to be a long night. Jose was parked across the street.

"Well, senor, how did you like it?"

"Jose, everything they say about Mexican lap dancers is true. Where to next?"

He took me to several other clubs. They were more or less all the same. Young women from various parts of the world with the same sad stories, using their bodies to survive the only way they knew how. Some were only one step above prostitution, if that. Some, like the poor unfortunate street waif in Boston who ended up on a slab, were only children. Alicia could be one of them.

We stopped at place called 'Foxy's', and another called the 'Cadillac', which brought back memories of a club I used to play at back home in the 'burgh'. It seemed like a hundred years ago and a million miles away, so much had happened.

I'd had five lap dances and spent $300 dollars with nothing to show for it but a hard-on. I wondered if my haphazard, seat of the pants method of investigation was a waste of time. Perhaps I should admit defeat and go home. According to Jose, however, the best clubs were yet to come. After all, this was only my first night.

It was almost two a.m., closing time in most establishments. However, 'The Hombres' Club' was open 'til four. According to Jose it had the youngest and most titillating girls in the city. I decided to give it a try. After all, there were worse ways to spend a night than having half-dressed, beautiful young women dance on your lap.

The room was dark like most of the others. It had swirling, colored lights over the stage, where a lone woman danced around a pole. There was no one to check me at the door. Perhaps the doorman had gone home. After all, it was past two a.m.

There were a few men sitting singly in small tables around the room. There was no one dancing on their laps. A few of them eyed me with hard stares. I instantly became alert. I hadn't seen looks like that since the last time I looked into the eyes of a killer.

I found a table off to the side and ordered a drink from the waiter, a short, swarthy Mexican who didn't smile. Maybe he had bad teeth. I got the distinct impression I wasn't welcome.

As soon as the waiter left, I was surrounded by a bevy of young girls, all eager to dance for me. Who could blame them? There wasn't much going on in the joint. They were obviously eager for some new blood - mine. For an instant, I had the weird idea that they were all vampires, and that would have suited me just fine.

I bantered with them, trying to decide which one to choose. It was going to be a tough decision. They were all attractive and in various

126

states of undress. Again, as in the other clubs, they were young girls from other countries, probably with the same stories.

"Can I get a two for one deal?" I asked, only half joking. They giggled. One put her hand on my knee. She became my first choice. Another put her arm on my shoulder. I almost forgot my reason for being there. I smiled at the first girl, the one with her hand on my knee.

"Girls, I'm afraid you will have to take turns. Who's first?"

They all chimed in, "Me! Me!"

"While I've got you here," I said, reaching into my jacket pocket. "Have you seen this girl? She's from Boston. We have reason to believe she's here in Mexico City."

That kind of put a damper on things. A few girls took a look at it and passed it around. Like before, they said there were no American girls there. They told me that she was too young for dancing, although not for other things.

"Hi," a sultry voice said from behind me. "My name is Jasmine. Would you like a dance?"

I turned my head and looked up into the face of a gorgeous, dark-eyed woman. She was tall and shapely, and obviously of Mexican descent. I sensed some European blood in the mix as well. She had high cheek bones and oval eyes. Her skin was dark and stunningly smooth. Her hair was jet black. It cascaded down her bare back like a velvet waterfall. She looked down on me and smiled. I almost fell off my chair. The other girls scattered as if blown away by her beauty. Finally, it looked like I was going to have a real Mexican lap dance.

I forgot all about Alicia. She could have been standing beside me and I wouldn't have noticed. I'd never been that close to a woman of such dazzling beauty before.

We talked briefly as she told me the price - the standard $40 (I would have paid $4000) – and her story. She was born in Mexico City where her parents and brothers still lived. The youngest of five, she earned more money than all of her siblings and father put together. She had been dancing for five years and was going to Hollywood as soon as she had enough money saved up. I told her she should. With her looks and poise she would do well.

She moved closer to me as a new song came on, opening the front of her chemise. She was flawless in every way. She put herself so close to me as I sat in my chair that her chest pressed against my lips. I kissed her lightly and started speaking the only words of Italian I knew.

"Amore. Bellissimo. Ti Amo. Sei Bella!"

I knew I couldn't touch her and sat stone still. I had kept myself in pretty good control all night. I hadn't let myself get fully erect – I have some pride, you know - but this woman was quickly getting the better of me. She turned away and sat on my lap, grinding herself up and down on my crotch. It was so erotic I almost laughed. Now this was a lap dance!

She turned back to face me, and brushed her breasts against my lips as she pressed her body against mine. I kissed them lightly and rubbed my thumb against her wrist, which was holding the arm of the chair. I think she was getting aroused. She pulled her head back and looked at me with a hungry smile that made my toes curl.

I was fully aroused now, in some weird alpha state that was almost like a dream. The room was swirling around me. The music throbbed in my ears. Her body overcame me. I became dizzy, like I was losing my equilibrium, and suddenly felt sick. I grabbed the chair and tried to rise. I had only taken a sip of my drink, but it must have been a strong one. Then, without warning, I was grabbed from behind. The girl jumped off my lap and screamed.

I felt like I was in a cloud, gasping for air. I had enough presence of mind to swing an elbow around and smash whoever was holding me in the side of the head a couple of times. He let go.

I tried to stand, but was immediately bowled over when someone tackled me from the side. I smashed into a table and chairs and fell to the floor with the guy on top of me. Everything was going in slow motion.

Others jumped on me. I was crushed beneath a pile of bodies. The last thing I remember was being punched in the back of the head.

Chapter 27

I woke to the strains of a Mexican love song in the back of Jose's cab. For a moment I thought it had been a dream, but it was all too real. My arms were tied behind me. There was a guy sitting next to me holding a gun.

"Hi, senor. How are you feeling?" said Jose from behind the wheel. "I hope those hombres in there did not hurt you too bad, eh. Do you like this music? It is Lois Miguel, singing 'No Se Tu'."

He sang a few lines of the song along with the radio.

"This is my cousin, Fernando," he added, smiling at me in the rearview mirror. "We were at his garage earlier, remember? He is not a friendly fellow like me, senor, so please do not make him angry. I am sorry we had to tie you up, but it is for your own good."

"Where are you taking me? Why are you doing this, Jose?"

"We are doing our job, senor. What are you doing, snooping around here where you don't belong?"

"Who are you working for?"

"Chihuahua, you have a lot of questions for a know-it-all gringo. You are looking for girls, si? We are looking for girls too."

"Who do you work for?" I asked again. The guy with the gun was looking at me in a way that made my throat constrict.

"He might be worth a lot of money," Jose said to his cousin. The man didn't say a word, but continued to look at me ominously. My hands were falling asleep from the tight ropes. I had a feeling it wouldn't matter.

"What are you going to do with me?" I inquired.

"There you go again, asking the questions," replied Jose, still smiling. I would have given anything to wipe that smirk off his face. "We will ask the questions, senor. Who sent you? What makes you think this girl you seek is here with us?"

"Do you know where she is?" I said. I wasn't going to give him the satisfaction of an answer.

"You mistake me for someone else, senor. I don't know anything about your little girl. All I know is what's going to happen to you if you don't tell us what we want to know."

He pulled the cab behind the deserted garage where we had stopped to get gas earlier that day. It seemed like weeks ago instead of sixteen hours.

He stopped the car and got out to open the sliding rear door of the building. His cousin, Fernando, never took his eyes or the gun off me.

"Get out," commanded Jose, opening the cab door. He wasn't smiling now.

I shimmied out of the car and pushed myself to a standing position. I had a good mind to kick Jose and run, but thought better of it when his cousin waved the gun at me. He motioned me away from the vehicle and got out. I had no choice but to do as they said and try to stay alive as long as possible. I always followed that old adage - as long as you're breathing you still have a chance.

Jose ordered me into the garage. His cousin followed, keeping me covered, and closed the garage door behind us. They talked in Spanish as we stood in the center of the room. I knew I should have taken that language in school rather than French.

A small, bare bulb hanging from the ceiling provided the only light.

Even though I didn't take Spanish in school, Suzy did. I had picked up a little from her, not much, but enough to carry on a conversation at the breakfast table. I couldn't understand everything they said, but I did get the gist of their conversation. I heard one word very distinctly – Russians.

Jose repeated that I was probably worth money and should be held for ransom. He thought whoever sent me would pay to get me back. He believed I would be eager to divulge that information after a little friendly persuasion. His cousin was having none of it. He wanted to kill me quickly and bury me in the corner of his deserted garage. I hoped Jose would win the argument. I didn't understand what Fernando said next, but it ended the conversation. Unfortunately, Jose's cousin had gotten the last word.

"I am sorry, senor," said Jose, looking genuinely apologetic. "But we have to do our job or it is us who will be buried in cement."

"If you're going to kill me, at least tell me if you have Alicia or not. Alicia Fleming. You may know her as Alicia Rossi, a fifteen-year-old from Boston. She was abducted a little over two weeks ago by a man calling himself Phil Sullivan. He has connections to the Russian mob."

"Yes, it is as you say. I will tell you this, senor, the information will not help you where you are going. My employers have a lot of young girls. They get them from all over the world, young and innocent, like the one you are looking for. Some come of their own free will, at least at first, until they learn the truth.

"Our clients pay top dollar, more than you greedy Americans spend on your drugs. American girls are in demand in some countries. I don't know why, since our Mexican girls are much prettier, wouldn't you agree? If I know our employer, your little girl, what did you call her, Alicia? She is long gone by now, more likely some place in the Orient or the Middle East. Those oil sheiks have a thirst for young American girls." He laughed. "And boys, too, for that matter."

He continued. "But why would they take her all the way down here if they grabbed your little girl in, where you say, Boston? They would have taken her right across the border to Canada. You came all the way here for nothing, amigo. She is not here. If they haven't taken her to the client yet, she's probably in Montreal. Not that it will do you any good."

He laughed again, sneering in my face. I might be dead in a minute, but I was going to take this bastard with me, hands tied or no.

I leaped at him with a front kick. Flying through the air, I covered the few feet between us in an instant, kicking him in the throat. He tumbled backward and landed on the ground clutching his gullet. Too bad I wasn't fast enough to dodge a bullet. I heard a gun go off and felt a sudden pain. Then everything went black.

Chapter 28

I woke up in a bed to the sound of a ceiling fan blowing cool air around the room. I thought I was in a hospital at first. The walls and curtains were white, but the room and bed were too big for a medical facility.

I noticed a computer on a desk in the corner. There were what looked like personal pictures and mementos scattered about the room. On further inspection, I appeared to be in someone's bedroom. The vague sense of perfume gave me the impression it was the Mexican lap-dancer, Jasmine's, room, but that was just wishful thinking.

I tried to get up, but got a sudden, searing pain between my eyes. It was accompanied by a flash of white light that almost made me pass out again.

"Take it easy," someone said. It was then I noticed I was not alone. "You've been out for quite awhile. I wasn't sure if you'd come to or not."

I tried to open my eyes and focus, but they were watering too much from the pain.

"I've given you a sedative," the voice informed me as I tried to clear my head. "I don't have much medicine here. You were lucky the bullet just grazed you. You were too fast for the punk who tried to shoot you. I've never seen anyone move so fast. Where'd you learn to do that?"

I tried to stammer something, but I had too many questions of my own to reply.

"I'm sorry," he said. "I see you're still a bit dazed. Don't worry. You'll be fine. I took care of the little creep who tried to kill you. The guy you knocked over with your kick couldn't talk for awhile. Hell, he was having trouble breathing. He expired during my questioning. He really didn't know much."

My eyes were finally starting to adjust to the light in the room, which was bright. The white walls reflected the fierce sun shining through the windows like aluminum foil. The fans were keeping the room cool, however. I focused my attention on the voice.

"My name is Dale Clarkson," he announced, introducing himself. "I guess you'd like to know how you got here."

"Yes," I mumbled. "What happened?"

Dale Clarkson appeared to be in his late fifties or early sixties, with short, snow-white hair and matching well-trimmed beard. He had a ruddy complexion and steel-blue eyes, and appeared to be an American.

"You were in quite a pickle there. I'd been following you all night. As a matter of fact, I've been trailing you since you arrived at the airport. You took a chance jumping into that taxi parked away from the cab zone like that. I thought you'd be kidnapped for sure. They apparently had other plans for you."

"Following me? Why? Who are you?" I stammered.

"Who I am isn't important right now," he answered. "What's important is what you know about these kidnappings. You're looking for Alicia Rossi, right? She disappeared from Boston a few weeks ago. You were hired by the mother."

"How do you know all this?" I whispered in a harsh voice. "Are you with the police?"

"Something like that. Like I said, I've been following you. You could say I had news of your arrival. I trailed you tonight from your hotel. I'd park down the street from your cab and then follow you to the next club. You've had quite a night for yourself, haven't you, Mister Lawless?"

"You know my name?" I croaked.

"I know all about you. And now you know me. You can trust me, Jason. Can I call you Jason? I'm your friend. I knew something was up when you went into that last place, the Hombres' Club. It was after normal closing time. The lights went off as soon as you disappeared through the door. When your cabby and his friend went into the place, I knew you were in trouble.

"I was ready to chalk you off for dead when they carried you out and dumped you in the cab. That was their big mistake. They should have taken you out the back. They were probably overconfident. I followed you to the garage and got in the place through a window. I was watching when you made your move. You're pretty good with that karate stuff."

He made a few karate chops in the air and laughed. He was sitting in a straight-back chair by the bedside, and talked in a friendly, casual manner.

"Pretty good," he said as if he found my life-and-death struggle entertaining. "Here take a sip of this."

He gave me a cup with what looked like clear noodle soup. I took a greedy sip and had an excruciating stab of pain over my eye. It shot around to the back of my head, making me groan.

"Easy now, easy does it," said the man, Clarkson.

"You saved my life," I said, finally realizing what had happened.

"Think nothing of it. Actually I was hoping you could help me."

"What? What do you mean?"

"We know why you are here, and that you got a tip from another young woman you rescued in Boston, Dominique Devereux. She told you something that made you come here."

"Yes," I replied, taking another sip of soup and resting my head back on the pillow. My breath was coming fast, as if swallowing had taken all my strength. I couldn't think for a minute. Then it all came flooding back in a rush.

"She said that there were two girls there before she got to the cottage. They had just left. She overheard the men guarding her mention they had been sold in Mexico City."

"Did the girl say anything else? Did she have any idea who the girls were?"

"No, like I said, she didn't see them. She only heard about them from her abductors. I assumed one of them was Alicia Fleming, the girl I'm looking for."

"Is there anything else? Did she say anything else?"

"No, but after she'd been rescued, I was sitting in the ambulance with her, waiting to go to the hospital to get checked out. She said something interesting. She told me that one of the kidnappers told her she looked like the girl who had just left. She said she felt bad there was a sister out there somewhere being subjected to God knows what."

"A sister? What do you suppose she meant by that?" asked Clarkson.

"That the girl looked like her. She must have been black, like Dominique."

"Here, take another sip of this," he advised. That was the last thing I remember.

Chapter 29

I came to some time later. It was still light. From the slant of the sun on the white walls of the room, I knew it was late in the day. I opened my eyes slowly and stared at the twirling ceiling fan. I began to recall the conversation I'd had with the mysterious stranger, Dale Clarkson. What did it all mean? As I lay on the floor, I tried to puzzle out the events of the past twenty-four hours.

I had obviously stumbled onto something, but what? Had I found Alicia's kidnappers or just a gang of desperados? My wallet was gone. Had it only been a mugging and robbery? And what had Jose's cousin said about a Russian? What did that mean? I began to recall their conversation. No, it was more than a coincidence, even if Alicia wasn't here. Jose seemed to know a lot about her.

Even more puzzling was who this guy Clarkson was. Was he some kind of Fed? He seemed to be quite knowledgeable. Who was he looking for? How did he fit into all this?

I finally tore my gaze from the ceiling fan. It was so soothing, it almost hypnotized me. I looked around the room. I was lying next to the bed. I slowly sat up and put my back against the bedpost. Holding my head, which throbbed with pain, I closed my eyes and called out.

"Mister Clarkson. Dale? Are you there?"

There was no response. I wondered how I had gotten on the floor. The last thing I remembered was lying in a bed. I ached all over, like I had fallen down a flight of stairs. Maybe I fell out of bed. Then I remembered. I'd been shot while in midair. Who knows how hard I landed.

I felt around. Nothing was broken. I decided to try to stand. I had a terrible migraine-type headache that made me nauseous. I had difficulty rising, but forced myself up using the bed for support.

Turning around to face the bed, I pushed myself the last few feet to a standing position, and froze in shock. There on the sheet was Jasmine, the Mexican lap dancer. She was looking up at the ceiling fan with a frozen, glassy stare and stark naked.

My knees gave out as if someone had clipped me. I fell to the floor like a spineless slug. I swore as I lay there. I shook my aching head back and forth. Again and again, over and over I swore. Finally, I pulled myself back up, using the bedspread as a hand ladder, until I was staring at her inert form.

It was happening all over again. It was six years ago. I was staring at the spread-eagled, nude body of a dead young woman. For a moment, I was back at that cold, wet beach, wondering if a demented, knife-wielding maniac had come back from the dead. Was he following me again? Old nightmares die hard. This girl had no slashing knife wounds, however, only a purple welt around her neck. Someone had choked her to death.

I leaned over the body and put my fingers to her neck. She was still warm. I felt for a pulse. There was none. She looked so surprised and scared, so vulnerable and helpless. I wanted to hold her, but she was beyond all comfort now. I hadn't stopped cursing, but went on repeating the swear words as if it were a mantra. I knew what I had to do. I calmed myself and began to apply CPR.

I had learned it years ago when I started my own karate school, soon after crapping out of college. I didn't want to be sued for negligence if one of my students got their trachea or a sternum crushed, so I took a course. I ended up teaching it to my black belts in case I might need it one day. I learned the old-fashioned way, mouth-to-mouth and chest message, no fibrillation for us. I did the same to Jasmine, alternately blowing into her mouth to get air into her lungs, and pushing on her chest to keep her heart going. I did it just hard enough not to break her ribs.

I worked on her like this for about twenty minutes before I collapsed on top of her, out of breath. She was no longer warm when I felt her. Rigor was starting to set in. I looked at her stark corpse and wanted to scream. I threw a blanket on her and ran out of the room instead.

It was dark again when I hit the street. I was in a residential area, where well-dressed people walked about on their appointed rounds. No one gave me much heed. I had no idea where I was or where I was going, but something told me I'd better get out of that room and pronto.

I was sick and confused. I had to find a place where I could rest and think things through. I had to figure out what was happening. Things were moving so fast around me I felt like I was standing still.

I had glanced in a mirror on my way out of the apartment and noticed the large bandage on my head. I couldn't be seen in the streets like that. I might as well carry a neon sign around with me. I still had on the same shirt and slacks I had gone out in the previous evening. Or was it several evenings ago? I wasn't even sure what day it was or how long I had been out.

I found a pair of sunglasses on a stand by the door, along with a baseball cap. Instead of the insignia of a ball team, it had the name of a popular Mexican beer. I picked up both items and put them on. There was also a small, light gray jacket hanging on a peg. I grabbed that too and slung it over my shoulder. I could almost pass for a Mexican. I left the building and limped slowly down the street.

My head ached. I was nauseous and dizzy. I hoped my wound wouldn't start bleeding or get infected. It may have been superficial, but it hurt like a mother and caused me no end of mental anguish. I knew I couldn't stay in the area. My instincts told me every minute I was there was one less minute I'd be free.

My instincts were right. I was no sooner out of the building and around the corner when three Mexican police cars drove up to the residence. They had their lights flashing and their sirens blazing. I didn't stop to find out what was going on.

Walking as fast as I could, I went down one busy residential street and then another, always heading toward what I thought was out of town. I didn't know what was happening, or what I was going to do. I only knew I had to keep moving, preferably away from the city.

I could hear sirens in the distance. They seemed to be sounding all over town. Maybe it was just a coincidence, but I had the unsettling feeling they were all after me. I quickened my pace. My mind was a blank. All I wanted to do was get as far away from that room, and what it held, as possible.

I hate to admit it, but as I left the apartment, I grabbed the dead girl's purse and pulled out almost five hundred dollars worth of pesos. The lap dancer had indeed had a good night. Too bad it had ended so badly. Yes, I had stolen from a dead person. My only excuse is that if I didn't think fast and act even quicker, I'd be dead too. I was careful not to touch anything as I left. I used a tissue to pick up the purse and extract the money. Unfortunately, my fingerprints were all over the dead girl's body.

I was too dazed to do anything but walk. The sun was setting in the west. I used it to head in a northerly direction, toward the U.S. border and home. I didn't know how many miles away it was, but figured it had to be at least a thousand.

Coming upon a filling station, I found a rack with roadmaps. I purchased one of them, and asked if there were any buses in the area going north.

"Hey, un autobus que va al norti?" I asked the attendant. The young man was obviously more interested in looking at the senoritas walking by than helping some gringo. He became much more attentive when I paid for the map and put twenty-five pesos in front of him.

After querying him several more times, I was able to determine that the local Camiones to Ciudad Valles went by on the next street corner every evening at 7:00.

"Vas rapido y ousted peudo cogerlo," he said, pointing me in the right direction. I took his advice and hurried out the door to catch the bus.

I waited at the next street corner, where a small crowd had gathered. There was no bus sign, but from the looks of it, I wasn't the only one waiting for a ride. A short time later, an old, dirty bus drove up, crowded with people. It made a coughing noise and belched black smoke. Then it slowed to a stop, making an even worse sound when it started up again.

I and several others had to stand. The top of the vehicle was crowded with baggage and boxes of all descriptions. Some of it was alive and in crates or cages. It was a regular cacophony of humanity, mostly country people going home from the market or their jobs in the city.

I stood for almost an hour as the bus made one stop after another. I thought it would never get out of the city. Once it did, it stayed off the toll roads and main highways, weaving its way north through a seeming endless vista of small neighborhoods and villages.

At some point I must have passed out. I woke up with a woman wiping my forehead with a wet cloth. The bus driver asked if I was OK. I told him I had wrecked my car and was trying to get to Monterrey.

"I'll be OK," I said, apologizing.

I was offered a seat by a farmer who was getting off at the next stop with his chickens. I rode the rest of the way to Ciudad Victoria in relative comfort. After a brief rest stop in Ciudad Valles, where I had a supper of sopa Mexicana and tortillas, we arrived at the town of Ciudad Victoria. It was around midnight. There was an actual terminal there, where I was able to pick up a second-class bus ticket to Monterrey. It left the next morning at 8:15. I had enough money to get a room at a small hotel. I asked the desk clerk to wake me up at 7:00.

My head was throbbing. I could hardly see straight or keep my eyes opened. I bought a small bottle of aspirin with codeine at a corner drugstore. I hoped I'd wake up and not slip into a coma.

I examined my bandage when I was in the room, after taking three of the maximum-strength pills. There didn't seem to be any blood. I pressed the wound. It was dry but warm. I probably should have been in a hospital. For all I knew, I was wanted by the police for murder. Perhaps I should have gone to them and told them what happened. With my history and the authorities, however, that seemed like a last resort.

Chapter 30

I didn't slip into a coma, though I didn't dream either. It was still dark outside when I woke. It must have been around four or five a.m. I had paid for the room in advance the previous evening. So I put the key and a few pesos on the dresser, and left some time around six without checking out.

I had breakfast at an outdoor stand near the bus terminal. Then I waited across the street in a park soaking up the sun on a bench until around 8:00 a.m. I had made sure the clock at the terminal was correct. With my baseball cap and sun glasses, I looked like any other Mexican waiting for the bus to Monterrey.

Still, I half expected the police to come charging in to take me away. Nothing like that happened, however, as I took my seat on the crowded vehicle. Because I waited until the last moment before boarding, I got one of the few remaining seats in the back. This bus was newer than the first one I had taken. Like the last one, it was crowded with mostly country people going to visit relatives, or going home from the city.

I was informed that the bus took mostly back roads and made frequent stops. I was also warned about the possibility of banditos in the back country. However, the bus company was quick to point out that outlaw activity had been low of late due to stepped-up police activity in the area. I thought nothing of it, being wrapped up and preoccupied with my own worries.

We were soon underway. I put my cap over my eyes and tried to get more sleep, or at least appear as if I was sleeping. The smells and sounds on the bus engulfed me.

I must have been tired. Despite the noise, congestion, and bumpy ride, I dozed off at some point. I woke with a start as the bus came to a sudden stop. We had come to a police roadblock. It was too late to do anything but hunker down in my seat and pull the cap over my eyes. A federale boarded the bus and began checking everyone's papers.

I considered my options, which were few, and they were diminishing fast. I counted how many armed men I'd have to subdue. I stopped counting at three. The Mexican policeman was almost at my seat at the back of the bus, when an altercation erupted outside right near my window.

140

A couple men, who had gotten out to check on their baggage, had gotten into an argument about who owned a certain valise. It soon came to blows. The two federales outside were having trouble subduing the men, who were going at each other with flailing fists. The officer in the bus ran out to help. They forgot all about checking papers as they arrested the two men and carted them off. The bus was soon on its way again.

I had been lucky. I wondered if I'd have better luck avoiding the federales if I hitchhiked to Monterrey. I looked at my map to see where I might get off the bus and make my way across country. I didn't want to get trapped by another police roadblock with no papers.

About fifty miles ahead, the road intersected several main highways. One of them went north, through some sparsely populated countryside. I considered ditching the bus there and trying my luck on foot and with my thumb. The way we were going, it'd be another hour or so before we got to the spot. I closed my eyes and sat back to relax until then.

I woke up about an hour later. We were in an arid area surrounded by high, flat mountains. There didn't seem to be a village or house for miles. I looked out the window as the bus started up a steep grade.

The terrain was rocky and desert-like. There were few trees and no water in sight. I was having second thoughts about leaving the bus and trying to hitch a ride. What if I didn't get picked up? I'd be walking through the desert with no food or water, nothing but a thin jacket on my back. I was pondering this dilemma when the bus started to slow down again. I was afraid it was another police roadblock.

I needn't have worried. It was not the federales this time, only a man in a sombrero holding a sub-machinegun. We were being hijacked!

All of a sudden, everyone in the bus was talking at once. Several people got up and peered out the windows trying to see what was happening. Someone rapped on the bus door. The driver opened it and put up his hands. A man jumped in and pointed his machinegun at him. Another came in behind him, also holding a weapon, and aimed it at the passengers. Other men with sombreros and machetes surrounded the vehicle.

The man facing us spoke in Spanish. I didn't have to know the language to understand what he was saying. In any case, a translator wasn't required. He repeated what he had said, this time in English.

"American tourists, please stand up," he said. "Please stand up if you are an American."

I sat stone still. He started walking through the bus, pointing his gun to the left and right as he went down the aisle looking at the occupants one by one. I sat with my head hung low like the other Mexicans, not making eye contact, although I watched his every move as he approached.

I was calculating my chances of subduing the two machinegun toting banditos without getting everyone in the bus killed, myself included. They were not good. To tell the truth, I just didn't have the heart for it. In any case, I didn't get the chance. He stopped a few feet from me and looked in my direction. He was too far away to get to.

"You, the one with the 'Corona' hat." He pointed the gun at me. "Who are you?"

"Mi?" I said, in my best Mexican accent.

"Si, uste." He started running off Spanish swear words at 120 words a minute. "Stand up!" he ordered in English.

I did as he said.

"Take off your hat and sunglasses, senor."

I obeyed.

"You are a gringo," he announced. He told me to get off the bus.

Out of the frying pan into the fire, I thought to myself as I got off the bus and stood in the middle of the road with my hands up. Now they had their gringo they didn't seem interested in anything else, and soon let the bus go. As the sun went down behind the western mountains, I found myself surrounded by six Mexican banditos with machetes and machineguns. I should have gone with the federales.

Most people would have been worried at this point, but I stayed calm. After all, I had been in worse situations. Instead of fretting about what was going to happen to me, I was already thinking about how I was going to get out of it.

Chapter 31

I wondered how they knew I was an American. Without further ado, the man with the machinegun ordered me to follow them along a dirt track that led into the hills. We soon came to a group of pickup trucks and early model cars. The men piled into them, after ordering me into one of the pickups.

We bounced along a rutted dirt road for half an hour, then stopped at a ranch house. It was really not much more than a couple shacks. Three of the bandits escorted me inside, while the others continued down the road.

One of the men with me was the man who had spotted me on the bus. He told me to sit in a chair and asked if I wanted a beer. I said yes. I was already bonding with my kidnappers.

"Give me your passport and wallet," he ordered.

"I don't have my passport or my wallet," I told him. "I've had, er, a sort of, um, an accident."

The man looked at me dubiously.

"Search him," he commanded. One of his associates frisked me and started going through my pockets.

"How did you know I was an American?" I asked as one man finished searching me and another gave me a beer.

"I would keep my mouth shut if I were you, gringo," the man advised. "You will be in a lot of trouble if the federales find you in this country without passport or papers. They will think you are some sort of criminal. How are we going to ransom you if we cannot contact the authorities?"

"Please don't contact the authorities," I pleaded.

"Oh? And why not?" he inquired.

"Because I'm wanted by the authorities."

"Ah, maybe they will pay to get you back then."

"I don't think so. The ones who are framing me run your police. They will take me from you without paying. You will be lucky if they don't kill you."

"Look around, gringo," he replied with macho bravado. "We are the ones who will do the killing."

"You can't stand up to the Russian Mafia. They're operating out of Mexico City. They're stealing girls from the U.S. and bringing them here and to the Orient."

He stopped and thought a minute when he heard these words.

"I have heard something of these Russians," he said. "It is not only American girls they are stealing. They have taken young, innocent girls from our villages as well. They are forced into the sex trade. Where did you find these people?"

I told them about the Hombres' Club. I mentioned I had seen very young girls there that could have been from their village. They were lingering at the edge of the room in the shadows. They seemed out of place, as if they didn't belong there. They disappeared at the first sign of trouble. I insisted that the girls looked as if they were of Indian descent.

So what if I stretched the truth? Who knows, maybe they really were from these banditos' villages. I needed some payback. I hoped these muchachos were as bad as they looked. I wouldn't want to be the blokes at the Hombres' Club when these combatientes showed up.

We talked late into the night and again the following day as a tropical rain pounded on the tin roof of the cabin. I told him everything I knew. I related what had happened to Jasmine and that I was being framed for her murder. The fact that a Mexican woman had been killed by the Russians seemed to enrage them. I thought it was more likely the mysterious Mister Clarkson, whoever he was, had strangled the young beauty, but I didn't tell my kidnappers that.

I still hadn't fit him into the equation. Although he had apparently rescued me from Jose and his cousin, I still didn't trust him. For all I knew, he could have been the 'Russian', though he looked and spoke like an American. He had pumped me for information and drugged me as we talked. He had probably killed the girl because she knew too much. He then used her to incriminate me so anything I said would be used against me.

But why would he quiz me about another girl, someone who had nothing to do with my missing person? It didn't make sense, unless he really was a cop. But who did he work for? And what kind of cop would be operating in another country like Mexico? Unless he was some sort of Fed, maybe even CIA. But what could they be doing down here? Perhaps they were after the same human trafficking ring I was after. If so, killing the girl and framing me for her murder was a funny way of going about it.

Later that night, after the rain had stopped and the sun had come out to go down behind the western peaks, my captor, Ernesto, and his compatriots met to discuss what I had told them. I repeated everything I had related to Ernesto, who turned out to be the leader of the ragtag band. They all agreed they had to pay this place a visit and see for themselves if that was where the village girls had been taken. If so, they would owe me a debt of gratitude.

I told them that was all well and good, but I had to get home so I could tell the authorities there what happened. My girl was still missing and I had reason to believe she was in Canada. Time was of the essence.

"That may be, senor," replied Ernesto. "But we cannot let you go until you have shown us this place."

"If there's a computer nearby, I can show you where it is without driving a mile."

He looked at me quizzically.

"There is one in the school. It is not far from where we are. My sister is the teacher. Come, I will take you there."

We got in the pickup and were at the school in twenty minutes. I remembered the address of the club from the night I was there and 'Googled' it. Zooming in on the location with the satellite view I had learned from Bud, we were soon looking down on the place as if suspended in air a few hundred feet above it, the streets and buildings in plain view.

I had a sudden pang of anxiety as Bud's image flashed across my mind. I had to find a phone and call him as soon as possible. That necessity filled me with concern. I prayed he was OK and that I would get back to him. I had to stop and get my breathing back under control - in through the nose, out through the mouth. Just breathe and concentrate on the task at hand, nothing more. Do not anticipate. Do not imagine.

I wrote out directions of how to get to the club from their front door.

"Be careful," I warned. "The police are with them."

"Don't worry, amigo," replied Ernesto. "We know how to take care of them." He looked at an older man, a farmer, standing next to him. "Juan, keep an eye on our friend here until we return. We don't want anything to happen to him."

Then he and the others left.

145

I was a bit miffed he had left me there under guard, though the fellow only had a machete. That was enough. I didn't like the way he looked at me, with a kind of, 'I'm not afraid of you, gringo', look. It made me want to shove the thick blade of the machete up his anus. I smiled at him as if he were a smart-ass little boy who was about to walk over a cliff. That made him even more macho and before long we were in a staring contest.

I stood up and began to pace the small room. He got up, too, and stood in front of the door with his arms folded across his chest. I went to a window and looked out. He watched me suspiciously.

"It sure is hot in here," I observed. "What you guys need is an air conditioner."

He didn't appear to understand what I said. He continued to stand blocking the door.

"Beautiful country," I commented, looking out the window again and admiring the view of the mountains. "You're lucky to live here."

I pointed to the surrounding vista and smiled.

"What do you do when you're not kidnapping American tourists?" I asked.

He looked at me with a blank expression.

"Que passa?" I asked.

He said nothing.

"I'd hate to be those hombres when your amigos catch up to them. I hope they find the little girls from the village."

He nodded his head and said, "Si, one of those little girls is my daughter."

The guy spoke English after all and was the father of one of the girls. I commiserated with him and told him what I had seen. I was almost sure now that it was the village girls that I saw at the club. I told him his daughter would be home soon. That made him smile and relax a bit. The ice had been broken. By the time the other banditos returned later that evening covered in blood, Juan and I were good buddies, having finished off a half bottle of cheap tequila together.

That night over a midnight supper of fried beans and tortillas, Ernesto told us what had happened. They had indeed found the girls from the village, and succeeded in busting up the dance club along with anyone who had tried to stop them. It had been a wild scene. The police had been lured away to another area. Ernesto and his gang were able to take the kidnappers completely by surprise just before the club opened up for the evening. They would not be back in business soon,

Ernesto assured me. When they were, there would be a lot fewer of them.

His gang of banditos had suffered only two casualties. One man was shot in the arm. One was stabbed in the side. Both would live. They were now under a doctor's care. I would read all about it in the morning papers.

"Now, what about you, senor?" Ernesto said, looking at me with a paternal expression. "What are we going go do with you, amigo?"

"I hope you are not still thinking of trying to ransom me," I said. "There's no one who would care that you've got me. If there was, they wouldn't have any money."

"You have helped us get our daughters back," Ernesto told me. "What can we do to repay you?"

"You can help me get home. I need to see my own boy and clear my name with the authorities back in the States."

"It would be our pleasure," he said, smiling broadly with a small piece of corn stuck in his teeth.

Chapter 32

The following morning the papers were plastered with grisly pictures and stories of the massacre at the dance club. Several men had been killed. Their mutilated, blood-splattered bodies were pictured, half-covered with tablecloths and white sheets. They weren't quite covered enough, however, to hide the grisly remains. A machete in the hands of an enraged peasant can be a terrible thing. Vengeance was wreaked that awful day. I was sorry I'd had anything to do with it. At least it wasn't me doing the avenging this time.

I had lost my appetite, but Ernesto ate with relish, recounting his deeds of the previous night.

"Hey, amigo, I want to show you something," he said as he finished his breakfast. "She is my pride and joy."

I wondered if it was a horse or a girl. I followed him outside and across the road to a small barn.

Ernesto's pride and joy was a candy-apple red, 'souped-up' Chevy pickup truck. It was spotless, with thick tires in the back and a raised suspension. I could tell the engine had been enhanced by the number of tailpipes sticking out behind the cab, and the oversized grill.

"Isn't she a beauty?" he crowed, standing back and letting the sunlight splash on the hood.

"Yeah," I agreed. "What kind of truck is it?"

"It's a Chevy Silverado. The best truck in the world."

"Nice. Looks like you've done a lot of work on it."

"Not me, the man I got it from. It's the fastest thing in these parts, a lot faster than those beat-up junk heaps the federales drive. I'll have you at the border in no time, amigo. In no time," he repeated, patting the fender of his pride and joy.

A few minutes later we were motoring down a backcountry road at seventy mph. Driving northeast for about an hour, we reached the small town of Ciudad Cerraivo. From there we continued northeast through high desert country.

"We're in General Trevino now," Ernesto informed me as we passed through a small, tidy village.

A short time later he said, "We are leaving the state of Nuevo Leon and entering Tamaulipas."

He took a detour across a field and down a bumpy dirt road to avoid a roadblock further up the highway. His police-band radio tipped him off. A few miles later he was back on the main road heading in a northeasterly direction toward the border. About a half hour later, he slowed the truck down at an intersection.

"To the right is the border town of Ciudad Miguel Aleman, but we are going east, toward Nuevo Laredo."

I looked at my road map.

"Isn't that a bit out of the way? Why don't we go to Miguel Aleman. It's a lot closer. I can cross there."

"How?" he asked. "You have no papers. You will only be arrested by the federales and right back where you started. Unless you want to try and cross over by yourself in the desert like a dirt-poor, ignorant peasant, is that what you want? You are sure to get caught or shot. There are patrols all along here, on both sides of the border. Plus there is a fence with razor wire on the other side. No, senor, you would not stand a chance. Stick with me. I know a way for you to get across."

He pulled into a small gas station and filled up his tank, taking the rest of the pesos I had stolen from the dead girl's apartment. I wouldn't have objected even if he didn't have a machinegun and a machete. He bought me a coke from the dispenser and some chips with the change. Then we started on our way again. He drove along Route 2 as it ran west, parallel to the U.S.-Mexican border. We soon passed the village of Guerrero and drove out into the desert.

There was not a tree in sight. The land was flat and rocky. Sand blew across the highway like snow in New England. Ernesto never slowed down below eighty. We were making good time, near the U.S. border town of Zapata, when Ernesto swore in Spanish.

"The federales have spotted us!" he yelled over the roar of the engine, pointing to the right toward the border. Two white vans with blue and gold insignias were racing toward us along a side road. He stepped on the gas. I was pressed to the seatback. The truck accelerated to 120 as if it had been boosted by a rocket.

We sped down the highway. I peeked in the rearview mirror. The police cars veered onto the road behind us and came in hot pursuit.

"Do not worry," Ernesto told me. Putting his foot to the floor, he made the truck go even faster. "They will not catch us."

"It's not the ones behind us I'm worried about," I replied, clicking on my seatbelt and holding on to the seat strap for dear life.

It was late in the day. There was not much traffic on the highway, but too much for the speed we were going. Ernesto zipped by the slower moving cars like a bullet with radar. We just missed several as he sped past, once on the shoulder.

We approached an intersection, where a police car was parked to cut us off. Ernesto made a hard right and cut across a field. Tearing through a barbed wire fence and bouncing across a dirt track, we skidded back onto the highway, this time heading due north. A road sign we streaked by said Rt. 85. Another one we tore past said Nuevo Laredo, 10 KM.

Looking back, I saw the two vehicles pursuing us try to take the turn without smashing. One drove through the junction, just missing the squad car blocking the road. It slammed on its brakes to stop well beyond the intersection. The other one skidded around the turn and almost tipped over before it rammed into the back of a pickup truck that had just passed through the crossroad. We gained another two minutes on them as they backed up their cars and continued after us. The third vehicle joined them with its lights flashing.

"What are you going to do?" I asked with concern.

"Don't worry," he assured me. "I do this all the time."

"So do they, but I think you've lost them," I said, looking behind me. I could see the federales receding into the distance.

By the time we entered the city they were far behind us and for the most part out of sight. After a few turns down some side streets and alleys, they were nowhere to be seen.

He slowed down. We were in a borough on the edge of town. Small squat adobe houses alternated with shops and stores of various kinds. If the federales had radioed ahead, I saw no sign of it.

We drove down a back alley and stopped behind what appeared to be a repair shop of some kind. As if on cue, someone opened the sliding door of the garage. Ernesto drove the truck in.

As he pulled a tarp over the vehicle, I peaked out the front window. The two police vans screamed down the street with their sirens howling. A third followed slowly a few minutes later.

"So much for the police," said my host. "They will go all the way to the border and find nothing."

"Now what?" I inquired. I still didn't see how I was going to get across. "Are you going to pack me in a crate of bananas and smuggle me across?"

150

"No, amigo, nothing like that," he replied. "We have a much better way of getting you home."

Chapter 33

It had grown dark by the time Ernesto hid his truck and led me into the house adjoining the garage, a white-washed adobe building with windows that needed a bath. I wondered what he had in store for me. We were in a small kitchen with cracked linoleum and garbage on the floor. Without saying a word, he led me down the stairs to the basement.

"Here, you will need this," he said. He turned at the bottom of the stairs and handed me a wad of U.S. dollars. I counted it.

"There's fifty dollars here," I announced. "What's this for?"

"Let us just say it is a small payment for your services in helping us get our girls back. Maybe it will help you get your girl back."

"What are we doing?" I asked, looking around the cramped, dark space. The basement walls were cinder block with bare dirt in some places. An old hot water heater sat in one corner, an old furnace in another. An ornate bookcase stood against the opposite wall, taking up most of the space

"You want me to wait here?" I inquired.

"No, senor, I want you to go." As he spoke, he grabbed the edge of the bookcase and swung it forward. It opened effortlessly, like a door. Behind it was a large Indian blanket. Behind the blanket was the entrance to a tunnel.

I stood in amazement. I had heard about tunnels under the border, but never in a million years ever thought I'd see one, let alone be traveling it. It was lit and clean, and wide enough to ride a golf cart through. I could walk with my arms extended and still not reach the ceiling.

"Wow!" I exclaimed. "Unbelievable."

I had tears in my eyes.

"How can I thank you?" I asked.

"For one, don't tell anyone about what you've seen. We will destroy it soon and build another, but I would rather not have the authorities know about it in the meantime."

"I swear I won't tell a soul, not even my son."

"I know. I would not have brought you here or helped you if I had not thought you were a good man, one who could be trusted. The tunnel is exactly 1.9 miles long. When you get to the other end, go up

152

the ladder and knock three times. The man there will let you up. Do everything he says. Here is a bus ticket to San Antonio. I trust you will not get hijacked on the way." He laughed.

I laughed too. Grasping his hand in friendship, I thanked him again.

I started walking down the tunnel as he closed the entrance. It seemed to descend slightly and then evened out. It was cool. The walls were dark red clay reinforced with wide planks. Thick beams that looked like railroad ties were spaced every so many feet apart to support the walls and ceiling. Water seeped through at places and splashed on the stone floor. There were several wires and pipes strung along the ceiling, and bare light bulbs every twenty feet or so.

I walked for almost twenty minutes at a good pace, until I came to the end of the tunnel. There was a ladder leading up through the ceiling with a latched door at the top. I knocked three times and waited. After a few minutes, a middle-aged man in his undershirt opened the door.

"Bienvenito!" he said. "I hope you have had a nice trip. My name is Ramone"

"Ah, wonderful," I replied, ascending the rest of the way up the ladder. I was in another basement room, this one furnished. "Thank you, Ramone."

"I hope you will stay and have dinner with us," he offered. "Ernesto told us what you have done. Any friend of El Jefe is a friend of ours."

"Gracias, Ramone. Your hospitality is much appreciated."

After my third dinner of beans and tortillas in as many days, Ramone told me I could stay in his room until morning. I was in a suburb of Laredo, Texas. When he went to work in the morning I would leave with him.

"I will take you to the bus station in town," he told me. "We will be just two more commuters going to work in the morning like everyone else. You will not be noticed. There's a bus for San Antonio leaving at 9:00 a.m."

I thanked him and got a few hours of much needed sleep, along with a shower, which I needed even more. Ramone also had a change of clothes for me. When we went to work the next morning at 8:00, I had on a white shirt and dark pants, much like he was wearing.

"Good luck, amigo," he said as he dropped me off at the bus station. I boarded the next bus to San Antone.

Chapter 34

I looked in the papers as we drove northeast up Rt35, but could find nothing about a murdered Mexican lap dancer or the goings on in Mexico City. At least my face wasn't plastered all over the front page. I had boarded the bus with no police escort.

I wasn't sure what I was going to do when I got San Antonio, but I had an urgent desire to call Bud. I wondered what had become of my cell phone and wallet. No doubt they were at the scene of the murder. Well, it wasn't the first time.

When I got to San Antone I found a pay phone at the airport. Unhappily, Bud's phone number was lost somewhere in what was the disorganized jumble of my brain. Bud had programmed my phone to call his at the push of a button. I never had to dial it after that. Other than the area code, I had no idea what his number was.

I tried information. They were less than helpful and told me they didn't have cell phone numbers.

"Where do I get a freaking cell phone number?" I yelled into the receiver. I got a dead line in response.

I was about to give up, when I remembered one number I could never forget, my ex-wife, Suzy's. It was indelibly embedded in my mind from all the late night calls I inflicted on her during our lengthy separation and final divorce. I could dial it even in a drunken stupor. I had plenty of practice.

Despite my misgivings, I dialed the number. I had twenty dollars worth of quarters in my pocket. I hoped it was enough. Mercifully, she answered on the third ring.

"Yes," she said. Her irritation and anxiety were noticeable from that single word. "Is that you, Bud?"

"It's Jay," I answered. "Hi, Suzy."

"Jay, where is Francis?" she asked, using his real name, her father's name, a name I couldn't stand.

"Where are you?" I countered. "What's the idea of dropping him off without telling me?"

"Don't start that now, Jay. I'm in no mood and don't have the time. Where's Francis?"

I wondered what had happened to the funny, happy-go-lucky, carefree girl I used to know. Then I remembered - she married me.

"I'm trying to get in touch with Bud myself," I told her. "Do you have his cell phone number?"

"What do you mean, you're trying to get in touch with him?" she replied. "Where are you?"

"Where are you?" I demanded. "When are you coming back?"

"I'm on my way back now," she explained. "We're on a layover in London. We're flying out for New York in a few hours. I was going to have him take a bus home and meet us there."

"You can't swing by and pick the kid up? You got to make him take a bus? I suppose you wanted me to pay for it."

"You're such a cheapskate, Jay. I can't for the life of me remember why I married you."

"Because you used to have a sense of humor."

"Yeah, that explains everything, I married a clown."

"Hey, it's not my fault you just went on your honeymoon with the circus. Now, give me Bud's cell phone number."

"He's not answering. I was getting worried. Where are you? You're not on one of your cases, are you?"

"As a matter of fact, I am. Some of us have to work for a living. He's with my landlord, Mrs. Corrado."

"Do you have her number?"

I didn't, but I gave her the address and told her to call information. Mrs. Corrado didn't have a cell phone, but had an unlisted number, which was sure to drive Suzy crazy.

I assured my ex I'd find out what was going on with our son and let her know. She didn't have to know I was 3000 miles away from him. Or that I had just crossed the Rio Grande like an illegal alien.

I had to look at a paper to find out what day it was. I was totally disoriented. I felt like I had fallen off the face of the earth and had just dropped back in. Then I had to figure out what time it was in Boston, and where Bud was likely to be at this time of day. Suzy had probably left him all sorts of messages. For all I knew she had filled his mailbox. I had no intention of leaving a message. What I had to say couldn't be said in a memo.

I found a kiosk and had lunch. I figured he'd be hanging on the street corner with his friends or between one of his classes at the YMCA. I wondered if he was worried about me. Probably not. I was a day overdue and hadn't called but once, which was par for the course

155

where his old man was concerned. It was likely he was screening his calls. Being miffed at his mom - I couldn't blame him — he was not picking up when he saw her number. Still, I began to worry that he might be in trouble.

Chapter 35

"Pickup, pickup, pickup," I begged later that afternoon when I called his cell using the number Suzy grudgingly gave me. I hoped he'd see the payphone number on his phone's display and figure out where it was coming from. At least he'd realize it wasn't his mother calling him.

"Hello," Bud answered. I breathed a sigh of relief. Then I started bombarding him with questions.

"Bud? Bud, is that you? I need to talk to you. It's your dad. Can you talk? Where are you? Bud, listen. Bud, Bud, are you there?"

"Oh, hi Cynthia," he replied in a nonchalant voice. If he was worried about his old man, he certainly didn't sound like it. As a matter of fact, he sounded like he didn't know who it was. Who was Cynthia?

"Bud, it's me, your dad. I need to talk to you. Something's happened."

"Yeah, I know all about it. Look, I can't talk now. Are we still on for tonight?"

"What?" I said, perplexed and in no mood for games. "Bud, it's me, your dad, Jay."

"OK, I'll call you at seven. You can tell me where to meet you."

"Bud, it's me. It's your dad. I need to..."

"See you tonight, Cynthia. Bye."

The line went dead. I sat trying to figure out what my crazy kid was talking about. Was it all some kind of joke to him? Maybe he couldn't talk. He said he'd call me at seven. I assumed he was talking Eastern Standard Time. That would be in three hours.

I occupied myself in the airport until then. I did what most people do, sit and wait. Unlike most of the folks there, however, I was waiting for a phone call not a flight. About ten minutes of four, my time, I stood at the phone with the receiver to my ear pretending to talk while I surreptitiously depressed the hook with my thumb. To my surprise and relief, the phone rang at precisely seven p.m. Bud's time.

"Dad, is that you? It's Bud."

"Bud, what was that all about? Why the cloak and dagger?"

"I couldn't talk. The police were here asking about you."

"What? What did the police want?"

"You tell me. Where are you? What's going on?"

157

"Just tell me what the police said."

"They came by Mrs. Corrado's place this afternoon, just before you called. They wanted to know if you were home. I told them you went to Mexico City, and that you were supposed to be back yesterday. They said the Mexican authorities were looking for you and told us to have you contact the captain when you got home. What's all this about, Dad?"

"I can't tell you over the phone. Did they see my number when I called?"

"No. I thought the cop was going to ask for my phone, but I was asking too many questions, so they left. You think they've bugged my phone?"

"I wouldn't put it past them, but I doubt they've gotten around to it yet. We'd better not take any chances, though. Can you call me back on a payphone?"

"Already ahead of you, Pop. Where did you think I was calling you from?"

"Good boy. Now you've got to help me."

"What's wrong? What happened? Are you OK?"

"I'm fine. I'm in Texas. I lost my wallet and passport in Mexico."

"Did you find the girl?"

"No, but I found out something about who took her and where she might be. I'm just afraid I may be too late to help her. That's why I have to get back to the east coast."

"Why don't you hitchhike? That's what I'd do."

"If I had a couple of weeks and was twenty years younger I'd try it. Anyway, it would take too long. I don't have time for that. I might get picked up. The police are looking for me."

"What did you do, Dad?"

"Nothing, but I got too close to the people who took Alicia. They set me up, or at least I think it was them. In any case, I need a quick way back home that's not going to cost anything."

"Hmm, maybe I can wire you the money."

"Where are you going to get money? I don't want you borrowing any from Mrs. Corrado. The $100 I gave you must be almost gone by now. Anyway, it's not enough."

"I can write a check."

"What do you mean, write a check?"

"I'll just sign your name on one of your checks. You keep your bankbook in the desk draw, right?"

158

"Never you mind about my bankbook."

"Do you want to get home or not?"

I thought for a moment, but couldn't come up with anything better.

"OK, but the bank will never cash it. They know my signature."

"Don't worry."

"What do you mean, don't worry?"

"I mean I ran out of money the first day. I can't be eating at Mrs. Corrado's every night. I don't know where you eat, but a measly $100 doesn't get you very far around here."

"Bud!"

"I'd have starved to death the first day if I didn't write a check. I've got your name down pretty good. Anyway, they know me at your bank. They've seen me a couple of times when I went in with you. Remember, I was with you when you withdrew that hundred dollars and gave it to me."

"Bud!"

"Do you want to get home or not? How much do you need and where do you want me to wire it?"

I wanted to berate him and tell him to show some respect, but I was in a slightly compromising position. I told him where to send the money.

Before I hung up, I told him I had talked with his mother.

"Call her," I said. "She's worried about you."

"She's not worried about me. She just wants me to go home and go back to school when it starts as if nothing's happened, but I'm not going back."

"Bud, I don't have the time for this right now. You've got to go back to school. If you want to live with me, maybe we can arrange things. That is if I get back. But it's probably too late to get you into school in Boston this year. And you can't miss the start of school. It's going to be hard enough catching up as it is. You don't want to fall behind."

"I won't fall behind. Anyway, have you ever tried living with newlyweds?"

"What do you know about newlyweds?"

"I hate them!"

"Bud, don't be like that. Call your mother and do what she says."

"What are you going to do? It sounds like you're in a lot of trouble."

159

"I've been in worse. Never mind about me. I can take care of myself. Just worry about yourself."

"You haven't killed anyone, have you?"

"What kind of question is that to ask your father?"

"A normal one if your father is Jay Lawless."

"No, Bud, I haven't killed anyone, nor do I plan to."

"Then what are you going to do?"

"I haven't worked all that out yet, but I don't want to have to worry about you while I do. So please go home like your mother wants."

He started to complain, when I had a sudden thought."

"Go home to the 'burgh'. I'll meet you there, but you can't tell anyone."

"What do you have in mind, Dad? Are you going to let me work with you?"

"We'll see, Number One Son, we'll see."

For all I knew Alicia could have still been in Mexico City, if she was ever there. Jose's story about the girls being taken to Montreal could have been just a lie to dupe the dumb gringo before killing him. Going to Quebec could be yet another wild goose chase, another phantom lead.

If my girl was in Mexico she was on her own. I could not go back. I had not only been discredited there, I was a fugitive from the law. I had nothing left but to follow the lead in my usual simpleminded way no matter how tenuous it was. It had worked before. Sometimes a simple mind can solve a crime – if he's dogged enough.

I was determined to do the only thing left to me, go to Montreal. There was always the chance Jose was telling the truth. After all, he thought I'd be dead in another few minutes. Why would he bother lying to me? At a minimum, I had established a connection between the gang in Boston, the group in Mexico City, and the Russians. It all confirmed Rossi's initial assessment.

And what about Clarkson? Did he save my life? Or was that just another lie? Is he one of them? Did he kill the dancer? It sure did appear that way. It would fit. They succeeded in discrediting me and making me the fall guy. Maybe they thought that would be better than killing me. The Montreal tip could just have been a way to throw me off track.

Clarkson was the wild card. Everything hinged on him. If there was even a chance he was a cop and on the level, following the same leads I was, then Montreal could be the real thing. I had to check it out.

Chapter 36

I took the red-eye to LaGuardia with the money Bud wired me. I wasn't happy about him forging my checks, but it was a sight better than hitchhiking. That's what I get for not taking my checkbook with me. I hoped this wasn't going to be a habit with him. The last thing I wanted was a con-man for a son.

I had decided to go to the 'burgh' on the spur of the moment and kill two yellowthroats with one raca. It was obvious I couldn't go back to Boston. That would be a one-way ticket to a Mexican City jail. Gracias, but no gracias. I couldn't just fly into Montreal either.

The 'burgh' was only sixty miles from there. According to Jose, if Alicia was still in North America, she'd be in Montreal. Better yet, if I brought Bud home with me Suzy would owe me big time. So I boarded a Greyhound at Penn Station and headed north.

After a seven and a half hour trip, the bus dropped me off at an inn in the west end of the 'burgh'. I got a room under an assumed name and paid cash in advance for a week's lodging. That didn't seem to raise any eyebrows. I needed sleep and crashed for the next twelve hours straight. The following day I did some shopping. Then I called Bud as arranged. He answered on the first ring.

"Where are you?" he asked.

"I'm in town. Got in last night around eight," I replied. "I don't want anyone to know I'm here, not even your mom, until I tell her."

"OK, don't worry. I won't say a thing."

"Where are you?" I asked him.

"In town. I got in yesterday afternoon. Mom's home. She was shocked to see me. I told her you made me come back."

"Good boy," I gushed. "You get a brownie point for that."

"Where are you?"

"I'm up at the Travel Lodge. Don't tell anyone. Remember our plan."

"I won't. You're going to let me work on the case with you, right?"

"You're going to be my man Friday, which means you stay put and do what I tell you. Stay by the phone."

"My phone's with me. It goes where I go."

"And you go where I tell you. This is like the army. You follow orders or you're cashiered out of the regiment."

"Roger that, general."

"You can call me sergeant, private. A good non-com is worth a dozen officers any day."

"OK, Sarge, sir."

"That's better. All kidding aside, Bud, no one can know I'm here. This is very serious. Alicia's life may depend on it. You need to act like everything's back to normal. Go back to school, do what your mother tells you. Don't attract attention. Keep me informed if anyone approaches you and asks about me. Be careful. These people are dangerous. They kidnap young boys as well as girls. It's even worse for them, if you can believe it."

"I can believe it," said Bud. "Can I see you?"

"No, not right now," I answered, "but we can arrange something for later."

"Do you want me to get you another cell phone?"

"No, it might attract attention. Too easy to trace if someone has a mind. I'll use pay phones for now. I've got a dozen rolls of quarters for just that."

We talked for a few more minutes, until I was sure he understood. I made plans to call him later that night. I had grave misgivings about involving Bud in the case, especially after what happened six years ago. Entangling my family in my detective work is what almost got them killed and led to my divorce. Now here I was involving my thirteen-year-old son in a dangerous white slavery ring – yes, I had missed his birthday too.

I tried to estimate the danger and found it minimal. But it didn't take much to imagine things getting out of control and the Russians, or whoever was behind the abductions, finding out about Bud. I'd die before letting anyone hurt him.

I only planned to use him to help me around town with logistics and supplies. The first thing I planned to do was regain possession of my checkbook. I'll write my own checks, thank you. Not that there was much left in the account. I had Bud withdraw all my remaining money.

After talking to Bud, I took some cash and went on a little shopping expedition. I stopped at various stores and shops around town, where I picked up a number of different items of clothing. These are things I've found useful over the years in hiding my identity while on a stakeout. I picked up some khaki work clothes and a used rake, as well as some jogging outfits. I also went to a uniform rental shop and bought a security guard uniform, as well as some accessories, like clear and dark glasses, different hats, and hair coloring.

I also bought a pair of baggy trousers and a non-descript sweater, also too large. I intended to use it to make myself look heavier and older than I was. With black-rimmed glasses and a little talcum powder on my temples, I morphed into a nearsighted, overweight fifty-year-old. It was not that much of a stretch.

I needed to find out as much as I could about the sex trade in Montreal, so I took a city bus to the local public library. All the computers were taken, but I didn't have long to wait. While I did, I read the current town paper. It appeared that Boston wasn't the only place where young women went missing. But then young women have been going missing since they first started crawling out of caves.

I surfed the web, looking for sex clubs in Montreal. There were plenty of them, so I started writing down addresses. Some of the ads were rather explicit, however. I was soon getting rude looks from people walking by. I sat closer and tried to hide the screen, but after one gross add, a librarian walked up to me.

"Sir, you can't view that type of material in the library. There are children around."

"I know, sorry. I'm doing research for a column I'm working on about the sex trade in Montreal, and how it leads to a moral degeneration in the surrounding area, including our city."

"That may be, sir, but you cannot view that kind of material here at the library. I suggest you get your own computer. What organization did you say you worked for? Mister...?"

""Mister Jack Dillon," I said extending my hand. "I'm a freelance journalist out of San Antonio, Texas. I just wrote an expose on the illicit sex trade in Mexico. This is a follow-up story. The kidnappers in Mexico have ties to those north of the border."

"I can believe it," replied the librarian, relieved I had closed down the results of the Google search on Montreal sex clubs. "There's been a number of missing person cases right here in town over the past few years. Just last fall a young girl disappeared from the fair. But it's hard to tell if they just run off or are abducted."

"Sometimes it's one and the same," I said.

"What do you mean?"

"Well, sometimes the girl takes off on her own, only to end up the victim of a kidnapping or abduction later. Sometimes they're lured away with promises. There are an awful lot of lonely, unhappy kids out there. Teenagers, especially young girls, but boys, too, are susceptible to melancholia and depression. They think being out on their own, out from their overly strict, abusive, or uncaring parents, will make them happy and solve all their problems. It usually creates more. It certainly opens them to a lot more dangers and unscrupulous people. There are all sorts of slavery."

"You sound like an expert," observed the librarian, a short, rather frumpy matron about my own age, mid forties.

"I am now. I've been working on this story for almost two years."

"Working for your Pulitzer," she said smiling.

"Exactly!" I laughed, "One period at a time."

"Well, I hope you get your computer soon so you can continue your research. It sounds like a very important topic."

"It is. I plan to have my laptop back by the weekend. What I really need to do is visit Montreal and stake out the clubs in person. See what's going on first hand."

"Oh, that sounds like a very interesting job. What does your wife think about it?"

"I'm sorry to say I'm divorced. She didn't care for all the odd hours and weeks away from home. I'm afraid I'm kind of boring to live with."

"You don't sound boring to me, Mister…?"

"Dillon, Jack."

I extended my hand again and smiled.

Chapter 37

I called Bud later that night.

"How's your mom?" I asked.

"OK. She's so happy I came home she's cutting me some slack and letting me go out tonight with my friends."

"Good. Say, how would you like to go to the fair tomorrow if it's nice?"

"The fair?" he echoed, as if I had asked him to get a job and support me. "I haven't been to the fair in years."

"This weekend's the end. There'll be some good bands from Montreal and the 'trotters' will be racing. Remember? We used to go all the time."

"That's when I was a kid," he replied.

"Well, you still like to go on the carnival rides don't you?"

"Sure, but…"

"I'll give you twenty bucks. You can bring a date."

"Make it forty and you got a deal. I've been wanting to take this girl out. If you promise to disappear as soon as we get there."

"You want me to give you forty dollars so you can take your girlfriend to the fair and then disappear so you can be alone. Forget it. I was just trying to be nice."

"OK, OK, twenty-five then, but you still have to disappear."

"Fine," I said. "It's a deal."

The next morning I picked Bud up near Suzy's house and headed out to the west end of town, to the county fairgrounds.

When I left the 'burgh' this last time, I had to leave my dad's Caddy behind. It was one of the few things of his I really wanted when he died suddenly of a heart attack. He filled up the church with his friends and acquaintances. A lot more people than will come to my going away party. I had already gone over those sad statistics when my younger brother Billy died. Billy and I will go to our maker alone, pretty much like we lived.

Dad left me the house and the Caddy. I gave the house to Suzy, but kept the car. She let me leave it in the garage, which was big enough for it and her Toyota SUV. The car had been under a canvas sheet for the past two years. It started up on the first turn of the key.

166

I had called Suzy at her agency from a payphone the previous day and told her I was passing through. I mentioned I was on a sensitive case and asked her not to tell anyone I was in town. The car was still registered to my father. I told her if anyone asked about it she could tell them I took it. I doubted anyone would notice.

I had to figure out how to get across the border without papers. In the meantime, I needed to learn as much as I could about Montreal's illicit sex traffic. I wondered if there was a connection between Montreal and the local missing girls. The fair was the last place the latest missing girl had been seen. It would be a good place to start looking for a connection, if one existed. Bud would be a good cover, as long as no one put us together. He met his girlfriend there and didn't introduce us.

I had on my good-old-boy outfit, with grungy blue jeans and a dirty t-shirt. I hadn't shaved in several days and wore a greasy cap with a John Deere logo on it. I hung around the real fair where the prize bulls and pigs were shown, but kept my eyes on the park across the way, where most of the kids gathered. I told Bud to meet me at the front entrance at four, and not to leave with anyone but me.

I walked up one lane and down another, past all the 4-H buildings and exhibition areas. I was looking for anyone or anything that seemed out of place. I was especially on the lookout for lone men, following or otherwise paying too much attention to young girls.

I had read that carnivals and fairs, as well as large sporting events, were notorious places for abductions. Although this was just a small county fair, a girl had disappeared from this very place last year at this time. Maybe whoever helped her go missing would come back for another victim.

After a while I moseyed over to the carnival area, where I walked around the rides munching on a cotton candy. There were a lot of young girls there, most in groups or on dates, but several by themselves. Some of them, though still quite young, dressed provocatively, with little belly-shirts and short-shorts, trying to attract attention. If they only knew what kind of attention they were likely to attract, they'd cover themselves up like it was the middle of winter in a blizzard. I looked around to see if any of them were attracting the wrong kind of notice.

I saw Bud. We passed without acknowledging one another. He looked me up and down with an amused smile. I hoped he didn't look at any real hillbillies like that. He'd be liable to get his teeth handed to him.

As I stopped and watched the Atomic whirl-a-loop ride, which Bud and his date had just gotten on, a man who was approaching caught my eye. He was tall and wore plain brown pants with a matching shirt and vest. The vest looked like something a fisherman might wear. He had a brown, short-brimmed hat and sun glasses and was eating a bag of popcorn as he walked along in the crowd. The only thing missing from his getup to complete the picture was a fishing pole and some fly hooks in his hat. He appeared to be observing his surroundings much like I was.

I glanced at him out of the corner of my eye as he walked by. He appeared familiar. At first I thought he might be someone from around town I knew, but couldn't place. Perhaps he was an old school chum, although it seemed I had met him more recently. Then with a start, I realized it was Dale Clarkson, the mysterious man I had met in Mexico City.

I almost jumped out of my skin. There was no way he could have recognized me in my get-up with a week's worth of facial hair. Still, the fact that he was here in the 'burgh' gave me quite a shock. I followed him discreetly. He was easy to spot, even from the other end of the fairground.

What could he be up to? What was he doing here, of all places? Was he one of them? There was a good chance he was the one who had killed the Mexican lap dancer. Was he here to kill someone else? Was he after me?

All these thoughts bombarded my brain as I followed Clarkson, staying well out of sight. We were in a large, circular park. I could almost stay in one location and more or less keep an eye on him as he wandered around the periphery of the fairground. He seemed to be trailing one of the young girls I had noticed earlier. She was a young blonde nymph, who dressed way too sexy for her fifteen-something age.

When it looked like he was actually talking to her, I started to move closer. I wished I had taken Bud's suggestion and let him get me a cell phone. I thought it would be too easy to trace. I could have used one now. Clarkson and the girl moved toward the parking lot. I followed. To my utter consternation, she got in his car with him.

Chapter 38

Running to my dad's Caddy at the other end of the parking area, I followed Clarkson and the girl as they took a left at the fairground entrance and headed west, away from town. My adrenaline was pumping.

Was I witnessing an abduction? Had he lured the young girl into his car? Was he now spiriting her away to a life of sexual slavery? Or were his aims more immediate? I had to keep them in sight whether he saw me or not.

They crossed a bridge near a small village next to the river and drove further into the country. It looked like Clarkson, or whoever he was, intended to have his way with the young, half-dressed girl far from prying eyes. He drove her toward the western mountains. At one point, they disappeared as their car curved around a tree-covered hill. I almost drove past them.

He had stopped and pulled over to the side of the road. They appeared to be talking rather animatedly. I drove up right next to him and rolled down the passenger side window.

"Are you all right?" I said to the girl. "Is this man bothering you?"

Clarkson looked up in surprise.

"What are you up to, Clarkson?" I asked. He took a closer look at me.

"Lawless!" he announced, recognizing me. He looked annoyed, but smiled. "I wondered what happened to you."

"I bet you did. Why'd you have to kill that dancer? What'd she ever do to you?"

As I said this, I threw open the door and rushed around the front of the Caddy. I was at the side of his car before he had time to answer. Alarmed by my sudden movement, he tried to open the car door to get out.

I threw a kick at his head. It missed, but then I hadn't intended to hit him. I only wanted to stop his forward motion and sit him back on his heels. It worked! He stopped half in and half out of the car.

I grabbed his wrists and pushed him back into the vehicle. Then I pressed him down, swinging my left leg up and over his as I did so. Sitting on him, I pinned him to the seat.

He tried in vain to swing his arms to punch me while I held him down. I had all the leverage. He had no upper arm strength to speak of. We tussled back and forth like that for awhile as he tried to break my grip, but he was easy to subdue. At one point he reached for the glove compartment where I suspected he had a gun.

"Calm down," I urged as we struggled. "I only want to talk to you. What are you doing with that young girl? Why'd you kill that dancer in Mexico?"

His underage passenger left as soon as the scuffle started. She was halfway back to the bridge by now. I hoped she would notify the police that she had been abducted. As it was, I was having trouble keeping Clarkson down. He was growing more agitated and struggling more violently by the minute.

Without warning, he crossed his hands and broke my grip, a move only a trained man would know. He grabbed me by the throat with his free hand in a grip I would call a tiger's claw. I swung my arm up to knock his hand away and hit him with a short left to the head. He jerked his body back, then quickly brought his forehead forward as if to head butt me. I smashed a forearm into his face as it came at me, snapping his head back into the seat rest.

I thought he was out, but he suddenly jerked his body forward and pushed me off. I tumbled backward out of the car and onto the pavement. Rolling back to my feet, I met him as he got out of the car. I had underestimated my opponent. It wouldn't happen again.

We started trading punches. He blocked my first three strikes and I blocked his three counterstrikes. He ducked my next punch and just missed my ear with his right. I countered with a quick ridge-hand that nailed him in the midsection. He looked surprised, but not hurt. He tried to take me off my feet. I replied with another series of hand strikes, which he blocked and otherwise expertly evaded.

I was facing a trained opponent, but he made a mistake. Taking my hesitation for fear, he charged me with a loud yell, trying to use his size advantage to overpower me. He was at least a couple inches taller than I was and outweighed me by fifty pounds.

He barreled toward me with his right arm pulled back to punch. I waited until he was almost on me. Then, before he unleashed his strike, I snapped a hard front kick at his chin. It was a close-in kick. He never expected it. I had timed it perfectly and delivered it with power. I was aiming at his chin, but my kick landed a little lower and struck him in the throat.

He went down holding his neck and choking. It was a little more than I had intended. I didn't consider our fight a life-or-death struggle. First of all, there was only a single opponent. Secondly, I knew him. It wasn't like I was battling an unknown assassin. Or was I? In any case, I wasn't trying to kick him in the throat. Still, he was wide open for a front kick of some kind. I had to hit him with something.

He was instantly incapacitated. The lethal strike was an accident, however. My foot slid up his chest and caught him right in the Adam's apple. I was afraid I killed him. I bent over him with concern.

"Calm down," I said softly. "Slow your breathing and relax. You'll be OK if you stay still and breathe easy. That's it. It was just a glancing blow."

I continued to examine his throat and neck as I tried to calm him.

After a few minutes he was able to breathe more easily and sat up. The fight had been knocked out of him, but he'd be all right.

"What's going on here?" I demanded.

"I'm a federal agent!" he croaked as he rubbed his neck. "My credentials are in my back pocket. Look and see."

"You'd better not try anything," I warned. "I'll break your freaking neck next time."

"No, no, I'm too old for this stuff," he replied, coughing.

"You're too old for that little girl too. Do you have a gun?"

"In the glove compartment of the car, but don't worry about that. Damn you kicked me hard. I'll never be able to speak again."

"Yeah, what stories were you telling that little girl?"

"None! I was just doing my job. If you would be so kind as to look in my rear pocket? In my wallet, please."

I helped him up. Leaning him against the car, I checked his back pocket. To my great consternation he had the credentials of a Secret Service agent.

"Now do you believe me?" he asked.

I returned his wallet. He rested against the car and rubbed his throat while I retrieved the gun from the glove compartment.

"That's quite a kick you threw there," he observed. "I never saw that coming."

"What are you doing here? Are you trying to tell me picking up little girls is part of your job? Who are you trying to kid?"

"No one. You just blew my cover and two weeks of work. She's one of them."

"What? That little girl?"

"Yes, that little girl is bait. She lures other kids her age to the kidnappers. She was about to tell me who she worked for. Now she's probably in danger."

"What were you doing in Mexico? Why'd you kill that dancer?"

"I can't tell you what I was doing, or why I was there. And I didn't kill the dancer. They did, after they drugged you and stuffed you in that cab. She was there on the floor the whole time we were talking. I moved you both before I left. I didn't want to leave her on the floor like that. They were the ones who set you up, not me. I just disturbed their little party before they finished with you. So I pumped you for some information. I needed to know what you knew."

"Why? What's going on? What are you doing here?"

"Working on a missing person case, just like you. We're trying to crack an international kidnapping ring, OK? Is that good enough for you? I've already told you too much. You've ruined my cover. It will take me weeks to gain her confidence again, if I can find her. I hope they don't hurt her."

"You mean to tell me these people are operating here in the 'burgh'?"

"Yes, they're working out of Quebec. That little girl you thought I was picking up is a young Russian immigrant, who until recently lived in Montreal."

"What were you doing taking her out here in the middle of nowhere? Why didn't you bring her into town and arrest her?"

"I was trying to scare her. It was working too. She was going to tell me everything she knew in return for asylum and a new identity. That is until you showed up. Can I have my gun?"

"No," I replied. "You can pick it up at the state police barracks."

"That's not too smart, Lawless. You're in enough trouble as it is for assaulting me. I could have U.S. Marshals on you so fast you'd think you were public enemy number one."

I handed him back his gun after removing the bullets.

"Well, what did you expect, picking up a young girl like that in public? You're lucky it was me who followed you and not some 'Statie'. I wonder what your superiors would think about your methods. They probably wouldn't have approved of your performance today. I kicked your ass."

He didn't take that too kindly.

"Fuck you, Lawless!" he replied.

For a minute, I thought we were going to go at it again, but he shouldered his empty automatic and got back in his car. I was glad he did. Fifty years old or not, I didn't want to tangle with him again.

"This is a federal investigation, Lawless. Now you know. Stay the hell out of my way. I'm letting you off the hook this time. Remember, you owe me for Mexico. So don't fuck with me. Next time I won't be so understanding."

As he drove off in a cloud of dust, I wondered if there was more to it than he was letting on. How much, if any, of his story was true? Was he really on a white slavery case, or was he just a pervert hiding behind a badge? And what was a Secret Service agent doing investigating this type of case? Didn't they guard the president? I decided to expand my investigation and investigate the feds.

Chapter 39

I picked Bud up at the fairgrounds around three and dropped him off near his house. I didn't bother telling him about my little side trip. He didn't tell me about his date. I got the distinct impression he had struck out. That made two of us.

I wondered about the Secret Service man, Clarkson. What could he be up to, hanging around our little town? What had brought him from Mexico City to the 'burgh'? I thought back to our conversation in the apartment of the dead dancer. He was looking for someone just like I was. Who?

I had been so tied up with my case and finding the missing girl that I had no idea what was going on in the world. I hadn't listened to a newscast in weeks. I couldn't remember the last time I had read the papers, unless it was the comic strips. I was completely out of touch. I decided to talk to someone in the know.

My cousin Pat lives at an assisted-living complex on the south side of town. It's not far from where the airbase used to be. The base is long gone. It was closed in the nineties. They say Perestroika put an end to the need for this particular SAC facility. I suspect it had more to do with the little fiasco I was involved in. It's still highly classified. Maybe the truth will come out some day.

Although Pat's confined to a wheelchair with Muscular Dystrophy, she's a fulltime social worker for the state. She's also a news freak. She's up on the latest information, caught from a variety of national and international broadcasts and websites. She's also abreast of the latest internet gossip and conspiracy theories. I figured she might be able to shed some light on things. I decided to contact her - incognito.

I wasn't too thrilled at being recognized - by a Fed no less! At the very least he could report me to the local authorities. The last thing I wanted was for them to know I was in town. For all I knew, there was an international APB out on me. I had to find out what my situation was. I felt like an illegal alien without my license or papers.

Later that day, I donned my green work clothes and took my new rake to Pat's apartment. I pretended to work on the park across the street while I kept an eye out for her. It was a nice Sunday morning. I hoped she'd take her motorized wheelchair to the nearby shopping center. There was a Dunkin Donuts there that she went to all the time. I didn't have to wait long.

I saw her coming up the walk from her building's front door. I crossed to her side of the street and pretended to work on a patch of grass a short distance up the block. As she approached, I stopped raking and took off my cap and sunglasses.

"Hi, Pat," I said. She stopped and stared at me, shaking her head in disbelief. I put my cap and sunglasses back on and started raking again. "How you been?"

"Jay? Is that you?"

"Yes," I replied. "But don't let on. I'm not supposed to be here. Come across to the park where we won't be watched. I want to talk to you."

We crossed the street. She sat in the shade of a tree, while I pretended to rake the grass.

"What's this, Jay?" she asked. "You've got a job working for the city? What's all the secrecy for?"

"I'm on a case. I don't want anyone to know I'm in town. Has anyone been asking about me? Have you heard anything?"

"What, about you? Why no, Jay. What's going on?"

"That's what I'm trying to find out. I got in a little trouble working on a missing person case. There was a slight problem in Mexico City. I lost my wallet and passport at the scene of a crime."

"Scene of a crime! What happened?" she inquired. Pat was used to my cases and their fallout. "I hope it's not like last time. I'm not sure the town's ready for another one of your cases."

"No, it's nothing like that. No terrorists involved."

"How'd you get back in the country without papers?"

"It's a long story," I answered. "You haven't heard anything about me have you?"

"No, you're not on the news if that's what you mean. I haven't seen your picture on the wanted posters down at the post office. That doesn't mean someone's not after you. If I know you, Jay, there probably is."

"I've been of out of touch. What's going on in the news, any big stories, missing persons, disappearances?"

"No, not that I've heard of, although a couple of local girls disappeared last year around this time."

"Yeah, I heard about that. As a matter of fact, they may be connected to the case I was working on. A fifteen-year-old from

Boston went missing last spring. I almost found her. I just missed her by a couple of days, though I found another girl who had been abducted. I ended up going to Mexico City based on what she told me she overheard the kidnappers saying. I wasn't able to find my girl, but I did pick up information about a human trafficking ring run by the Russian mob. It has ties with Boston and Mexico City. I'm here following up the third piece of that puzzle in Montreal."

"You sure do get yourself in some pretty good messes. So what happened in Mexico City?"

I wasn't sure I wanted to get my cousin involved or how much I should tell her. She was my cousin, but she was also a government employee.

"I'm not sure you want to know."

"I'm not sure how much I'll be able to help you if you keep me in the dark."

"I was set up. I was attacked after asking some questions in a dance club where they have young women. I was brought to the place by my cabby who turned out to be working with them. They somehow knew I was coming and picked me up at the airport. Maybe Sullivan got the word out. That's one of the guys we caught in Boston. He probably did it through the prison system, who knows. That's where he is now.

"I woke up in one of the dancer's apartment. She was dead. She'd been murdered. I was set up. I was lucky to make it out in one piece. I was aided and abetted by some very friendly banditos, who not only helped me get across the border, but put my assailants out of business. It seems they had kidnapped some of the girls from their village. I wouldn't want to be the kidnappers when these machete-wielding hombres caught up with them."

"Gee, Jay, you sure do get yourself in some fixes."

"I know, you said that. The thing that's got me worried is one of the people who were involved down in Mexico City has just turned up here in town."

"Who? One of the mob guys?"

"I don't know. He has the credentials of a Secret Service agent. He was in the dancer's room with me when I woke up. I thought he had saved me from the kidnappers, but now I'm not sure. He asked me a lot of questions. I think he drugged me. When I woke up again, he was gone and there was a dead girl in the room."

"Oh, my God, Jay, that's terrible!"

"Yeah, tell me about it. Have you heard anything? Anything unusual going on on the street?"

"No, like I said, nothing unusual. Things are pretty quiet, although I guess the police are still looking for those missing girls."

"I wonder if it has anything to do with what I'm involved with."

"Why would the Feds be interested in a couple of local teenage girls?"

"Maybe someone's kidnapped the president's daughter," I said joking.

Pat stopped and stared at me with a look of shocked surprise.

"Jay, I just remembered. It's just a vague rumor, one of those internet conspiracy theories. It's probably nothing, but the president's daughter hasn't been seen in a couple of weeks. The White House put out a story that she was sick at home. Then they came out with one that she was back in school. It seems none of these stories have been confirmed, however. There's nothing in the news indicating there's a problem. There have even been newscasts showing her, but there's some question how recent the pictures are. Everyone's being evasive. The internet quacks think she's been kidnapped by psycho White Supremacists. I thought nothing of it until you mentioned it."

"I was only joking," I said, wondering if she was on to something. "How can I get across the Canadian border?"

Chapter 40

After talking to Pat and making arrangements to meet later in the week, I headed back to my room. I wasn't sure of my situation, so left the car in the mall parking lot and walked the short distance to my motel. I kept to the back lots and out of sight as much as possible. As I got closer to my building, I checked out the surroundings, looking for police cars or men in dark suits. Nothing seemed out of place.

I watched my room for a short time from across the street. I found no sign that it was being observed. It looked like Clarkson had kept his mouth shut. He probably didn't want anyone to know he was in town anymore than I did, especially the authorities. What could he be up to?

Once I was sure it was all right, I went back to my room. Now that someone knew I was in town, I didn't feel comfortable staying there. I was registered under an assumed name and wasn't sure how anyone could track me. Still, it wouldn't have been that hard for someone who knew about those things. I thought about trying to pick up Clarkson's trail again. If I could do it, so could he. After all, he was a trained federal agent. I wasn't going to make it easy for him.

Even though I had paid for the room a week in advance and had several more days left, I decided to leave it that night. I could get another place and keep both in case one of them turned out to be hot. I would also be easy to spot driving my dad's old car around town. If one of his friends didn't notice it and start asking question, one of the city's veteran cops would. I decided to sell it.

There were several people in town, acquaintances of my dad, who had wanted to buy the Caddy. A couple of them put up very substantial offers. I decided to take one of them up on it. He was someone I was sure wouldn't inform the cops. As a matter of fact, there was all likelihood that no one would ever learn how he got the coveted Lawless automobile.

Jake Lamont would normally have been the last person I'd have thought of. He was a year ahead of me in high school, in the same class as my older brother Tony. He had a well-earned reputation as a troublemaker and bully. Like most bullies in town, I had had a run in or two with him. Although I didn't get beat up, they were encounters I'd just as soon forget. But Jake Lamont was hard to forget, especially if you were a little kid about to get beat up by him. All that was water under the bridge.

My dad had helped Jake get into the Marines. After he was discharged, Dad got him into the local Marine Association. Though none of the other men in the group could stand Jake, Dad liked him, and that was enough.

I drove out to Jake's place. He had a small log cabin by the lake about fifteen miles north of town. He had a few chickens and ducks, and a goat or two out back in pens. He also kept a horse in a small fenced in corral next to his house. He was a survivalist, and acted as if he lived in 10,000 miles of Alaskan wilderness rather than a small town in Upstate New York. He got along with animals better than he did with people. He grew a small vegetable garden, and lived off his produce in season. He sold the surplus in a small stand by the side of the road in front of his cabin. Few people were brave enough to stop and buy from him, however. Everyone knew Jake always kept his shotgun close by.

"Hi, Jake," I said pulling into his driveway unannounced. He was sitting on the porch of his modest domicile. I wondered where his shotgun was. "How you been?"

I had washed the car and shined it up with a new coat of wax. It probably looked as good as it did when it was still on the showroom floor.

"What do you want, Lawless?" he asked in a sullen tone. He had long, dirty-brown, shoulder-length hair, and a short, trimmed beard of the same color. He was thin and dressed in greasy jeans and t-shirt. He didn't smile.

"I see you haven't changed much," I observed. "I thought you might want to buy my dad's Caddy."

"Since when has it been for sale?" he inquired, standing up and stepping off the porch to get a better look. "What are you selling it for?"

"Make me an offer. I was hoping to get five or six grand for it."

"No, I mean, why are you selling it now? I thought it wasn't for sale, that you wanted to keep it for yourself. Why do you want to sell it to me?"

"I need the money. I've got no need for it. It's just taking up space in Suzy's garage. She asked me to get rid of it. Anyway, I remember dad saying he wanted you to have first nibs on it."

"Really?" he replied.

179

"Sure," I lied, hoping to grease him up. "You know, one gyrene to another."

"No kidding. Your dad was a great guy. She sure is a beauty."

"I tell you what, give me $3000 and your VW and she's yours. I brought the deed with me. You can have it today, right now."

He didn't have to think about it for long. He wrote me a check on the spot. I cashed it in a bank just before closing time that afternoon. Afterwards, I got a room at another motel on the north end of town by the beach. The place brought back memories of my last case, the one that led to my downfall. I hoped this time things would turn out better.

I decided not to sit around and reminisce.

I could get around town unnoticed now in my new secondhand Jetta. It was four years old, but only had 50,000 miles on it. The motor was almost brand new and Jake had done a lot of work on it.

It didn't take me long to track down Clarkson. I had memorized his license plate number. His vehicle was indelibly imprinted on my brain. I found it in a motel parking lot at the west end of town. It wasn't far from my original room, which still appeared to be unwatched.

I grabbed a quick supper at a fast food joint nearby and sat in my new car observing his place. He came out a few hours later, around seven, just as it was getting dark. I followed a short distance behind him as he made his way east toward the lake. Then he turned off onto the thruway and headed north toward the Canadian border.

I followed him to the border, turning off just before the custom station. I stopped and watched as he passed through the gate and entered Canada. It looked like Mister Clarkson, Secret Service agent for the U.S. government, was not only going out of town, he was leaving the country. I wondered if he was going there to abduct a young girl, or rescue one.

.

Interlude

Alicia woke in the small, dark room not knowing if it was day or night. She had been deprived of all contact with the outside world. She didn't even know what day it was or if it was summer or fall. Her waking hours were filled with terror and torment, her sleep with nightmares and worry. She had only to open her eyes and they were filled with tears of anguish and pain.

The fact that it was her own actions that had brought her here only made her despair deeper. Oh, if only she could die. Yet, the fear of death, which sat on her shoulder like a vulture, made her knees shake and her stomach weak. She prayed for deliverance.

Then suddenly one day, she was cleaned and bathed and soothed with expensive oils and perfumes. Dressed in alluring and expensive lingerie, she was placed in a room, where leering men behind a glass panel bid on her. She was so high on drugs she wasn't sure what was happening. It was all like a terrible dream.

Soon after that, she was brought to another room, where the highest bidder had his way with her. He was fat and old and ugly. He spoke some language she didn't understand. He pressed his sweaty, bad-smelling body on her and kissed her with fat, wet lips. Long into the night, he assuaged his most beastly and vile lusts. She wished she had died a thousand times as the nightmare continued, but when the man finally left, she was still breathing. Alone again in her tiny cell, she washed her face over and over, rubbing her skin so hard it bled.

She wondered how her innocent dream to be a model, to be up on a pedestal and loved, could have turn out so badly, so filled with horror. She wondered when it would end.

Chapter 41

The longer I stayed in town, the more chance there was of being picked up. Pat had been able to confirm that I was wanted in connection with the murder of a girl in Mexico City. The authorities there had requested my extradition. The FBI wanted me for questioning as well. If apprehended, I was to be arrested and shipped back to San Antonio, Texas. From there I would most likely be escorted back across the border by U.S. Marshals.

I didn't have that many friends, it's sad to say, and none of them were in high places. In any case, there didn't seem to be any reason to hang around the 'burgh'. Trouble was, getting across the border where everything appeared to be happening would be tough without papers.

I met Bud for lunch at a Michigan joint near the beach, which was about to close for the season.

"What do you want for your birthday?" I asked as we shared a couple hotdogs smothered with hot Michigan sauce served on a bed of diced onions and a soggy bun.

"A computer would be great!" he said enthusiastically.

"Eh, I thought you already had a computer," I replied. I hadn't actually been thinking of anything that expensive. I had in mind a computer game, not the whole damned machine.

"Yeah, but it's almost two years old now and obsolete. There's a nice one down at the computer store in town for only 1200 bucks."

"1200 dollars!" I exclaimed. "I wasn't thinking of a new computer." He looked disappointed. Maybe I could take out a small loan. "I'll see what I can do. I'll go down and take a look at it."

"If you want, I'll give you my old computer," he told me as he splashed more ketchup on his hotdog. "You can use it in your detective work, you know, to Google things. You'll never have to go to the library again."

"I don't go to the library now," I replied.

"Well, you should. You could learn a lot, stay up on things."

"What do I need to stay up on?"

"Oh, I don't know. You're supposed to be a detective. You must need to know facts and things. Like did you know the President's daughter is missing?"

"That's just a rumor. Pat said it's one of those urban legends. She's been seen recently in public."

"That's what the government wants you to believe, but she's really been kidnapped. The newspapers are covering it up."

"That's absurd. They couldn't cover something like that up."

"That's what you think. Anyway, if you had a computer you'd know what was going on. Now you have two reasons to buy me one."

I realized I didn't have any idea what I would do once I got across the border to Montreal. I could try staking out the strip clubs there like I had in Mexico City. The chances of finding Alicia that way, however, were slim to none. They didn't abduct the Charlestown teenager to have her dancing on men's laps for peanuts. According to Jose they had better things in mind for her, like a personal sex slave to some Middle Eastern sheik or rich Malaysian prince. I had to act fast. I had a lead, although the slimmest and most tenuous of ones. According to my tried and true methods, it had to be followed and substantiated, or discarded.

Ever since my experience in Mexico City, I'd been looking for an angle, something that might give me better results than the blind, needle-in-a-haystack method that almost got me killed. This thing about the President's daughter had cropped up several times. Conspiracy theory or no, I was starting to take the possibility seriously. What if someone really had kidnapped the Chief Executive's kid? Certainly the Feds would be involved, some Secret Service guy like Mister Clarkson, perhaps. Could Alicia be with her? What were the odds of that?

That evening, I went down to the local computer store and bought Bud a computer. It wasn't exactly the overpriced one he wanted, but the geek who sold it to me assured me it was just as good. He even put the two machines side-by-side and showed me how they ran the latest popular games. I couldn't tell the difference, although the expensive computer screen looked just a bit snazzier. There was hardly a noticeable difference to my eye in speed or performance, however, certainly not enough to warrant the $460 price difference. I'm sure it's all twenty percent technology and eighty percent hype.

I called Bud on his cell and told him I had his computer at my motel room and to come over and check it out. He knocked on my door fifteen minutes later. I had taken it out of the box. I was less than gratified by his response.

"This isn't the one I told you to buy," he observed with a frown.

"The salesman said it was just as good. It's the one he'd buy."

"The guy doesn't know what he's talking about. I can't run half my stuff on this."

"Well, it's the one I bought and I'm not taking it back. It's a heck of a lot better than the two year old box you've got, which I want by the way."

He was somewhat mollified when we hooked it up and saw how well it ran his favorite games, which he brought along to try out. He had to admit it was a damned sight better than his. It helped that I had also bought him three of the latest games, also suggested by the know-nothing geek.

"You can't take it with you tonight," I told him. "I've got a box from the post office to make it look like I sent it from Boston. You can pick it up here tomorrow. Say you got it at the post office. Your mom will never know."

"Don't bother. Mom knows you're here. She saw Jake driving granddad's Caddy through town. He told her you sold it to him."

"That big mouth. The only reason I sold it to him was because I thought he'd keep his mouth shut. It's OK. I told your mother I was here, but made it seem I was just passing through. I don't want her to know I'm still around."

"Well, everyone's going to know you were here. Jake's driving it all over town showing it off. He's telling everyone how you told him your dad wanted him especially to have it. Don't worry. Mom doesn't know you have a room in town. But she's cool. She won't tell anybody."

"Just tell her you got the computer in the mail."

"What are you going to do if everyone finds out you're in town."

"It doesn't matter. I'll be leaving soon. Here, before I go, I want you to do something for me."

Chapter 42

I needed help, the kind my thirteen-year-old kid couldn't provide. I decided to call an old friend. I hadn't talked to John Rothburg since he left the college and the town. I heard he had recently moved back. We got out of touch the last few years, John with his academics and symposiums, me with my criminals and terrorists. My life was too outrageous for most people. That's why I left the 'burgh' in the first place. John was one of the few who remained a friend.

His specialty before he retired from the college was radio astronomy. My problem had nothing to do with radio astronomy or computers – one of John's other hobbies. Still, he was the smartest guy I knew, full of information on just about every subject. I decided to elicit his services. His number was in the book. I tried it.

He answered on the second ring as if he'd been waiting by the phone.

"Hi, John. It's Jay Lawless."

"Jay! Why you old son-of-gun. I was just thinking about you. How they hanging?"

"Not as high as they used to. How you been?"

"Not bad, same old same old."

"Say, I've got a favor to ask you," I said without preamble.

"Ain't that just like you, Lawless. I haven't talked to you in years and the first thing out of your mouth is, 'I want a favor.' No, hi John, how's the family? How's retirement? How you been? Just do me a favor. What, you want me to off someone for you? Or is it something more trivial like breaking into a bank? What, you need a new driver's license? Where the hell are you? Where the hell have you been? They said you were dead, and I for one believed them. Weren't you voted most likely to kill or be killed in your high school year book?"

"Yeah, something like that. I've been in Boston. Suzy and I are divorced. You missed that ugly fiasco."

"'I'm lucky like that. How's Little Bud doing?"

"He's doing well, despite the poor excuse he has for a father, and he's not that little anymore."

"Don't be so tough on yourself, Jay. It takes two to fuck up a marriage."

"Well, all I've got to say is good thing kids are resilient. I'm on a case."

"That can't be good. I heard that last time you were on a case you killed half the town."

"It was only four or five and they were trying to kill me."

"I know. Your old girlfriend, Mary, told me. I was sorry to hear about your dad. Say, what happened to Jerry LeGrande? No one seems to know much"

"I'm surprised Mary didn't tell you. She knows as much as anybody. You're not going out with her are you? How's she doing?"

"She's doing well. Don't worry, we're just friends."

"Glad to hear it. You had me worried there for a minute. She married my dad, you know."

"I know. She told me all about it. She also told me the official story about Jerry, but what really happened? How did he buy it?"

"If you help me out, maybe we can get together and I'll tell you about it. It's not something I can talk about over the phone. I can barely think about it let alone recount it. But you and me and Jerry go way back. You deserve to know as well as anybody."

I told him I was lying low and didn't want it known I was in town. He wasn't surprised. He told me that if he had my reputation, he wouldn't want anyone knowing he was in town either. I didn't tell him I was wanted for questioning in two countries for a homicide. We made plans to meet at his cabin in the mountains later that night.

Even though John no longer went to the observatory at the top of the mountain, he had bought a piece of land just below it at the end of the lake. It's a lovely spot, with the mountain as a backdrop and the bowl-shaped lake for a view. Only problem was, it's a twenty-five mile drive. The last three miles of it are on a winding dirt road through dense woods. At night, like I was trying to find it, it was just about impossible. I had my brights on and drove five miles per hour, and still almost missed it. I finally found the spot after coming to the abrupt end of the road and backtracking a half mile. He lived alone.

"Boy is it great to see you," John gushed as he greeted me at the door. He had a beard, and his once long hair was almost gone. Just a thick smudge of gray-brown at the sides and back of his head was all that was left. He was thicker at the midsection than I remembered, but just as simian as ever. His long arms had gotten hairier, his shoulders rounder. He wore glasses now, and had the same old enthusiastic manner and expressions. He grabbed my hand and pulled me to him for a bear hug. I let him smother me for awhile before unwrapping from his large, hairy embrace.

"It's good to see you, too, John. You must be slaphappy from being alone for months out here in the middle of nowhere."

"I know. That's the way I like it."

"If I knew you hated people so much and how hard it is to get here, I would have sent you a letter."

"It's not that I hate people. I just love nature more. It's incredibly peaceful and beautiful in these woods, along the lake and the mountains."

"I know. We used to spend a lot of time out here. But that's not why I came to see you."

We were on our second beer by the time I told him about Jerry and finished my story. Then I explained my plan to follow the trail to Canada. I also mentioned my hunch, as preposterous as it sounded, about the President's daughter.

"Damn! I knew it!" he swore when I finished, jumping up and startling me. I knew my story was compelling but I wasn't expecting this type of reaction.

"What? What did you know?"

"That the president's daughter has been kidnapped. They're trying to cover it up, pretend everything is OK, but there's a lot of information on the internet that indicates otherwise. Now with what you've just told me, I know it must be true. Who was this guy you met down in Mexico, Clarkson?"

"He's a Secret Service agent. He showed me his badge when we had that little tussle."

"And you say he was here in the 'burg', and that you saw him go across the border to Quebec?"

"That's right. Pretty interesting, eh?"

"I'll say. It just goes to confirm my suspicions. What do you plan to do when you get to Montreal?" he asked.

"I don't know. That's why I've come to talk to you. I don't think checking out all the sex clubs would be that fruitful."

"Why not? Sounds like fun. It worked before."

"Yeah, because whoever it was somehow got wind of my coming and set me up. I was lucky to come out alive. Not only that, I was really no closer to Alicia than when I started, maybe even further away from finding her. I need to figure out something better than a needle-in-the-haystack method."

"OK, let's assume the internet conspiracy theorists are correct and the President's daughter is missing, perhaps abducted. Let's also assume the kidnapped victim you rescued was correct. One of the girls there before her was a 'sister', interpreted to mean a black girl, and just for argument's sake, that she's the president's daughter. And suppose you're also correct to assume your missing girl was there too, and that cabby who told you so much before they were about to kill you, was telling the truth. That the girls were brought across the border to Montreal."

"So far so good, we're on the same page. Those are the very assumptions that have brought me to this point, as farfetched as it sounds."

"OK, so someone has abducted the President's daughter," continued John. "Taking such a high-profile person surrounded night and day by Secret Service agents would be next to impossible at best. You'd need the cooperation of the victim for starters, at least at first. From what I've heard about these precocious, troubled teens that wouldn't be too difficult. It'd be easy to lure someone like that away from her keepers. Like you say, it's probably what happened to your girl. A hunky guy or a group of young girls from the in-crowd, or a promise you'll make her a model, is all it would take to set the trap. It would be easy enough for a pampered teenager to elude her protectors, especially if she knew their routines and habits."

"But how would you hide someone like that? Even presuming you could keep them drugged up or otherwise sedated, they would still be recognized. What, put a paper bag over their head?

"Something like that," replied John. "I know what I'd do."

"What?"

"I'd drug her, put some bandages over her face, and smuggle her across the border in an ambulance. If my guess is right, you won't find your girl in a sex club. You'll find her in a clinic or hospital specializing in plastic and corrective surgery."

"I don't know, John, that's quite a stretch."

"I'd say so too, but there are a number of things, which alone mean nothing. When you add them together, however, they become an interesting hypothesis. Fact can be stranger than fiction."

"You have a point. That would be a good way to keep someone's face covered. It should be easy enough to test that theory. There can't be that many places up there that specialize in that type of surgery."

"I think I'll do a little research," volunteered John.

"Great. This is just the kind of break I was looking for. In any case, it's better than blindly searching the streets and strip clubs in a foreign city."

I had already despaired of finding Alicia. I was certain that even if she had been in Montreal, she had been spirited away by now. She was probably already a sex slave in some godforsaken third-world country. There was still a slim chance I was close, however. It was all the chance Alicia had. So I continued to pursue the trail, while I tried to elude capture myself. I didn't know what else to do. I'm not the kind of person that gives up and cries uncle. Life would have been a lot easier if I was. Despite all the lessons I should have learned, I still hadn't changed. I wouldn't give up. Someone's life was at stake.

Chapter 43

Instead of disintegrating into thin air with the light of day the next morning, John's hypothesis took hold and began to sprout wings. My vivid imagination and vague grasp on reality started to weave a rich web of what-if's.

Rather than a list of strip clubs, after a few days of research, John had a list of private clinics in Montreal. Following his hunch, we concentrated on those that specialized in plastic surgery. A few days later we met at John's place in the Mountains.

"I did some digging," began John after we had settled down on his front porch with our brews. "I hacked some of the hospital systems to get the inside scoop. Not the bullshit on their web page and advertisements they want you to believe.

"For instance, one place, this Mont-Royal Clinique de Chirurgie Plastique, popped out immediately. Their web page said they've been in business for over twenty years. However, their financial records and internal emails only go back two years. There's nothing before that. They didn't exist.

"The place's list of staff and affiliates is kosher enough, all French and English sounding names. There are a few Indians and Chinese, as well. The normal mix, you know. But many of the names on the company emails and private letterheads of management are, get this, Russian."

"Quite a coincidence," I responded. "Your vague speculations are becoming more solid."

"Have you looked into that little matter I asked you about?" he inquired. "Is there any record of medical emergencies or transfer of patients across the border? Or anything having to do with female patients having bandages over their faces? Accident victims, people requiring plastic surgery or other cosmetic surgery? Something like that would require special clearance or papers. There has to be a paper trail if it occurred."

"I talked to my cousin Pat. She told me about something that happened in town a while back, about a month ago. One of the guys down at the station told her an ambulance came through town escorted by two official-looking vans. They had government plates. At least that's what the cop who told the story to Rudy, Pat's friend, said. He heard it from a friend of his at the Sherriff's office. The ambulance was supposed to be on its way to Montreal.

"They had papers that allowed them to zoom right across the border without even stopping. The papers said something about an accident victim needing emergency plastic surgery in Montreal."

"That's interesting. I'll follow up. See if I can determine where they went. When did you say this was?"

"A little less than a month ago."

"Hmm, another coincidence, and another nail in the lid of our theory. That's right around the time rumors of the President's daughter's disappearance began cropping up."

"I still don't like the idea of taking Pat along," I stated. "The risks are too high. I don't even like the idea of taking you."

"What I have in mind can't be done without her," John answered. "And what you need to do can't be done without me and this plan. You already said she wanted to do it. She's the perfect cover for reconnoitering the hospital. Even if there's a tenth of a chance of finding and rescuing your missing teenager, you have to take it."

"No, it's too risky," I repeated after considering it some more "Even if Pat agreed, I just can't risk it. I can go in alone like I've always done, find out what I need to, and summon help."

"Like you always do? What, are you going to bust in there like a commando? That's the worst thing you could do if they have the girls. They'd kill them and you. No, Jay, this time you're going to use some finesse for a change. If we do this right, the only kung fu fighting you'll need to do is with your shadow in the bathroom."

"Hmph," I snorted. "That is if we can pull it off. You're asking an awful lot of my forty-year-old, wheelchair-bound cousin. We're not all con artists like you."

"Everyone has a little actor in them. I know you do with all your dramatics. I bet your cousin's no different. All this will be is acting. Just follow my script and everything will be fine. We'll get in, find out what we need to know, and get out. No one will be the wiser. They won't know what's happening until they're behind bars."

"You sound awful confident. Have you done something like this before?"

"All the time, amigo. Ask the mining company that just got closed down for illegal dumping of contaminants into the river. Your terrorists have nothing on these guys, I assure you. No, by the time I'm done with these baby snatchers, they won't know what hit them, but

191

we need someone on the inside. I thought that's what you wanted. It's the only way."

"It's too risky, even if we're wrong and they're not the kidnappers. No, we can't do it."

"Why not? You said your cousin's van practically looks like an ambulance. With a little work we could probably fix it up even better. You're good with disguises. I'm sure you could dig up a medical uniform."

"I don't want you or my cousin involved."

"You've already got us involved, and from the sound of it your thirteen-year-old kid."

"Don't remind me."

"We can say we need an evaluation prior to some procedure related to her condition. I'm sure we can think of something convincing."

"It's not getting into the place that I'm worried about. It's getting out. Pat would be in there all alone and defenseless."

"Maybe we can figure out a way to have one of us stay in there with her."

"I'm not sure that would work."

"You got any better ideas?"

I didn't answer, but sat lost in thought.

What better way to infiltrate a suspected medical facility covering for a kidnapping ring, than to pose as a patient and her doctor looking for some complex advice. John not only looked like a doctor, he was one. They didn't have to know his PhD wasn't in medicine. As a matter of fact, he happened to be an expert on my cousin's particular malady. His sister had it. But could we pull it off and what would happen to us if we didn't?

"I don't know," I said, still undecided.

"You're such a wimp, Lawless. You were going to call this place and make an appointment, weren't you?"

"Yeah, I guess so."

"And what were you going to say?"

"I was going to say what you told me to say."

"Why not let me say it. If I don't convince you I'd make the perfect doctor, you don't have to take me."

John had a good point. I hadn't even thought about calling ahead for an appointment. Although it would have occurred to me eventually, hopefully before I got there, I wouldn't have known what to say.

192

We talked for a short while more. John explained the ins and outs of scapular fixation and current stem cell research to me. After listening to his spiel for about ten minutes, I agreed to let him at least make the initial call.

I had to admit, the thought of having John along gave me an added sense of security. Although John wasn't a martial artist, he was big and strong and smart. Not a bad combination of assets to have when you're going into harm's way. Still, I had to make sure he knew what he was getting into.

"John, I appreciate what you're trying to do, but these people are killers. If we're right, then the stakes are high, high enough that they wouldn't hesitate to kill you and my cousin."

"If we do this correctly, the risk will be minimal."

"But what if something goes wrong? And it always does. I wouldn't underestimate our opponents, whoever they are."

"Then don't underestimate me. I know exactly who I'm dealing with. I know how they think. This is a sophisticated, professional organization with the latest tools and technologies. We're going to use those tools and technology against them."

"There's liable to be a lot of security."

"If there is, it will all be electronic. They can't risk too many eyes. They'll have a small security detail. I'll hack into their system. By the time we enter the building I'll own it."

"How are you going to do that?"

"Don't worry," he answered. "When I'm through setting this up, we'll control every method, function, stored procedure, and web service on their network. In the meantime, here's what I want you to do."

Chapter 44

When I first decided to consult with John and drove up to see him, I had no idea that I'd end up doing his bidding as if I was under his command. To my great surprise, it felt good to have someone else calling the shots for a change. I just saluted and obeyed orders like a good soldier.

We talked to Pat a short while later. I couldn't ask her to do what John had in mind for her. Even though I agreed to his plan, I couldn't bring myself to actually ask my cousin to participate. It was just too dangerous, and as many would say, crazy. I asked her to meet us at a little diner a few miles west of town. There, I let John explain his idea and ask if she would take part.

I tried to talk her out of it. I informed her of the dangers and risks involved, and told her that she didn't have to do it.

"You really think they've got the President's daughter?" she asked.

"We think so," replied John. "Our whole plan is based on that premise."

"Then why don't you go to the police, or the FBI, or that Secret Service guy, what's his name?"

"Clarkson," I volunteered.

"Do you think they would believe us?" answered John. "It's a long shot at best. They'd just deny she's missing like they've been doing for the past three weeks. Even if they believed us and decided to follow-up, they'd probably end up pinning the whole thing on Jay. No, just the paperwork alone would take weeks. Any cross-border investigation of this type is as cumbersome as an oversized load on a curving highway. We need speed and surprise. They won't see us coming."

"Let's hope not," I added.

"Count me in," said Pat. "That's exactly what I was thinking of, but Jay wouldn't agree. He's such a big protective he-man."

The two of them proceeded to gang up on me. They didn't let up until I agreed to go along with their audacious plot. And I thought *I* was crazy!

A few days later, with Pat and me standing nearby, John made a call to the Mont-Royal Clinique de Chirurgie Plastique. He had them on speaker phone.

"Oh, by the way," he said as he looked up their number on the internet. "I followed up on Pat's story about that ambulance. There's a record of a crossing around that time on the State computer. The paperwork involved doesn't give the name of the facility they were going to. However, the address given was 13 Rue Mont-Royal, the address of our clinic. I checked the admission records of the clinic for that time period while I was hacking their system. There is no record of an admission for the same time. Highly unusual."

"Downright suspicious," I commented. I was sure we were on the right track.

"Hello," he said, dialing the number of the clinic in Montreal. "My name is Phillip Simmons. I'm working with a patient at the Albany Medical Center who has a severe case of FSHD. My colleague, Bob Fisher, at John Hopkins University suggested I call you. He told me your facility is the best of its kind for the procedures my patient needs."

There was a pause on the other end of the line as the French-speaking female digested this bit of information. She responded in English.

"Yes, Doctor Lummis will be able to answer all your questions."

John looked up at us and moved his eyebrows up and down to signal he was making progress.

"Yes, hi, Doctor. My name is Doctor Phil Simmons. I work here at the Albany Medical Center with a female patient who has facioscapulo-humeral muscular dystrophy. I heard you were doing some amazing things up there with scapular fixation and stem cell procedures. You come very highly recommended by my colleague, Doctor Fisher, at John Hopkins in Maryland. I was wondering if it would be possible to schedule an appointment for me and my patient to discuss the possibility of having her evaluated for possible treatment at your clinic."

There was a pause at the other end of the line, which seemed strange. I expected a glib response full of assurances, eager to take our money. A rather hesitant, soft-spoken voice answered with a less than enthusiastic sales pitch.

"Well, that's very nice, but we have a backlog of patients waiting to get in. I'm not sure we'd be able to accommodate you at this time."

"Yes, of course, I understand. You must be in demand. After all, there aren't many facilities that offer such advanced procedures, and so close by. All I'm asking for is an evaluation. We can come on a Monday and leave on a Tuesday. I'm sure you'd be able to answer our questions after a brief examination and discussion."

"Well, something as complex as FSHD can't be evaluated in a half hour, or an hour for that matter. It might take days for the tests and results to be obtained and examined. Our facility is small. We only have room for twenty patients at a time, and we are booked for the next two years solid."

John was ready for this. Their resistance only confirmed our suspicions.

"I'm sorry to hear that doctor, and so will the Canadian Medical Association. I have several close friends on their executive committee. I've written several articles for their journal. I have no problem writing another about how you're keeping this valuable information from people who need it. I assure you my patient can pay your fees. Money is no object."

Pat and I looked at each other with skeptical expressions. I wondered where John was going to get all the money. Then I realized he probably had access to the clinic's bank accounts. The voice on the other end of the speaker phone responded quickly.

"There's no reason to be threatening, Doctor Simmons. I assure you we will do everything in our power to help your patient. It's just not as easy as calling up and booking a room. Each of our patients gets individual and specialized care, customized to their precise condition. We work as a team with each patient to guide them through the whole process from beginning to end, and afterward."

"That's precisely why I'm calling you. I promise we won't take up much of your time. It's not like you have to start from scratch. I've been working with Pam for some time." He looked up at Pat and winked. She now had a new name, which we would use for the duration of our little charade.

"I'll be able to answer any of your questions and provide all her test results and financial information. That should greatly facilitate things. I'll be able to determine if your facility is the right one for my patient after a day. At least help evaluate her. I'm sure you have many patients, Doctor, but perhaps none that are so needy. She is willing and able to pay for the privilege of getting ahead in the line. I'm sure both your facility and my patient will benefit from the meeting."

John gave him a pitch that would have been hard to turn down without seeming suspicious. Although it would be risky to see us if they were really a human trafficking ring, turning us down after such offers and threats would have raised even more suspicions.

"I'm sure something can be arranged for such an interesting case," came the reply. "We are always open to the special needs of our patients. I'll have our receptionist arrange a meeting for later next week. Make sure you bring all her tests results, as well as her medical history for the past ten years. Can you do that?"

"Certainly, no problem," answered John. He gave us a thumbs-up to signal his success, even though we had already heard it on the speaker.

"We're in," he said, clicking off the speaker and picking up the receiver, which he put to his ear as he wrote down the date and time.

"Next stop, Montreal," he announced, as he hung up the phone.

Chapter 45

John kept us busy that week getting ready, while he hacked into their computer system. The first thing he obtained was a floor plan of the clinic itself. It was located on the seventh and eighth stories of an office building on Rue 13 in the Mont Royal district of Montréal. The fact that it was on the top floors made our task seem that much more difficult.

We concentrated on the central part of the building where the service areas and electrical boxes were maintained. This area was accessible from several locations. It also had its own set of elevators. They stopped at the seventh and eighth floors, as well as the basement, where there was a large garage.

"I feel like I've been there," stated Pat, now known as Pam, looking up from the computer screen.

"Good," said John. "I want you both to know every inch of it like the back of your hand."

John had come up with a dozen ingenious ways to smuggle things in with us using Pat's chair. My getup included hidden pockets and compartments in the cuffs, among other things, for items we might need like lock-picking tools and masking tape.

He also gave me a wide, thick leather belt of his own devising. It had a sharp, heavy metal buckle that made the thing a lethal weapon. It even had secret pockets for shuriken, the Chinese throwing stars.

"I thought you said we wouldn't need any of this kind of stuff," I commented. "What's all this?"

"Just a precaution, my friend. We have no idea what to expect. I just want to be ready." That's when he showed me his live video show.

"Look at this," he said as he turned on the display and flicked a switch. The screen came alive. It showed a grainy, black and white image of a hallway and a guard station next to a double door. At some point an elevator opened. A man and woman in white jackets came out. They flashed badges to the guard and walked down the hallway, disappearing through the swinging doors. I realized what I was looking at just as John explained it.

"This is the seventh floor reception area of our clinic, Clinique de Chirurgie Plastique du Mount Royal."

"Cool," I said. "Now I really feel like I've been there. How'd you do that?"

"Their security system is all computerized, like I figured, with digital cameras. I just hacked this system like I did all their others. We can not only watch them, we can make them see just about anything we want them to through these cameras. I'll keep an eye on who goes in or out of the place. Maybe we can get some ids on these people, see who they really are. Who knows, we might even observe a bandaged young woman being wheeled in."

I was finally starting to believe in John. Even though I knew he was a genius and a bit unscrupulous, if he could pull this off he could do anything. I started to relax a little. I shouldn't have.

That weekend Bud reported he'd been questioned by a plainclothes State Trooper – the worst kind. He also told me that my room at the other motel was being watched. I had asked him to observe the place from a distance. My instincts were correct. Either Clarkson had blabbed or the cops had figured it out on their own. They were on to me!

"We have a slight problem," I told the others. After I explained the situation, John sat scratching his head like he used to do during one of our epic chess matches.

"We need to divert them away from Jay," he stated.

"I got just the thing," Pat confided. "I have a friend who needs to get to Boston for a new job. It starts next week. I can tell him Jay will let him take his VW down and use it until he goes back later."

"That's perfect," I answered. "Jake Lamont has told the whole town that I traded my dad's Caddy for his VW. I'll tell Bud to tell everyone he knows that I'm leaving town next week to go back to Boston."

"Perfect," said John, "just what we need to get them off your back. Hopefully, whoever is tailing you will follow the car down to Beantown. Now we can concentrate on our parts. Pam and I will just be ourselves. I'll work with her on exactly how to answer their questions. It will be easy because everything we say will be true. It's just our motives that are false."

"But good," I added.

"Thank you, Jay, but it's your part I'm worried about. Can you somehow become a mild-mannered Clark Kent? Is there some way you can be a little less intimidating when you walk into a room?"

"What do you mean?" I objected. "I'm mild mannered. At least until I get riled."

"You have a way of coming into a place like you can kick the ass of any man in the room."

"The hell I do!" I replied a little louder.

"There, see, that's what I'm talking about. You have a chip on your shoulder. Why do you have to make eye contact with every big tough guy in the room? Why can't you enter meekly?"

"You mean with downcast eyes and tiny steps?"

"Exactly, Grasshopper. We are going to turn you into a meek girly-man. Accentuate the beer belly and cut down on the brawn. We won't let them see those muscular arms and legs."

I snorted a laugh. Pat, who sat next to me in John's cabin, squeezed my biceps and said, "Ooh!"

"I can be as prissy as you like," I told him. "I'll even wear glasses."

"That won't be necessary. Just forget for once that your body is a deadly weapon."

"So is your breath, meat mouth."

"You slug."

"You maggot."

"May you eat worms in your sleep."

"May you eat ..."

"Boys, boys, calm yourselves," pleaded Pat. "I'm trying to enjoy my lunch."

We were sitting at John's kitchen table.

All the planning and background work had been done. When the clinic checked John's credentials at the Albany Medical Center and his references to John Hopkins, they'd find just what they expected to find. His connection with the Canadian Medical Association completed an impressive array of qualifications, associations, and awards. All of this compliments of John's computer dexterity, which to me bordered on the miraculous. I thought he was good before, but like a fine wine, John Rothburg had improved with age.

"Monday will be the perfect time to cross," he informed us. "Most of the senior guys will be taking advantage of their extra vacation time and privileges to take a long weekend. The border will be staffed with junior men. They will have the Monday morning blues and resent the prerogatives of their more senior colleagues. Their overworked supervisors will have all they can do to keep their men in line without worrying about us. They see medical patients going to Montreal for treatment all the time."

Though there was not that much risk in the crossing, any international situation with false identification presents a risk. I was using Pat's driver's passport. He owed Pat some favors and actually looked like me once my mustache grew in. That's why she hired him. Despite all my experience in the field - or maybe because of it - I didn't get much sleep the next few nights as we prepared for our assault.

Chapter 46

"We're ready," announced John a few days later. He held up his glass of wine to the sun as we sat on his front lawn. "It's now or never, into the breach, my friends."

"Into the mouth of the whale," I replied, hoping I wasn't making a mistake getting my friend and cousin involved in my case.

Monday morning we packed Pat in the Van and headed north to the border. John gave us last minute instructions as we sped up the Northway in light traffic. I was dressed in a white medical suit. I had on a white jacket with an emblem reading, 'Albany Medical Center', sewn on by Pat the previous evening. Pat sat in the back in her wheelchair, which was strapped onto the floor and paneling. I drove. John sat in the passenger's seat with a legal briefcase full of Pat's medical records.

"No, no, that will never do," John had exclaimed when he first saw me in my outfit. "Can't you walk into a room without looking like Cato from the Green Hornet?"

"What do you mean?" I asked. "What are you talking about?"

"First of all, you swagger around like you can't wait to throw a kick or a punch at someone."

"Not someone, just a bag or something. There's nothing like kicking a heavy bag to get your aggressions out."

"Secondly, even though you say you're getting out of shape, you carry yourself too straight. Slouch a little, stick out your belly. You're holding your stomach in."

After that scolding I worked a little harder at developing my part. With a little padding here, a bit of stuffing there, and some time in front of the mirror, I morphed into another person. I gained twenty pounds around my waist and lost an inch or two from my already small stature. I even practiced avoiding eye contact, as if I were afraid of the world.

"OK, that's better," said John, after I reappeared the next day transformed into a disgruntled, overweight employee, who I hoped would attract no notice.

When we got to the border, John did all the talking.

"What brings you to Canada this fine morning?" asked the Canadian official after we were waved through the American side with little fanfare.

"We're here on business," answered John. "We have an appointment this morning at the Clinique de Chirurgie Plastique du Mount Royal. This is my patient, Miss Pamela McGuire. I'm Dr. Phillip Simmons."

He handed the bored border guard their fake papers. I did the same.

John had been correct. The guard, who was an older man, hardly looked at the documents. He kept glancing up to see what the other border guards, all younger men, were doing. They appeared to be on alert.

"Why isn't that line moving?" he yelled in French to the junior guard in the lane next to us. "If they don't match the profile…" He didn't finish, but mumbled something to himself under his breath and stuck his head in the van to talk to the passenger.

"Good morning, Mademoiselle. "Commo t'allez-vous?"

"Fine," said Pat, "Merci."

"I am sorry to hear you are not well. But happy our country can be of service to you. We have some of the best medical facilities in the world in Montreal."

"Yes, I know," replied Pat, "and much easier to get to than driving all the way down to New York or Boston and dealing with the traffic. Things are so much better up here. I love Montreal, although I don't get a chance to visit that often."

"Well, I hope you get to see some of the city while you are here."

"Oh, I will, if my doctor will let me."

"We'll see," said John. "We have an appointment to make first."

With that, the border guard returned our papers and waved us through.

"Bonne journee," he said, with a smile. He had already returned his attention to the rookie in the next lane, where a long line of vehicles waited to get through.

"Just as I thought," observed John turning to us with a smile. "Piece of cake."

"I just hope the rest of the trip goes as smoothly," I commented. "Who do you think put out the alert?"

John didn't answer, but looked at me with a wry Cheshire cat grin.

"What, you did that?"

"Sure, nothing like a little diversion. They're looking for a man and a woman who robbed a liquor store in Champlain. They were last seen in a stolen pickup truck heading for the border."

I looked at John with wonder.

"You, you, you're good," I said in my best Robert De Niro impression.

"You have no idea," he replied in his usual self-satisfied way. Normally, I would have snapped a few light punches at his head, or beat him at a game of chess to show him just how vulnerable he was. I stayed in character, however, and said nothing.

I had the route to the clinic memorized from the directions and map John got from the Internet. I had no problem finding the place in the light mid-morning traffic. We were in the Mount Royal district of the city.

I had vague memories from my childhood of coming here with my parents. They'd bring my younger brother Billy to one of the big hospitals for treatment of a rare hip disease he had when he was ten.

After my family visited the hospital we would go to the impressive St. Joseph's Shrine on the hill. This was dedicated to the famous Brother Andre, who used to cure sick people from all over the world. There was a place in the church where the crutches and braces and canes from all the people he healed with his touch were piled. There, my parents prayed for my brother's recovery.

He recovered all right, at least his hip. I guess we were praying for the wrong body part. I'm sure that accounts, at least in part, for the way he turned out. He had enough things to overcome without a disease that put him in a cast for four years. I guess he felt he had missed something, been cheated out of his childhood. So he tried to make up for it by living fast and furious, trying to take shortcuts to happiness. It only got him an early, ugly death, but we won't go over that again.

Thoughts about my dead brother were the last things I needed to be thinking about. I concentrated on my part, an unhappy driver who resented having to work for a bossy doctor and his complaining patient.

We drove up to the building, an eight-story brick job on a tree-lined street in a ritzy area at the foot of Mount Royal. It looked like embassy row. I entered the lobby. The place apparently housed several offices for various businesses and corporations. The receptionist told me to go around the rear to the basement entrance of the clinic. Someone there would help us.

I didn't care for her attitude or the way she stared at my bulging midsection with unconcealed mirth. I felt like a short, overweight menial slob, which was exactly what I wanted to appear as. I resisted the temptation to suck in my stomach and standup straight, staying in character, practicing for the main act.

Chapter 47

Doing as the receptionist instructed, I drove around to the rear of the building and was soon wheeling Pat though the parking garage to the elevators. It was just like in the floor plans we had studied. I felt like I had been there before. John was already in character. It was going to be a long day.

"Pick it up, Mister LaRue. We have an appointment for ten o'clock. We don't have all day. I don't want to be late."

"Yes, sir," I answered, moving a little faster. I was already hot and uncomfortable. I didn't have to do much acting to be the slow, reluctant employee I was pretending to be.

We reached the elevator. John pushed the button for the Clinique de Chirurgie Plastique. As we ascended to the seventh floor and reception area, John talked to Pat as if every eye in the clinic was on him.

"I'm sure Doctor Jarvis will be able to help us. They have some of the best people on the continent here. Their stem cell research is second to none. Even the top specialists from Europe come here to learn. I just hope they'll be able to take you. You're very fortunate to be able to afford it."

"Yes, I feel fortunate in a number of ways, despite my illness. There are so many wonderful people who are trying to help me."

"Let's hope the folks here will be as helpful," said John as we reached the seventh floor.

The doctor greeted us as we stepped out of the elevator.

"Hi, Doctor Simmons. And Miss McGuire," said the tall, forty-something man with the dark suit and glasses. He had thinning hair and a rather large mouth, which was full of white teeth and smiling. I was totally ignored.

As the doctors talked and informally discussed Pat's case, I casually took a look around. It was just as I remembered from the security videos. There was a long hallway with a security station at the end of it and large, double, swinging doors beyond that. Half a dozen rooms marched along each side of the hallway. The doors were all closed, and as we knew, locked. Some led to administrative offices. Some led to stairwells and the central service area of the building.

I was told to wait in a glass-paneled lounge. John, Pat, and the doctor went down the hallway, past the guard station, and through the swinging doors.

The hardest part of the whole day was sitting in that room, even though there was a TV and magazines to read. After about an hour, I was already going bonkers, and my wait hadn't even begun. I was there six hours in all before John came down to give me an update. As soon as he came in, my character let him have it.

"You said it would only be a couple of hours. I've been waiting here over half the day!"

"Don't worry, Mister LaRue, you'll be paid."

"I want time-and-a-half."

"Don't be ridiculous. You'll get paid exactly what we agreed on, fifteen dollars an hour and not a penny more."

"I'm not sitting here all day for a lousy fifteen dollars. I should be making a lot more than that."

"It's what you agreed to, Mister LaRue."

"I don't care. Just try getting a lift back to Albany and see how much it would cost you. A hell of a lot more than what you're paying me. It'd cost you three or four thousand with all the equipment your patient requires."

"Are you trying to blackmail me?"

"I'm only trying to get what's fair. You're taking advantage of me because I work for the Medical Center. You made me think it wouldn't be much more than my normal shift. So my usual salary seemed OK. Now that I see what's really involved, I believe I'm entitled to more. I should at least get what you would have had to pay a private driver.

"If I wanted to pay that kind of money I would have hired a private, professional driver. I hired you because you offered to do it for less. And I must admit, you haven't been exactly satisfactory."

"What do you mean?" I exclaimed. I was getting into my part, although I had to be careful. I had almost said the 'burgh' instead of Albany as our starting point. I didn't want to get carried away and make a mistake. I had no doubt that we were being closely monitored.

"Never mind," said John. "I don't want to argue with you. I need to get back to helping them with Pam. I'll raise your salary to twenty dollars an hour for the duration of the trip. I don't have to remind you, you're getting paid even when you aren't driving, which I think is a pretty good deal. Do you agree?"

"Make it twenty-five and you have a deal," I replied, sticking out my hand and smiling.

"Mister LaRue..." John said, staring hard at me and not returning my handshake.

"OK," I agreed reluctantly, looking at the floor then up at him with a resigned expression. "Twenty dollars. I want it in writing."

"OK, I'll put it in writing when I'm done with Pam. In the meantime, you'd better shape up if you ever want to work for me again."

He turned on his heels and walked away, back up the hallway. I flipped the bird at his back and picked up a magazine, which I pretended to read. So far so good, if anyone was watching us I was sure our little act had fooled them. It was the next act I was worried about.

Chapter 48

A short while after our conversation, John returned to inform me Pam would be staying the night. He had a room nearby. I could stay in the waiting room. I started to object – I wasn't acting. John replied by telling me where I could find the vending machines, before walking away.

So far things were working perfectly. The next part of the plan, however, was the dicey part. I still wasn't sure I could pull it off.

A short time later a woman in a nurse's uniform came by to give me the promised pillow and blanket. She even brought me a sandwich and a cup of coffee.

"You'll be comfortable in here," she assured me. "The guard down the hall will help you if you need anything."

"I'd rather have you help me," I quipped. I figured my deadbeat, uncouth alter ego would have said such a thing, not that I wouldn't of.

She glanced at my wrinkled white suit and bulging midsection. I had extra padding tucked into my waistband and pants, which gave me a decidedly fat-assed appearance. She smiled condescendingly.

"I only work with the patients," she replied and walked away.

I watched TV for awhile, until around 8:00, when I heard John whisper in my ear. He had brought a wireless communication unit, smuggled in Pat's chair, along with a small handheld computer. I had a tiny receiver, also compliments of John, tucked inconspicuously in my ear. Even though I had been waiting for him to contact me, I almost jumped out of my seat when his voice came over my small earphone.

"Jay, over, can you hear me?"

I clicked the pen he had given me twice, the signal for yes. Apparently, the clicking of the pen broke some wireless circuit to transmit a series of signals, like dots in Morse code, only simpler. One click for no, two for yes, with a simple twelve-word vocabulary made up of combinations of clicks. Not much, but better than nothing. It would have to do.

"Can you get into the service area to the eighth floor?"

There was a pause. I looked out the door of the waiting room and down the hall. There were two guards at the station at the end of the corridor. They had a clear view of the hallway. There appeared to be no way to leave the room without being noticed.

"No," I clicked.

"Then on to plan B," he announced. I didn't respond. Plan B was a last resort.

I stretched and walked out of the waiting room into the hallway toward the guards.

"Hey," I said, walking up to the desk.

"Bonne nuit," one of them replied.

"Would you have a cigarette on you?" I asked. "I'm dying for a smoke." I made a smoking gesture with my hand to my mouth in case they didn't understand English.

"Ne pas fumer," the other guard informed me, pointing to a sign in plain view behind them.

"Oh," I replied looking at the sign. "You gotta be shitting me. How do they expect me to sit here all night without having a stinking butt?"

The first man chuckled and stood up, saying something to his buddy who laughed.

"Come with me," he said. "I was just about to have a stinking butt myself. I'll show you where you can go. My name is Charles."

"Jake," I told him, almost forgetting my fake name.

I followed the guard back up the hall to a locked door, which he opened with his badge. We walked down a wide corridor and through a double door. It opened into a cavernous room with a large generator humming in the center of it. We walked along the high wall to another door and into a rest room. My guide went to a window along the far wall and cracked it open.

"We're not supposed to do this, but there's no one around after eight. Here," he said. He took out a pack of Camels and flipped one out for me.

"Thanks," I replied, taking the cigarette and sticking it in my mouth while he gave me a light. "So how long have you worked here?"

"Not that long," he answered, "only a month or so. I work for a security agency contracted by the clinic. We're separate from the building security."

"I could tell, you guys are much more professional looking."

"Yeah," he answered. "We're all ex-military. Not like those little boys downstairs."

"You speak good English," I observed.

"Most Montrealers speak English, that is when they want to. I studied English all through school. Anyway, you have to if you want to work for our agency."

"You must be the cream of the crop to work here. It looks like a tit assignment."

"It's steady and pays good if that's what you mean."

"Are there many of you on duty here?"

"No, just my partner and me. One of us patrols the floors while the other watches the station. There's another man on the ground floor and one in the rear."

"Gee, sounds nice. How do I get me a job like that?"

"Have you ever been in the service?"

"No," I answered.

"Can you speak French?"

"No," I responded.

"Have you ever done security work? Do you know any martial arts?"

"No," I lied.

"Well, if you can say yes to all those questions and prove you're a Canadian citizen, you may have a shot."

"I guess I won't quit my job, though I'm getting sick of driving demanding invalids around."

We finished our cigarettes while I complained about my employer and job. I bummed another smoke from him for later, even though I only pretended to inhale. I hate the things, but they make a good prop.

"How long you on for?" I asked as I followed him back to the corridor.

"Till midnight. Then the other shift comes in."

"I'll probably be asleep by then, but I'll sure enjoy this in the morning. Thanks again."

I turned and walked back to the waiting room. A short while after that the lights in the corridor went off. Only the floor lights remained on for illumination, and the lamps at the guard station. I soon turned off the light in the waiting room, along with the TV. Then I tried to get a few hours rest before I began my reconnaissance.

Chapter 49

"Jay, Jay, are you there?" I woke to the sound of John's voice squeaking in my ear like a mechanical Jiminy Cricket. "Jay, can you hear me?"

I sat up quickly and clicked the pen in my shirt pocket twice for 'yes'.

"Time to get moving. I've temporarily diverted the guards downstairs to the basement. The floor you're on has the administrative offices, the six examination rooms, and the labs. All the examination rooms and labs are through the double doors. Pat and I saw most of this today. They have the patient rooms on the eighth floor where we think they might be keeping the girls.

"It's funny they didn't bring Pat up to spend the night. They're keeping her down on the seventh in one of the examination rooms. Said it was because they were all occupied upstairs. They told me they'd be testing her early tomorrow morning. I want you to check out the eighth floor. Can you get to the service elevator?"

I clicked twice.

"Where's the door. Left or right?" John asked through my tiny earphone.

I clicked once.

"Left?"

Click, click.

"How many doors from the entrance?"

I clicked three times.

"OK, let me know when you get there."

I walked into the darkened hall, looking up and down in both directions.

The guard station was empty.

I walked down the hallway, clicking twice when I reached the door. A moment later it snapped open as if I had swiped a keycard in front of it. I slipped in and moved toward the sound of the huge generators. Instead of pushing open the swinging doors to the generator room, I entered a small door to the right and stood in front of the service elevator. I hit the 'Up' button and waited.

I had a simple excuse if caught. I was looking for a place to have a smoke. They couldn't shoot me for that, could they? I wondered if

John had managed to compromise their security system to the point that I was invisible. I trusted that if anyone looked at a video display from a camera, all they'd see was empty corridor. Still, I expected to be greeted by a couple of security guards when the elevator door opened to the eighth floor. The corridor was empty. I wondered vaguely what John could have done to get everyone downstairs. He told me I'd have twenty minutes when I got to the top floor. Five minutes of that had already elapsed.

Walking through a set of double doors, I entered a wide corridor with rooms on both sides down its length. All the doors were shut. The one nearest me, like all of them, had steel meshing over a small window. It was thick and locked. It looked more like a cellblock in a mental institution than a hospital ward. There were no nurses or doctors on duty.

I tried another door. It too was locked. The rooms appeared to be empty. So much for the place being fully occupied. I took a quick look behind me through the double doors into the elevator corridor. It was still deserted. John had gone strangely quiet. I didn't like the silence.

Continuing down the wide hallway, I moved back and forth, from side to side. Trying each door in turn, I peered inside. When I had almost reached the end of the passage, a face appeared suddenly in the small window of the door. Only inches from mine, it stared madly through the glass pane like a deranged person. It appeared so quickly and stood so close to the panel that I was startled almost out of my shoes. The face was covered with white bandages like a mummy, with only her eyes and mouth visible. Then everything happened at once.

I jumped back in alarm at first. Then I started clicking the pen like crazy to attract John's attention. I wondered what he could be doing. At the same the, the girl began to scream hysterically.

"Help me! Help me! Please help me," she wailed.

I couldn't tell if she was Alicia or not, or even her race, with the white cosmetic surgery mask over her face. I tried to calm her down with soothing words she probably couldn't hear and gestures she obviously didn't comprehend. Foolishly, I tried to open the door. It was locked like the others, but this one was alarmed.

Lights started flashing and sirens began to sound as if someone had pulled a fire alarm. The face in the window disappeared. I figured I'd better try to do the same.

I ran down the hall to the double doors just as the elevator arrived to eject four men dressed in security uniforms. Unlike the guards earlier, these men were armed.

I hurried back to the other end of the corridor where there was a large window. It was partially open to let in air. It gave out to a small terrace that held a few antennas and a satellite dish. The roof of the building was only twelve or fourteen feet above the terrace, which was only meant for workmen. I climbed out of the window.

When I took the elevator to the eighth floor I had no intention of climbing around outside of the building. I hate heights. The view from the terrace was more than high enough. Even though the roof of an adjoining wing was only four stories below, not the full eight, I was having vertigo. I now found myself out on a narrow ledge over a hundred feet in the air. I controlled my breathing, concentrating on footing and handholds rather than the terrifying gulf between me and the ground.

I had two choices, up or down. A metal ladder led to the rooftop where I would probably be trapped. Down led to the seventh floor where I might be able to get back in unobserved. I could hear them in the corridor behind me. They would soon be at the window. Perhaps they would open it and look out. I had to move fast.

I edged myself to the corner of the terrace and peered over. There was another platform below the one I was on. The height made me giddy. I heard the guards approaching the window and the shrieking of the girl.

I swung myself down and off the small terrace, holding on with my arms and elbows, while I felt for the ledge below with my feet. There was nothing but air beneath me. At that moment someone threw open the window and leaned out. They looked left and right and then up. I let myself down, hanging from the bottom of the terrace by my hands with my arms fully extended. Finally, I touched the railing of the platform below me with my tiptoes.

I hung there for some time, until I managed to move one hand down and grab an out-thrusting cornice. Then I swung myself down onto the terrace below. From there I slowly started edging along the ledge toward the corner of the building. Just then someone flung open a window only a short distance away. Turning inward, I crawled around the corner of the building hugging it like a lover, and shimmied out of sight before being seen.

I was breathing rapidly, but controlled. Clinging to the building face first, I focused on each footfall and handhold. Then I noticed an open window not six feet away from me.

For a moment I thought a head would pop out of this one too. It was higher than the others and smaller. I soon realized from its position that it might be the window to the seventh floor bathroom, where I'd had a smoke earlier. I edged toward it carefully and reached up to look in. It was indeed the bathroom. Better yet, it was still open.

I hadn't heard from John since I entered the door to the elevator. I figured I was on my own. Gathering my strength and nerve, I began to pull myself in.

I had used all my arm strength to pull myself up to the window. My legs dangled uselessly in the air. I was so exhausted from clinging like a bug to the outside of the building that I was completely spent. No matter how hard I tried, I couldn't pull myself in. I hung suspended between the window and the ledge, which I could no longer reach.

The strength drained out of me like a seeping can. I felt myself slipping. At that moment I saw my miserable life pass before me. My misspent youth, my failed marriage, the string of dead adversaries, nothing much to show for myself except failure and regret. Then I thought of Bud and how I had let him down as well. But thoughts that would make some people want to jump only made me mad.

The anger welled up inside me like a giant wave. With a scream of rebellion at my miserable fate, I half crawled, half pulled myself up like the clinging, grasping animal I really am. Scraping my knees and elbows in the process, I threw myself onto the small bathroom floor. I lay there for some time until my wits were slowly gathered about me.

The first thing I did was stagger to the sink to bathe my head where I bumped it coming through the window. I could hear footsteps running down the hall in my direction. Just before they burst in, I noticed the ashtray overturned on the floor where I had knocked it over. Next to it was a pack of matches and a couple half-smoked butts. I grabbed one and lit it up just as two nervous-looking security men rushed in.

"What are you doing here?" demanded one of them, pointing his revolver at my head.

"Having a smoke," I answered. I didn't have to fake the alarm in my voice. I held up my hands and dropped the butt. "The other guard said it was OK. We had one together earlier. I didn't mean any harm. Please don't shoot."

"You're not supposed to be in here," announced the other one. "The whole place is in lockdown. You'll have to come with us."

Chapter 50

I thought my act had worked at first. When they brought me back to the waiting room, however, John was standing there. One of the security men with him had his handheld computer.

"You'll have to come with us," announced the man in charge, someone we hadn't seen before. He had a distinctive Russian accent. "It seems you have not been entirely honest with us. You have been hacking into our systems and disrupting our security operations since you got here this afternoon. I'm afraid you are going to have to be detained until the authorities arrive."

"And when will that be?" asked John, after giving me a look to stop me from cracking the trachea of the man standing next to me and using his gun on the other three. I relaxed after computing my chances of taking all four of them out before they shot one of us. The odds were not good. I didn't hear a reply to John's question if there was one.

I was relieved when they took us to Pat's room, then left. She was awake and knew something had happened when the alarms went off, but was unharmed. She had guessed it was something her bumbling cousin had done. We all stayed in character. John had drilled this into our heads while preparing us for the deception.

"What happened?" John asked me.

"I only went out for a smoke," I replied. "What's this about hacking? What are you up to, Doc? You didn't say anything about having to stay overnight. I quit. Get me out of this place."

"You're just being melodramatic. They found my tablet, that's all. I was reading some medical journals over the web. I must have interrupted their security system somehow by mistake. It's more than likely a glitch in their software. Just a misunderstanding, that's all. You'll probably have to testify in court when I sue them."

"Well, I just might do some suing myself and it will be you I sue," I yelled and stomped off to the other end of the room.

I had the distinct feeling there wouldn't be any authorities coming in the morning. In fact, I doubted we'd see morning if we didn't figure something out and quick. John didn't seem particularly concerned. Perhaps he had a plan. Pat looked at both of us expectantly. I felt like saying, 'Don't look at me'.

John motioned with his eyes in the direction of the corner by the door. A small, pen-size camera was mounted on the ceiling. I assumed a listening device was planted nearby as well. He made a casual gesture toward Pat. It must have been some pre-arranged signal. She began complaining loudly about her treatment and her doctor. John and I stood in the corner with our back to the camera.

"Do you think they can hear us?" I whispered.

"I doubt it, not over Pat's complaining," he answered just as softly

"OK, what's plan C?"

"I haven't got a plan C," he answered.

"Well, we better do something quick. I've got a good idea what they've got planned for us and it won't be pretty. I don't think they'll do anything here. They've probably already sent for someone, a team maybe. I don't want to be here when they arrive."

"I can open this door if that helps," said John. "They haven't taken all my toys." He pointed to the large, plastic watch on his wrist. "But that's about the extent of my powers at the moment. You'll have to do the rest. They're armed, you know."

"Don't remind me. We have to move fast. Unlock the door."

He touched a few icons on his wrist pad.

I turned abruptly and walked toward the door. Then without warning, after a glance and a nod from John, I threw it open. The hall was dark and empty. There was no guard by the door as I half expected. They must have been observing us from the guard station. I could hear someone shouting just down the corridor beyond the doors to the lobby.

I was halfway down the hall when the guard burst through the swinging doors with his pistol drawn. Taking three long steps, I leaped through the air just as he pointed his gun in my direction. Without touching the ground, I lifted my left leg up and outward in a sweeping motion. The reverse-crescent kick knocked his gun arm away just as he fired. The shot went wide.

I came down on top of him. As I did, I hit the side of his neck with a vicious chop, cutting the blood flow to his brain. The gun flew out of his upraised hand. His eyes rolled to the back of his head. He hit the floor hard. Picking up the gun, I threw it to John, who was already coming out of the room with Pat in her chair.

"To the auxiliary elevator!" I yelled. "Follow me."

We ran back up the hallway and through the swinging doors to the lobby. John pushed Pat in her chair. As we reached the guard station, the regular elevator arrived.

"Through that door!" I ordered, pointing toward the one to the generator and the auxiliary area. "I'll be right behind you."

They reached the door just as the main elevator opened. A man came rushing out. I didn't give him time to react, but nail him with a powerful thrust kick to the midsection. It knocked him back into the man behind him. They both tumbled backward.

The first man lay on the floor gasping for breath. The second man tried to get to his feet only to have the heel of my shoe smash against his jaw. His head snapped back violently, smashing his brain back and forth against the inside of his cranium. He went down semi-conscience with a soon-to-be-diagnosed concussion.

Stepping past the first man, I smacked him in the head with the inside of my foot to keep him down. Then I followed John and Pat through the door to the auxiliary elevators.

"Don't ever make fun of my kung fu again," I said looking at John hard as he stood waiting for the freight elevator. He grinned and bowed with his hands together in supplication. We didn't have long to gloat.

Suddenly, another guard burst through the door from the generator room. He was in his t-shirt with his pants half zipped, and unarmed. He had obviously been caught in the john when he heard the ruckus. He stopped dead when John raised the gun.

I glanced in John's direction and toward the doors to the hallway where the other guards were surely gaining consciousness.

"The elevator's almost here," I observed.

While John kept the man covered, I used the masking-tape we had brought to gag and tie him up. He tried to resist at first, so I cold-cocked him with a short jab to the jaw. It was much easier to wrap the thick tape around his arms and legs after that. I applied several layers of it to his mouth and shut it up tight.

So far things had gone fairly smoothly. None of my opponents were particularly well trained. All of them were caught by surprise. I had taken them out, but so far I hadn't seriously hurt anyone. That is unless you call a few broken bones and contusions serious. At least I hadn't killed any of them. I couldn't count on that kind of luck for long.

Finally, the auxiliary elevator arrived. John handed the gun to Pat as we piled in.

"Don't shoot me by mistake," I pleaded.

"Don't worry," she replied. "I used to go to the shooting range all the time, until my hands got too weak. I bet I could still use one of these if I had to."

"Let's hope you don't have to."

The fact that one of us was armed did not give me much comfort. I knew they'd have more reinforcements soon, if they hadn't already arrived, and they'd probably have more firepower than we did.

The elevator seemed to be going down even slower than it had come up. The floors crawled by as we descended to the basement.

Pat and I glanced up at the display panel nervously, trying to will the thing to go faster. If she could have, I'm sure she would have been pacing back and forth across the elevator like I was. John seemed unperturbed.

Finally, we were getting to the lower floors. I was just breathing a sigh of relief when we jerked to a stop at the third level.

"Crap," I swore. "What happened?"

"You weren't expecting to go to the basement, were you?" asked John. "Surely they'll be waiting for us, don't you think?"

"I don't know. You want to get out of here, don't you?"

"Yes, but not that way. They'll have it covered."

As John said these words, the elevator door opened. He rushed out pushing Pat's chair and yelled for me to follow.

"Hurry, we don't have much time. In a few moments they'll realize we haven't descended to the basement as the control panel lights are indicating. They'll know we stopped off on some other floor. Quickly, to the stairwell."

"Stairwell?" I stammered. "What about Pat's chair? How are we going to take her down three flights of stairs and out of the building?"

"We'll be her chair," John answered as we reached the entrance to the stairwell.

Pushing Pat's chair through the doorway, he stopped at the small landing. A series of steps led both up and down.

"Here," said John crossing his arms and holding them out to me. "We'll do it Boy Scout fashion. Cross your arms and grab mine. Pat you sit on our hands."

"You've got to be kidding," she objected.

"You can stay here if you want," I told her. "Just do it."

"We did this all the time when we were kids," said John calmly, giving me a look. "My sister used to pay us to carry her around like the Pharaoh's daughter. We never dropped her once, although I was tempted."

Pat reached up and grabbed our shoulders. We stooped before her with our arms crossed and our hands grasped to form a crude chair. Pulling herself up, she sat on our hands with her arms over our necks as we slowly rose to a standing position. We had her comfortably balanced between us. She didn't seem to weigh much. Because of our difference in height, however, John had to walk in a somewhat stooped manner.

"Now I know why I hate short people," he quipped.

"Bite me, Rothburg," I answered.

We went like this, carrying Pat between us, down to the second-floor landing, exactly twenty-two zigzagging steps.

John had programmed the elevator control console to make it appear we had gone all the way to the basement. Whoever, if anyone, was waiting for us there would have by now figured out we weren't coming. They'd be sending out patrols to check each floor and the stairwells. We didn't have much time.

I was completely disoriented by now. I didn't know what side of the building I was on or where the exits were.

We continued down, side by side with Pat between us. As we reached the first floor landing we could hear the footfalls of several men running up the stairs from the basement. We stopped and tried the door to the corridor. It was unlocked. We slipped through.

Chapter 51

What happened next is a blur. We put Pat down behind a chair a short way down the hall. John crouched next to her with the gun. I ran back and stood with my back against the wall just at the entrance to the stairwell. I could hear them running up the steps. They must have known where we were because they busted right through the door without stopping.

The first man ran into the hall with his arm extended holding a gun in front of him. I remained calm. It was as if I had been training for this moment all my life. I did not anticipate, but saw what was about to happen as if it had been choreographed. I guess if you do something often enough, it becomes ingrained. Your brain's synapses become hardwired to perform and perceive things in a certain way.

I became the moment. I didn't see their guns or their numbers or what they could do to me. I saw a series of targets to be hit and reactions to be triggered with a precise series of moves and counter moves. If these were executed with speed and accuracy, they would lead to the desired end - all three men lying on the floor.

I grabbed the first man's arm by the wrist and elbow as he stepped through the door. I grasped him from the side before he was even aware I was there. Striking and locking his elbow and wrist with the heel of my palms, I snapped my hands together. His arm broke at the elbow with a crack. He howled in pain and dropped the gun, going down on his knees. At the same time, I side stepped into the next man with a thrust kick, driving him back through the door into the man behind him. God, I love it when they line up in single-file like that. I followed with a front-thrust kick that sent them both toppling over the railing onto the pavement a floor below.

The first man was recovering. Using his good arm, he raised his gun to point it at me. Before he could fire, I stepped into him and grabbed his gun hand, raising his arm out and away. At the same time, I brought the blade of my hand down on his collarbone like it was a two-by-four in a demonstration, snapping it with a great deal more than the required forty-psi. The man dropped the gun and went down holding his useless arm and shoulder. I slid the gun away. He tried to get up, but couldn't without the use of his arms. I kicked him in the head just the same for trying.

I ran back into the hallway breathing hard.

"Quick," I wheezed. "This way. I think the coast is clear for now."

Every siren in the place was sounding. Men were running back and forth on the stairs. I stopped for a moment by the door, trying to decide which way to go. I expected to be discovered and shot at any moment.

"To the lobby," yelled John. "We've got to get to the main lobby."

"But the ambulance is in the basement," I replied. "We've got to get out of here."

"No, that's just what they expect us to do. They'll be waiting for us down there. The lobby's our only hope. If there're any cops around, that's where they'd be."

The lobby was all the way at the other end of the hallway, at least fifty feet away.

"Can you carry her?" I asked.

"Sure," said John. "On my back."

"Good, get her to the lobby. I'll stand here and watch the door."

Pat reached up and put her arms around his neck from behind while he rose to a standing position. As he did, someone burst out of the doorway, not two feet in front of me. I stood facing him as the others moved rapidly toward the lobby.

The man lunged at me with a truncheon. I dodged the strike and skipped backward.

He was large, about six-two with broad shoulders and thick legs. Well-built and muscular, he was obviously trained from the way he stood.

He raised his weapon, ready to come at me again. John was jogging down the hallway behind me with Pat on his back. Whatever it was in the lobby John wanted to get to, I aimed to see he made it.

As the guard rushed me, I unbuckled my belt and slipped it from my waist. I could feel the weight of the heavy, sharp buckle, and swung it around like a chain. He paused in midstride and reconsidered the situation.

As he hesitated, I accelerated toward him with a burst of speed. Whipping the belt, I struck him in the head with the buckle. He went back on his heels. I hit him with a side-thrust kick, striking his floating ribs. He went down, but got back up swinging the truncheon frantically at me.

Holding my belt in both hands, I grabbed his arm with it as he lunged forward again. Employing an aikido move, I used his

223

momentum to pull him forward, then quickly snapped him back, flipping him head over heels backward into the wall. The weapon flew from his hand. He crumpled to the ground and didn't move

I could hear sirens in the distance and wondered if they were coming for me. Had John been able to contact someone on the outside? Were they coming to rescue us or arrest us? I could only guess.

I dragged the unconscious man into the stairwell. I thought of throwing him over the landing to fall to the basement below, but decided against it. I figured one crack in his skull was enough. He wouldn't be bothering us again, but he was still breathing.

I headed for the lobby. When I got close I could see John standing between two city cops and a phalanx of security guards. Everyone had their gun drawn. Pat lay on the floor at John's feet in obvious distress. He appeared to be explaining that he and Pat had been kidnapped and held against their will. The guards were saying they had trespassed and were trying to steal drugs. I decided to stay out of it and moved back to the stairwell door unobserved.

I suddenly realized that the kidnapped girls might be in danger. I decided to go up to the eighth floor and try to free them. If things went south, the girls would probably go south with them, which meant they would disappear, perhaps permanently. Their kidnappers couldn't afford to let them be found to tell their stories. Alicia might be one of them. I had to help her.

Chapter 52

Going back to the stairwell, I started running up the stairs. I was afraid something bad might be happening to the girls.

Breathing heavily by the time I reached the fourth floor, I was winded by the sixth. I slowed my pace and tried to catch my breath. Climbing slowly, I warily made my way up the remaining two flights.

I opened the door to the eighth-floor corridor a crack and peered into the lobby. It was empty. I heard something through the swinging doors to the patient rooms. It was a rustling noise, and the sound of someone whispering. A moment later a security guard entered followed by three girls wearing white robes and white plastic surgical masks. They were trailed by a tall black dude in jeans and a sleeveless t-shirt.

"Stay together," said the black dude. "The fire's on the sixth floor. We'll go down the staircase."

I didn't have time to hide. They came straight through the lobby toward the door where I was concealed. I watched them approach, hidden by the darkness, waiting until the guard was at the door with his hand on the knob. He had his head turned toward the girls and was talking to his partner.

As he opened the door and turned to enter, I attacked. I hit him with five straight, hard punches to the head, right-left-right-left-right. The last one landed right between the eyes. Blood sprayed from his mouth and nose. His head snapped back and forth like he was shaking it. His cheek split. His forehead cracked. He went down heavily. The girls screamed. The black guy came around them with his fists flying.

I circled away to my left, blocking and dodging. I tried to keep him at bay with short, hard kicks to his knees and groin. As I fought the man, I yelled for the girls to run down the stairs to the lobby where the police were. They only half obeyed. They stood at the doorway screaming and hugging each other. Then they ran back to their cells. I couldn't believe it, but I had my hands full.

The black dude was whistling rights and lefts by my head like a whirlwind. He was tall and lanky, with long arms. He threw right hooks that looked like they were being fired from a slingshot. Even when I blocked them they hurt. They came so fast, from so many angles, that I was unable to counter other than with my feet. Even with that, he was able to reach me with long-armed jabs.

I made him pay for each punch, with kicks to his legs, pelvis, and midsection. Still, I was at a disadvantage. This guy was well trained, perhaps part of a squad called in to clean up the mess we had caused.

We circled the room in a deadly dance as we fought. His reach, speed, and skill were starting to tell. He had hit me in the ribs a couple of times with wide, arcing hooks. My arms were sore and weary from blocking his punches. Another blow like that last right, and I'd be fighting with broken ribs. Not a handicap I could afford given the ones I was already working with.

My nose was bleeding from one of his left jabs, making it hard to breath. I was sucking in air through my open mouth, which he had also cracked. I was doing little damage with my defensive kicks. He was too tall to try to kick in the head. Then he nailed me with a left hook to the eye that sent me reeling and left me half blind.

All the while, as we fought, he bad-mouthed me, making fun of my stature and inability to hurt him.

"Oh, Kung fu boy, eh?"

He'd make Bruce Lee sounds and laughed at my kicks. Every time he hit me he stopped and made a comment.

"There's one for Brother Malcolm. White men can't fight, chump."

That's when he got a little careless. Smelling blood, he stepped in to finish me off with a right hook to the head. I saw it coming – out of my good eye – and maintained a strong stance. Leaning back, I let the blow brush past my jaw by a hair's breath.

His right arm was extended across his body in an awkward position. All his weight was on his forward foot. Before he could recover, I locked his arm, and using pressure on the elbow, forced him forward off his feet. He landed on his face with his arm extended behind him.

Flipping over it onto my back, I grabbed his wrist with both hands and pulled his arm out straight. Then I locked my knees tightly around his shoulder and applied pressure to his hyper-extended elbow with my pelvis - a classic jujitsu arm bar.

Leaning back and raising my hips, I increased the force on the elbow. If I couldn't quite break his arm, at least he couldn't break my lock. I could sit like this all day if I had to. I hoped I wouldn't have to.

He had been overconfident. Now that I had him in a hold he couldn't get out of, he was even more belligerent. He insulted my parenthood, my race, my fighting ability, my looks, and age. He was helpless, off his feet, but not defeated.

I resisted the temptation for some payback. I knew he was just goading me, trying to make me do something foolish. But I had no intention of letting him get back up and start swinging those right hooks at my ribs again. I satisfied myself by applying as much pressure as I could on his arm. He didn't squeal like I would have liked him to, but he groaned and stopped the trash talk.

I considered taking a chance and letting the arm bar go to try for a choke hold. I was confident that if that failed and he was able to get to his feet, his left arm would be less than useful. He couldn't hurt me while I had him tied up on the ground like this. However, I was just as much a captive as he was, even if I was the one administering the punishment. Just then I heard footsteps on the stairs.

It was the cops.

Two policemen in uniform with their guns drawn entered from the stairwell. They pointed their weapons at me and told me to put up my hands. I hesitated, not sure what to do. I started to explain.

"Now!" shouted the closer of the two officers. He shoved his gun in my face as I lay entangled with the black dude. I did as ordered and put up my hands. My assailant started talking fast. He told them I was an intruder and had attacked the other guard, who was still lying unconscious on the floor. Mumbling a garbled defense, too winded and hurt to speak, I tried to explain that there were three kidnapped young girls in the next room.

The cop got out his handcuffs and walked toward me, while his buddy kept me under cover. I tried to get my frazzled brain and vocal cords to work so I could explain. All that came out was hysterical gibberish. I must have seemed insane. The black dude sat on the floor next to me, rubbing his arm and accusing me of trespassing and assault.

"Didn't you talk to my friend, John?" I finally managed to stammer. "Down in the lobby. He can verify everything I told you. I've been tracking this girl from Boston for four months now. She's been kidnapped! She's in there with…"

"Fermer la bouche!" yelled the Canadian cop angrily. "We have seen what you have done here. The hospital is full of your victims, salaud! You like to break people's bones, eh? You're a tough guy from New York, eh? I will show you how we handle tough New Yorkers."

He went to hit me on the side of the head with his flashlight as I sat on the ground with my hands behind my head. Being one who always expects the worst as well as the unexpected, I anticipated just such a move. When I saw him fondle the long, heavy shaft only moments before, I got ready. My hands were in a perfect position.

As I flipped my left hand up to block his arm, I brought the ridge of my opposite hand up and smashed his elbow, snapping the arm and forcing his head down. The gun went flying to the floor. I didn't have time for niceties. As he went down I used his motion to propel myself to a standing position, leaping to my feet.

The other cop, who still had his gun out, was coming toward us to help his partner. He was only a few feet away, but I had risen from a sitting position so fast he was taken completely by surprise.

Side-stepping into him suddenly with a thrust kick to the midsection, I knocked him backward and off his feet. He dropped the pistol. I punched him hard between the eyes as he tried to get up, and knocked him out cold. The other cop sat up holding his arm, moaning.

During the struggle with the police, the tall black dude had gotten to his feet. I was vaguely aware of him, but too busy to give him much heed. When I looked up again he was gone. So was one of the cop's guns. I glanced around for the other one and not seeing it, went after him anyway.

I was worried about what he would do to the girls. For some reason I didn't even think about myself. I must have been in some kind of zone, because normally that would have been my first thought. I was beyond fear now, in a place that knew no trepidation, a deep place that's forever fearless.

I ran through the double doors into the corridor where the girls were being kept. The last three rooms stood open. Moving rapidly down the hall, I glanced in each cell. They were empty. I was too late.

Wondering where the girls could be, I noticed the window at the end of the hallway was open. Running to it, I stuck my head out and looked up just as the kidnapper slipped over the rooftop. An iron ladder rose up the side of the building where he disappeared. It had grown light since I was last outside clinging to the side of the building.

Without thinking, I jumped out of the window onto the small platform and climbed up after him. As I reached the top I saw a blur and instinctively raised my arm to block. I'm not sure why he didn't try to shoot me. Perhaps I was too close and caught him by surprise. Maybe he didn't want to attract attention by discharging the firearm. Whatever the reason, instead of shooting me, he tried to smash my skull in with the butt of the pistol.

Again and again, he struck me. I held onto the metal ladder with my right as I blocked his strikes with my left. Twice, three times, then a fourth in succession, I blocked each one, but I was losing my grip. One more blow. I blocked again. This time I brought my fingers around his wrist in a sticky-finger technique. Grabbing him, I pulled him forward. He went over my head and off into thin air. At the same time, I let go my grip and fell backward.

Chapter 53

I thought I was dead and screamed bloody murder. Instead of plummeting to the pavement below, however, I landed on one of the antenna wires secured to the eighth-floor platform. Miraculously, it held, and I was able to drop to the small patio, where I caught my breath. The kidnapper was less fortunate. He went over the ledge to drop eight stories to the ground. He didn't make a sound the whole way down.

Gathering my strength, I slowly ascended to the top of the building again. The three girls were cowering in the corner of the roof not far from the ladder. They were in white gowns. They all had cloth masks on. Only their eyes and mouths were exposed.

"Alicia?" I said looking at them. "Is that you? I'm here to help you."

No one answered. Whimpering and hugging each other, they appeared hysterical and in a state of shock. I finally got them to follow me to the entrance of the stairwell by taking one of them by the arms and pulling them forward. I was almost at the door, when two metropolitan police busted out. They were mad as dogs, and would have shot me outright if I hadn't grabbed one of the girls and held her in front of me.

"These girls have been kidnapped!" I yelled. "They've been drugged and held against their will."

The girl I held was short and had long, brown, curly hair. It brushed my face as I held her. I could see her ears. Could it be Alicia, after all this, could it really be her?

"Alicia?" I whispered into her ear.

The Canadian cops yelled in French for me to let the girl go or they'd shoot. They were royally pissed off after what I had done to their comrades. I hoped they would soon realize I was telling the truth. It didn't look like that was happening, however.

"Wait, wait!" someone yelled from the stairwell. I breathed a sigh of relief. It sounded like John Rothburg.

A moment later, John walked out onto the rooftop. He had a police captain at his side

"Hold it," the officer ordered. "What's going on here?"

Things got crazy after that. The girls were crying and wailing. The cops were swearing and threatening me. John was trying to explain. The security detail had disappeared.

Despite my heroic efforts, the police wanted to arrest me on the spot for assaulting two of their men. John had all he could do to convince the captain I was on their side. Once things calmed down, we turned our attention to the girls.

"Alicia?" I asked again as the three girls stood before me. "Is that you? Everything is going to be OK. Alicia?"

No one answered. We started to gently unmask them. The last one was Alicia. She seemed to be shell shocked and did not respond to her name. I put my white medical jacket over her shoulders. A physician and two EMTs arrived soon after. As the girls were being led away to be examined, John asked them if there were any others being kept there.

"There was another girl," said one of kidnapped victims, a tall brunette. "I think she was black. She was taken away early this morning. I overheard them bragging about how they had sold her to some sheik in Saudi Arabia for a million dollars."

"Lockdown the whole building," ordered the Captain. "Arrest all the security personnel and employees of the clinic, including doctors and nurses."

The Montreal Metropolitan Police scattered to do as commanded.

John and I remained on the rooftop alone.

"Boy was I glad to see you!" I told him, pulling him into a bear hug. "I don't know what those jokers would have done to me if you hadn't showed up when you did."

"I'm happy to see you, too, Jay," he replied. "But we have a problem. I think the one that was taken away earlier to be sold in Saudi Arabia is the president's daughter. We've got to help her."

"What? Are you sure?"

"It makes sense. That assumption is what brought us here in the first place, remember? The girl said she was a black girl. It has to be her!"

He took out his smart phone and took a deep breath, telling himself to relax.

"Let's see if we can find out where she is. There are only so many airfields you can fly out of from here to a place like Saudi Arabia. I'll just check the airports and schedules for international flights leaving the city. I doubt they would have used a commercial airline. That should limit our search."

He started Googling flights to Saudi Arabia from private airfields around the city.

"It's early, not even eleven yet," he observed. "There's a good chance she's still in Montreal."

"I hope so," I said.

It didn't take John long to come up with the answer. He didn't even have to hack a computer.

"The only flight from the city to Saudi Arabia today is out of Montreal Saint Hubert Longueuil Airport. The place is like an air dock for the filthy rich. Private jets take off from there all the time. The flight's scheduled to depart at 1:00 p.m. We've got two hours. It's across the bridge in the northeastern part of the city."

After giving me directions, John left to report this information to the captain. I knew that by the time John got their attention and got them to believe his story, the President's daughter would be in the Arabian Desert, the sex slave of some Saudi prince.

I ran to the basement of the building. Like the last time I was compelled to go that extra mile to save Jerry's wife and grandchild, I felt it was my duty. I had to go on until it was finished. It was the least I could do as long as there was still a young girl in captivity, president's daughter or not.

Pat's van was still where I had parked it the previous day. I was also still in my white medical uniform. That might come in handy for what I had to do. Backing from the space, I squealed tires and peeled out of the garage.

Chapter 54

Driving northeast through the old city, I headed for the La Ronde bridge. From there I went southeast to 116, then due east to the airport. I got snarled in traffic after the bridge and lost almost an hour. It was quarter-to-one when I reached the airfield. Driving around to the rear, I sped to where the private hangers were located. From there I headed toward the field where signs said 'No Trespassing'. There was a fence between me and the runway. I drove to a closed gate. A jeep came up with an armed guard at the wheel.

"You can't be here," he said. "This is for authorized vehicles only."

"This is a medical emergency," I informed him. For some reason I thought he'd believe that before he'd believe the President's daughter was being kidnapped. "Someone has had a heart attack during take off. They're going to taxi the plane here and transport them to my ambulance."

"I haven't heard anything about a medical emergency," the guard replied.

"It just happened," I insisted. "Call it in if you don't believe me."

He went into the guard station inside the gate to verify the information, leaving the gate open. When he did, I backed up and gunned the van. Scraping by his jeep and sweeping through the entrance, I accelerated toward the runway. It was just one o'clock.

I wasn't sure what I was going to do, but I've been in that position before. I had to somehow prevent that plane from taking off. I figured it would be just about impossible. I would more than likely end up killing myself and everyone on board. But that didn't stop me. I had to do something! I had to try.

Suddenly, I heard a buzzing in my ear. All this time, even with all the fighting, the tiny earphone John had given me was still there. I had forgotten all about it. He was now talking to me through it.

"Jay, are you there? Where are you?"

I still had the pen in my pants pocket. I was going to use it to stab out the black dude's eyes, but never got the chance. I clicked it twice."

"Have you gone after the President's daughter?"

I clicked it twice again.

"I've talked to the police. They are going to try and help, but I'm afraid it will be too late. It's already one. Are you by chance at the airport?"

Click-click.

"Jay, you hot shit. You never cease to amaze me. The plane is taking off on runway C21. That's at the southwest end of the field."

Click-click.

"What? You're there now?"

I clicked twice.

"You son-of-a-gun! They're in a Beechcraft, twin-engine turboprop. It's a twelve-seater. The number on the side is N36DB. It should be taking off any minute."

At that moment, the guard drove up in his jeep with its blue light flashing. The good thing was he hadn't drawn his revolver.

"What's the big idea of skidding past me like that? You broke my taillight. Who the hell do you think you are? I talked to the tower. There's no medical emergency. The police are on the way. So you better just settle back and relax."

I was about ten feet away from him. I contemplated rushing him and leaping in the air with a flying kick. I was sure I could hit him before he drew his gun.

"I could take you out in two seconds, you know," I told him. "I'm trying to save the daughter of the U.S. President. She's on that plane. I would just as soon risk a bullet than see her taken away. But I need you. I can't stop them by myself. You've got to help me."

"What style?" he inquired.

"Heh?" I replied a bit confused.

"You're going to take me out from ten feet away. You must know the martial arts or something."

"Kenpo," I answered.

"Me too," said the man. "You never would have made it. But I think I can trust the word of another kenpo man, however crazy it sounds."

"Will you help me?" I asked again.

There was a long pause.

"I can radio the tower," he suggested to my relief. "We can have the plane brought back to the pad."

"Then please do it!" I said. "We don't have much time."

I gave him the information John had relayed to me. He contacted the tower and gave them the details. A short time later, I saw a plane like the one John described taxi onto the runway. It was getting ready to take off. At that moment the guard came back and told me that the plane was not responding to their transmission.

"It's not acknowledging any of their requests."

"And it won't come back after it takes off. We've got to stop them."

"How?" he asked.

"I know what I'm going to do."

I Jumped back in the van and headed out to the runway. I was soon moving at speed directly toward the Beechcraft, which was starting its take-off. I looked back. The jeep was right behind me with its lights flashing.

I picked up speed. I was playing chicken with an airplane! I had to intercept it before it gained enough velocity to lift off. The jeep and van were now neck and neck, zooming down the tarmac in a race to the turbojet. It didn't look like it had enough room to take off. We were headed for a head on collision.

At the last minute, the jeep veered off. I did the same a fraction of a second later, but stayed close enough to nick the tailfin of the aircraft. It smashed my windshield as the plane whizzed by. I screeched the van to a stop, almost fishtailing.

The aircraft careened off to the left across another runway and into a ditch. The landing gear flew off. A wing was sliced away. The plane skidded across a gully on its belly and came lurching to a stop against a dirt bank.

Turning the van around, I raced toward the wrecked aircraft. I jumped out and reached the door just as the pilot opened it to bail out. Hitting him in the temple with a right, I followed up with a sharp left to the solar plexus. I finished him off with a hand-sword to the back of the neck He fell heavily, lights out!

Another man ran down the steps at me. As he reached the last step, I took him by the balls and throat in midstride and threw him up and over my head. It all happened in one fluid motion. He landed head first on the tarmac and remained still.

A third man jumped me from behind. Bending my body sharply as he grabbed my shoulders, I flipped him over my head. Then I stomped him in the face. His head smacked back against the cement.

A moment later, before I could turn and face my next opponent, I was hit in the back by something that sent me flying forward. I had never been struck like this before. It was an odd sensation. Whatever had hit me was small and solid, but it was the most powerful blow I ever felt. It seemed like my entire shoulder was shattered. I lay on the ground motionless. I felt nothing. I heard nothing. Then all was black.

Chapter 55

It's taken awhile for things to get back to normal. Hell, it's taken forever just to get out of the hospital and back across the border to the good old United States. Like most of my adventures, I'm relating this one from a hospital bed, this time in Montreal. I'm recovering from a bullet wound to the shoulder. I'm lucky I can even use my arm, let alone practice karate. However, the doctors assure me that with patience and perseverance, it will be as good as new. I'll have to take their word for it. It hurts like a bastard.

I wouldn't even be here if it wasn't for Dale Clarkson. He showed up at the clinic a short time after the rescue. He was apparently in the city looking for the Chief Executive's girl, following the same leads I was, when he heard the news. The president's daughter had indeed been in the plane on her way to a life of slavery. After talking to John Rothburgh, Clarkson sped out to the airport to help. The kidnapper was about to put another slug in me when he took him out, saving my life a second time. At least it wasn't me who killed him. I didn't kill any...

I guess that's not true. I almost forgot the black dude. I didn't intentionally kill him, but pulling him over the ledge of an eight story building certainly didn't add to his life expectancy. He was trying to bash my head in, however, and would have probably killed the girls if I hadn't stopped him.

I was still wanted for the murder of the Mexican lap dancer. My hospital room was under guard. Hmm, why do I find this all so familiar? Clarkson promised to testify on my behalf, so it should all be cleared up soon. Eventually, the truth will be revealed and I'll be vindicated. Then I will have all I can do to prevent them from making a national hero out of me. Hopefully, I can get my life back, as mediocre as it was.

All the girls are at home now, including Alicia and the President's daughter. All four of them were highly traumatized. It might take years for them to fully recover, if they ever do. They not only underwent brutal physical treatment, but significant emotional and psychological abuse as well. This was all in an attempt to make them malleable to their captors' wishes. They had been sexually mistreated repeatedly, and kept high on drugs the whole time, forced to wear the masks except when they were servicing their clients or their guards.

The case is still under investigation. Not all the facts are known. All those involved have been arrested and charged with kidnapping and human trafficking – the transportation and sale of young women for prostitution. This includes the security guards, the doctors and nurses, and the hospital staff. Dr. Peter Noskov, the man in charge of the clinic at the time of the arrests, was named as one of the chief conspirators. Also named was his associate, Nocoli Roskolovich. Both have ties to the Russian underworld. Doctors Lummis and Javis, the ones we talked to, were also arrested at their homes.

Alicia was returned to her mother in Charlestown, although all is not well. My last conversation with Mrs. Rossi was gut-wrenching. It left me depressed for days. If the family had problems before, they were only magnified in the aftermath of Alicia's abduction.

She's like a emotionally-damaged war casualty, only a shadow of her former self. There's nothing behind the eyes but a vacant stare. They're thinking of putting her in an institution. There hasn't been much to celebrate. The only thanks I got was a half-hearted thank you between her mother's sobs. There was nothing I could do or say to make it better, so I said and did nothing. I'd just as soon forget the whole business.

Speaking of thank you, no one in the White House bothered to contact me afterward. I didn't get any medals or commendations. Like I said, I wanted to avoid that sort of thing, but a note of thanks for saving the daughter of our nation's leader would have been nice.

Then a few days ago I got a letter in the mail. It had no return address, but the postmark was from Virginia. It was handwritten and obviously done in a hurry. At first I had trouble reading it. Then when I got the gist of its meaning, I focused on it like a laser, reading it a second time. It was a thank you note, and a very gracious one at that. It was for saving the most valuable thing in this individual's world. Although circumstances precluded any formal, official recognition, the writer wanted to express his most heartfelt and sincere gratitude. It was short and to the point. My bravery and heroism would not be forgotten. It was signed with the President's initials. Of course, the author will deny writing it if asked.

I had to put my John Hancock on a paper saying what occurred never happened. It's not the first time I've had to do that. It probably won't be the last. They threatened me with a prison term for saying otherwise. I really can't complain, however. I survived and so had my friends. Too bad they aren't allowed to visit me in the hospital.

Bud thinks I'm a hero again. As nice as it is to be a hero, it is not enough to outweigh my reputation back home. I still can't return to the 'burgh'. The rumor of what happened in Canada and Mexico City just adds to the stigma. Even Suzy wouldn't have tolerated me. So I'll go back in Boston, to my apartment in the North End.

Even if the chief of the local precinct won't be happy to see me, Mrs. Corrado will, and that's good enough for me. I'll get back up to fighting weight with heaping helpings of her pasta dinners every night.

Even though there was no media publicity of the events that took place, word gets around. I'm already getting calls for my services, not only the detective business, but my self-defense classes as well.

One of my first students will be the swimming teacher at the YMCA, Judy Sales. Of all the people I want to see during my forced convalescence, she's the most longed for. She's the calm in my stormy life. Thinking of her makes me feel warm inside. Her image gives me hope. I lived to see her again. That's the only thing I had asked for in my time of distress.

Once I get out of here I plan to see Judy every chance I get. From our last phone conversation, I don't think she'll mind. This could be the start of something big, a whole new Jay Lawless. Think of it!

Epilogue

Semyon read the communiqué one more time, getting madder with each word. Their incredible coup, months of planning and legwork, had been wrecked. Worse then that, their entire eastern U.S. operation had been disrupted. Then there was the fiasco in Mexico City that threatened to compromise that operation as well. Their international network had been all but destroyed, as well as their reputation. They valued their reputation for ruthlessness almost as much as the riches it brought them. In that, they were like their ancestors on the plains of the Russian steppes, rapacious where wealth was concerned. They were also insatiable when it came to vengeance, vendetta, an eye for an eye. His business had been hurt, perhaps permanently. Someone must pay.

Why hadn't he been notified sooner? Thanks to Sullivan's tip from prison, they were ready for the interloper in Mexico City. Sullivan was paid for his tip with a shiv in the belly. That's what happened when you failed, when you let yourself be traced and caught. The others had suffered similar fates, although in different times and places. He should have been notified sooner.

It would have been the biggest coup of the century. Think of what the Arabian princes and East Asian potentates would have bid for the president's daughter. Imagine what the U.S. government would have paid to get her back. It would have been a king's ransom, an accomplishment talked of for decades. His reputation would have been sealed, the man who had bested the great United States. It would have been worth all the effort and more, if only they had succeeded.

He still wasn't sure exactly what had happened south of the border. It was supposed to be a diversion. They had succeed in drawing the Secret Service off the track, but when the private detective showed up they tried to take care of it themselves. All hell broke out. A girl had been murdered, not even one of his. The two men running that fiasco had been killed. The club had been wrecked and several of his men hacked to death with machetes. He didn't learn anything more, but shortly afterward the same private dick showed up in Montreal and wrecked the whole operation. That was no coincidence. Somebody in Mexico City must have talked. The man had become an annoyance. Semyon looked at the dossier again and wondered how someone with such a name could be allowed to walk the streets everyday – Jason Lawless.

Reading the long bio that his team had provided, he wondered why this guy wasn't working with the U.S. government. Although he seemed to have a healthy contempt for authority, he had helped them on several occasions. Who knows, maybe he was with the mob. After all, a notorious Boston gangster had hired him.

Maybe his dislike for authority could be used to their advantage. Perhaps with a little leverage, they could even get him to join their side. Stranger things had happened. With enough incentive, anyone could be bought. It didn't always require hard currency. Others things could be bartered.

He looked again at the personal information his men provided, and focused on another name below the troublemaking detective's, the name of his thirteen-year-old son, Francis Robert Lawless. Then he smiled.

The End?

About the Author

Joe was born in upstate, New York, where he grew up and went to school. He holds a Bachlor's Degree in music composition from Berklee College of Music, and a Master's Degree in Computer Science from Boston University. Joe lives in Hudson, Massachusetts with his wife Kathy. Until his retirement a few years ago, he programmed computers for a living. Joe studied Chinese Kenpo karate in Acton MA, obtaining his black belt in 1977. He took over the school (Acton Academy of Self-Defense) when his instructor left for the west coast. Joe ran the school for several years, obtaining the rank of nidan in the process. He has won first place in kata and second place in sparring in local tournaments. Joe also studied aikido and tai-chi over the years. Although he no longer goes to the dojo, he still does all his forms (fifteen of them) and continues to teach from time to time. As Joe used to tell his students, "The Martial Arts is a way of life."

ALSO BY JOSEPH BEBO

www.ingramcontent.com/pod-product-compliance
Lightning Source LLC
Chambersburg PA
CBHW070920180626
46817CB00003B/1150